Randomization

No one gets away with murder ... or do they?
Karma takes care of what the law does not.

Randomization

A novel

STEVE MULLANEY
Author of TWISTED

Wilmont & Wilshire
Book Publishing

Published by Wilmont & Wilsher Book Publishing
Delaware | Georgia

www.wilmontwilsher.com
Copyright @ Steve Mullaney, 2022

Hardcover ISBN: 979-8-9875288-9-1
Paperback ISBN: 979-8-9875288-8-4
eBook ISBN: 979-8-9875288-7-7

Dedicated to those that believed in me, and to those that didn't.

Preface

It should be noted that Matthew never intended to become what it is he became. It was just one of those things that happened, an evolution of sorts. Oh sure, he did it the first time just to see what it would be like. After that, well, he just got better and better.

People say to forget the past, to keep it where it belongs—which is to say in the past— and just move on. Countless self-help books, along with many so-called professionals and people who just mean well, confidently assert *cleverisms* such as *"our future does not depend on our past"* or *"your past does not define you or your future."* But sometimes, the past can do just that, and quite subtly too. Other times, it defines our present and, in Matthew's case, the present is quite terrifying.

Chapter 1

Would he actually go through with it? He really did not know, but he was certainly eager to find out. And so, here he sat. Waiting. Patiently. The one hundred and eighteen car train led by four diesel electric engines traveled along the steel rails, making its way through central South Carolina. After lumbering through the small town of Chapin, the variable frequency drive system increased the speed of the metal mechanical centipede as it traveled through Irmo.

It was somewhere between 11:15 and 11:30pm. He had last checked the time when he glanced at his watch at 11:15 as he sat in the edge of the woods. The passage of time was distorted in his mind. The anticipation was making him very antsy, even nervous, making seconds feel like minutes. Conversely, the excitement had him hyper-alert which was having the opposite effect and making minutes seem like seconds. All he knew was the freight train would cross Rauch-Metze Road somewhere between 11:15 and 11:30. Well, at least he thought it would. He had checked out this site for the last several weeks and found that was the normal time for the train. But this was not Switzerland where renowned Swiss precision had trains on a very precise schedule, down to the minute and, at times, seemingly to the second. He had visited Switzerland for snow skiing several years ago and the train between Zurich and the Swiss Alps was very precise. If the Swiss said a train was going to be somewhere at 6:23, it was indeed going to be there at 6:23, not a minute earlier and not a minute later. Even the trams to the ski areas were precisely and accurately timed.

"Toby! Toby! Toby!" came the taunts in his mind.

He hated that name. During show-and-tell in the second grade, Matt had presented the DVD *Toby Tyler* to the class. He gave a nice review of the movie, and even said it was one of his favorite movies. Neither of those were a problem. But when he said he wanted to run away and join the circus like Toby did, the class burst out in hysterical laughter. He simply stood there. He turned to the teacher for help, but even Mrs. Palmer was laughing, though she was at least trying to hide it by holding the palm of her hand over her mouth. He first felt the tears streaming down his cheeks, and then he felt something else; the urgent need to urinate. Was he peeing himself in front of the class? He did not know; he only knew it was time to go. Dropping the DVD on the floor, he ran out of the classroom, struggling with the door as he made his way into the hallway, leaving the laughter behind. He kept running until he reached the bathroom. Fortunately, his pants were dry; he had not yet started peeing. He locked himself in the stall for the next ten minutes until Mr. Lohman, the science teacher in the classroom next to Mrs. Palmer's room, came into the bathroom to retrieve him. The next day, the kids in the class were referring to him as Toby behind his back, but it only took a matter of days until he was openly referred to as Toby. The name stuck.

"Eat it! Eat it! Eat it!" the taunts continued.

Matthew held the live goldfish between his thumb and forefinger, about six inches above his wide-open mouth. His head was tilted back while the fish dangled in Matthew's right hand.

"Toby! Toby! Toby!"

It started as a dare. Less than two weeks ago he was dropping the *Toby Tyler* DVD on the second-grade classroom floor and running out the door, and now, here he was at Susie Hendershot's birthday party on a Saturday afternoon. Kelly, the cute little brunette with a smattering of freckles on her cheeks, innocently asked Matthew why he wanted to join the circus. He liked her; she was always nice to him. Matthew replied that he liked animals. Teddy Thompson said, "Well, if you like animals, then eat that goldfish. I dare you."

"I double dare you," added Fred Miller.

This was a party of course and, being a bit of a loner, it was not often that Matthew was invited to parties. And, he had just been dared, doubled dared. What was he supposed to do? All he really wanted to do was fit in. He was always an outsider; now was his chance to change that. So, to the chorus of "Eat it!" he reached into Susie's fish bowl and snagged the lone goldfish. At first, he was not sure if he would actually eat it or not, but once the chants of "Toby" began, his mind was made up, and now here he was, holding the wiggling fish above his open mouth. He was going to be a cool guy; he was going to be part of the group. He surely would get some respect for this.

He released the fish and it fell into his mouth, sliding straight down his throat. It was a weird feeling, it almost tickled as the goldfish wiggled all the way down Matthew's esophagus and into his acid filled stomach where the fish was very short lived.

Susie cried and screamed hysterically. Kelly stared at him in disbelief. Some of the kids were laughing, laughing *at him*, while others shook their head in dismay. Teddy said, "Wow, what a jerk," and Fred said, "I can't believe he did it."

Mrs. Hendershot called his mother, while Mr. Hendershot promptly loaded Matthew into the car and drove him home without saying a word the entire trip.

Ed Hendershot pulled into the Stockmore's driveway. Matthew slowly got out of the car, and quietly uttered a single word, "Sorry."

Frank Stockmore was waiting when his son walked through the door. "You are a real piece of work," he said as he sat his fifth beer of the afternoon down on the coffee table.

"Frankie, don't do—"

Frank turned and glared at his wife. Then he pointed at her as he spoke and Katie knew it was going to be an unpleasant evening, "You. Shut. Up. Now." Pausing for a moment, Frank took a deep breath, and calmly added, "I will take care of you later." He turned his attention to Matthew.

Matthew did not go to school Monday or Tuesday.

He felt the rumble of the train before he heard it. The memories of second-grade and goldfish and childhood beatings quickly evaporated. His heart rate increased and he quickly got to his knees. Sweat formed on his brow. The steady gentle hum of the engines grew closer. Matthew had read online about the engines. He knew each of the 270,000 horsepower train engines consisted of a large V-12 diesel engine running at a constant speed. Those engines drove an electric generator, with the alternating current output of the generator powering four variable speed electric drive motors. The output of each generator was enough to power approximately 1,000 homes.

The red crossing lights on each side of the tracks began flashing while the bells began simultaneously dinging. The crossing arms lowered as a car came to a stop at the white stripe painted on the southwest side of the tracks and the lead engine came into view. He was on his feet now. The excitement was unreal. The tingling he felt was almost like electricity coursing through his body. Fifteen seconds later the train began crossing Rauch-Metz road.

He wiped the sweat from his face. Reaching into the waistband at the back of his pants, he removed the small Springfield XD sub-compact semi-automatic 9mm pistol. He walked towards the stopped car, approaching diagonally from the left rear of the vehicle. Extending his arm, he held the gun about a half of an inch from the driver's side window. The driver was oblivious to the figure dressed all in black on the other side of the glass as the gun fired. The sounds of gunshots were mostly drowned out by the clickity-clack of the steel wheels on the steel rails and the screeching of metal on metal as the train made its way past them. Though the gun held thirteen rounds plus one in the chamber, he did not use all of them. He fired five shots through the safety glass of the window into the driver's head.

Matthew "Toby" Alan Stockmore had just taken a human life. He was now a killer, not only of animals, but of people too.

The train cars kept rolling past while Toby disappeared quietly into the woods.

Chapter 2

He was wide awake by 6:15. Matthew was still trying to process things as soon as he had awoken.

Wow! What a rush! What a thrill! He still had a bit of a tingling sensation running through his entire body. He was amazed he was able to sleep at all. He wondered for a moment if last night was even real. Did he do that? Did he really just do that? Wow! He guessed he did.

"Wow!" he said aloud to the open empty room. "I just killed someone," he said to no one, bursting into laughter. "And you know what else? It felt grrrrreat!" and his laughter resumed.

"I just killed someone." What was that song? By some country singer. Something about being in love with a waitress and not even knowing her name. "I just killed someone and I don't even know her name." Know her name? It occurred to him he did not even know if it was a her or a him. He did not know how old he or she was. He did not if he or she was white or black or brown, or heck, even red, yellow, blue or green. What difference did that make? All he knew is it was fun! Okay, he thought, maybe it might be nice to see the person the next time. "The next time?" he said aloud. "The next time?" His very next thought was, of course there will indeed be a next time. There has to be. That was fun.

Last month is what really got the ball rolling. He had been helping a friend in Chapin do a few repairs on a house. He was not exactly an expert by any stretch of the imagination, but he was a bit handy and could handle simple repairs. And, he was pretty good at following directions if someone told him what to do. Internet videos were often a great help; he could watch them for instructions on how to do things, and he could also see someone else doing it.

One evening he was painting a bedroom and a hallway. The woman he was helping left after about half an hour to go on a date. He knew Christie had no interest in him, but it still seemed a bit insensitive and inconsiderate. The thing that did bother him was that she said nothing about it, she simply said she needed to leave for a bit to go meet a friend. Oddly, her teenage daughter came home and was surprised to see Matthew there working. "I can't believe you are here working while my mom is out on a date. She should really appreciate that. No other guy she knows would help her the way you do. Have you ever consider—oh, never mind."

He did not need to hear the end of the sentence to know what she was asking. He had perhaps thought about it. But it did not really matter what he thought. What mattered is what the other person thought. It always mattered what someone else thought. He just found it funny was all, that she of all people would be asking. It was no secret the daughter did not like him. In fact, her mom had told him that several times before. The curious thing is when he was over here doing work one day last week, Christie said something completely out of the blue about her daughter. "Trish thinks you're ok." Matthew responded that he thought Trish did not like him. He was surprised to hear, "That was definitely true, she really did not like you, but she thinks you are okay now. She and her friends were talking about you, about how hard you were working on the porch. Remember, they were all sitting on the driveway for a while? She said her opinion of you really went up. She lectured me after you left about how I did not really appreciate you and that maybe I should open my eyes." Open her eyes? Right. She was not the only one. Most people ignored him. Somehow, it seemed he just always blended into the woodwork. It was okay for people to sometimes ask him for a favor, but he knew that if he could not do something to help them, they probably would not give him the time of day. And really, he guessed he was kind of okay with that for right now. Well, no, not really, but what choice did he have?

But oh well, he was there to paint and paint he was going to do. Five hours after starting, he was done with both the painting and the cleaning up, and he was walking out the door at 11:03 pm.

Just after 11:15 he turned from Highway 76 onto Rauch-Metze Road in Irmo. About a quarter of a mile down the road was a set of train tracks. As Matthew approached the tracks the red lights began flashing and the bells began ringing as the crossing arms lowered to block the roadway on either side of the tracks. He pulled up to the crossing arm and stopped. There were no cars on the other side. Looking in his rearview mirror, he saw there were no cars coming down the hill behind him.

He heard the sound of the train's horn and saw the beam from its undulating headlight just before the train came into full view at the crossing.

Matthew instinctively began counting cars. It was a habit he picked up when he was a kid. Counting four engines, he figured it was going to be a long train and he was going to be here for a while. He was not sure where he had heard it, or perhaps he had read it, but he seemed to recall that a train engine was about seventy-five feet long, while the length of a rail car was about sixty-eight feet long.

He turned the car's ignition off. Thirty seconds later both the radio and the car's headlights automatically shut off.

It was dark. Very dark. He was no longer able to reliably count the cars. It was sometimes difficult to make out on this cloudy night where one car ended and the next one began. The only sound was that of the train lumbering along the rails. The sound of the cars themselves, the rumble of the wheels, and the metal-on-metal screeching of the steel wheels on the steel rails.

Unable to count train cars, Matthew's thoughts drifted. He thought about something that had happened a few weeks earlier, about a dog he intentionally killed. It may have been spontaneous, but it most certainly was intentional. Oh sure, he had eaten a goldfish, had killed a few fish in a lake with his dad, and had accidentally killed a cat. But those were different. He was curious what it was like to intentionally kill something. He had almost forgotten about the squirrel and the pellet gun, but that was when he was a kid, something like eleven or twelve years old.

He was out walking along Riverfront Park in Columbia one day, just minding his own business. Out of nowhere a little white poodle came up to him, wagging its tail. He reached down to pet the little dog. The dog seemed happy, and then stood on its hind legs, putting its front paws on Matthew's shin, as if it wanted to be picked up. Matthew obliged. The small dog was happy being held, and Matthew rubbed its little head. Surely this little dog belonged to someone. Looking around, he saw no one, not a single person. He stepped off the paved path and to the edge of the trees. Glancing around, he still saw no one. He grabbed the little dog by its hind quarters and swung the little white head against a tree. The dog was immediately motionless. Smiling, Matthew tossed the lifeless dog into the trees.

"Excuse me. Have you seen a dog, our little white poodle?" he heard the young couple asking passersby five minutes later. Ignoring them he continued back to the parking lot, trying unsuccessfully to suppress a wry smile.

Suddenly, he was back to watching the train cars pass by.

A thought occurred to him. As dark and deserted as this place was, someone could easily walk up to his car and shoot him. It was dark, it was loud, the car was off, even if it was not off, there was no place to go because there was a train in front, and there was no one, absolutely no one, around. This was a great place for a murder.

Three days later he was again doing some work for Christie. He noticed she was extremely cordial. She cooked dinner for him and even had some of his favorite beer. She seemed to occasionally brush lightly up against him; perhaps it was innocent, perhaps not. Regardless, he told himself it was. And she seemed to smile at him, a lot. It almost seemed like she was flirting with him.

Matthew surmised that her date the other night must not have gone very well. Either that, or her daughter had lectured her again. Either way, it was not his concern. He certainly was not going to make himself available to her just because her current situation did not work out. She would be looking for someone else soon enough and then she would be done with him — that is just what women like her did. Nope, he was having no part of that merry-go-round.

As he did three nights earlier, he arrived around 11:15pm at the crossbucks heralding the train tracks crossing Rauch-Metze Road. Roughly 8 minutes later the crossing arms lowered preparing for the over a mile-long mighty freightliner of the rails.

Again, the darkness of the place was impressive. About fifteen seconds after his car's headlights automatically turned off, he saw the glow of light bleed underneath the train. Matthew instinctively knew this was from the headlights of a car stopped on the road on the opposite side of the train.

As the last car of the train passed, Matthew could see three vehicles on the opposite side of the tracks. There were none behind him on his side of the tracks. It was time for a test.

Keeping his car off, he simply sat in the driver's seat and waited, staring straight ahead, and waiting, simply waiting. The crossing arms raised up, the clanging of the bells stopped, and the cars began crossing the tracks before the arms returned to their full upright position just before the red lights stopped flashing.

The three cars drove past, one at a time, and still Matthew did not move. None of the cars stopped to check on him, none of the cars slowed down so their drivers might look at him. Instead, the cars with their occupants anxious to resume their journey after having been inconvenienced by a train for the past three minutes and forty-seven seconds, accelerated. He shifted his gaze into the rearview mirror where he watched the taillights of the cars move up the hill and fade out of site.

This is a great place for a murder, he once again thought. This would indeed be a great place.

Matthew pondered for a bit. Some people kill for a specific reason: money, revenge, hate, spite, sex, and self-preservation, among others. He had no reason, other than to see what it would be like to kill a human being.

He wondered if he killed someone else—if? No, it was a matter of when, not if. He wondered if the feeling would be the same. Would he get the same rush, the same thrill? He had to know; he had to find out.

Another thought occurred to Matthew. So, when he killed someone else, would that make him a serial killer? Hmm. He needed to look that one up at some point. Heck, why not now?

Picking up his smartphone from the nightstand next to the bed and opening a browser, he searched for "how many victims before someone is classified as a serial killer." Selecting *Serial Killer Victim Selection* at crimemuseum.org, he began reading. *"To be defined as a serial killer, an individual must satisfy a few criteria, specified by the Federal Bureau of Investigation. The person in question must have murdered a minimum of three individuals (not simultaneously), there must be a period of time in between the murders (to prove that multiple victims were not killed during a single fit of rage), and the circumstances of each murder should indicate that the killer felt a sense of dominance over the people they have killed. The victims must also be vulnerable to the killer in some way, a characteristic which indicates that the killer has sought to achieve a feeling of superiority."*

Well, three people I could do. I think. If I kill two, I might as well kill three, he mused. I think. We will just have to see. If the second is as much fun as the first, then why not do another?

But the rest of that stuff, the part about a sense of dominance, the superiority, and the victim feeling vulnerable to him? None of that applied to him. He did not even know the person in the car last night. The person in the car felt nothing towards him. Heck, they did not know he even existed and they certainly never saw it coming. As for dominance or superiority, he felt none of that. The only things he remembered feeling were excitement and anticipation in the minutes before it happened, and a sense of excitement, a definite thrill, afterwards. Dominance or superiority? Nope. He did it just to see what it would be like. He guessed he would not be allowed into the serial killer club after all. That was okay. They would probably charge a membership fee, have a secret handshake he would need to learn, and he would probably feel compelled to buy a club t-shirt. He had enough t-shirts, thank you very much.

Nonetheless, if he was going to do this again and, who knows, maybe again and again, he needed to be smart about it. He needed to make sure each one would be different with no way to link them together.

His modus operandi would be that there would be no real modus operandi. The only thing the killings would have in common is they would have nothing in common. Okay, maybe there would be something in common: someone was going to die. Okay, and maybe one more thing: Matthew would do the killing.

Reading a bit further in the crimemuseum.org article, "*It is generally accepted that most serial killers feel a strong urge to commit acts of murder. They are, however, thought to be extremely cautious people who will not choose a victim unless they feel the chances of success are very high.*"

Now that, that he agreed with. He liked the thrill of the first, and he wanted to see if he got it again from the second and third and fourth or however many. And if he wanted to be successful, of course he would need to be cautious.

Chapter 3

Matthew "Toby" Alan Stockmore was restless. He was anxious. He was trying to figure out his next move. Matthew saw the small cat at the edge of the parking lot as he was filling his motorcycle with gasoline on the way to work. He could not help but think about a cat he once briefly had.

One day, two or three years ago, a little stray kitten had wandered onto his front porch. After a few days, he decided to put some water and food out for the cute little thing. About a week later he let the calico kitten inside. The kitten he named Gwen seemed to love him. It was as if the kitten knew how good she had it and was very appreciative.

Every time he sat down, the kitten Gwen hopped up in his lap and went to sleep. There was something that was calming and relaxing about this. Frequently, if he reclined the sofa back, she would climb up on his chest purring and rubbing her little face on his chin. He usually thought this was so cool, so adorable.

One Wednesday evening about six months after he brought the kitten inside, Matthew was sitting on the sofa, with the back reclined, drinking a beer and eating a slice of delivery pizza from the box sitting next to him. Gwen tried to climb on his chest. He pushed her away. Undeterred, she tried again. Matthew was just raising the glass of beer to his mouth when she hit the glass, causing him to miss his mouth and spill beer on his chest.

His temper erupted and he threw her across the room. Hitting the wall, she fell motionless to the floor. He took a drink from the glass of beer. "Hey cat." The feline remained motionless on the floor. "Hey Gwen." Still no movement. He got off the couch and walked over to Gwen. The kitten lay motionless on the floor with her eyes open. He noticed the pool of urine beginning to form as the kitten's bladder let go. "Oh great." He picked the kitten up and placed her little body into a plastic shopping bag he had saved from the grocery store. He felt no remorse for having killed the kitten. It really was no different than dropping a cookie on the floor, picking it up and throwing it in the trash. It was merely a momentary annoyance.

He walked outside and deposited the bag into the trash can. "Well, I guess that sucks." By tomorrow the bag and the kitten would be just another part of the county landfill.

Walking out of the office after clocking in, Matthew made his way through the warehouse and into the breakroom.

Alfonso and Ted were sitting at the table, drinking coffee and apparently guarding what was left of a dozen donuts.

"What happened here? Is there a hole in the bottom of that box, or something? Did all the donuts fall out, or what?"

"More like a hole in Ted's mouth. He ate like three of them."

"Man, why do you want to tell lies against me? No respect, I get no respect, man."

"What, did you really eat *four*," Matthew said as he sat down at the table.

"Don't you know it, man," Ted said chuckling.

"How's it going, Matt?" Alfonso asked, never taking his gaze from the three remaining donuts.

"Ah man, it was a weird night last night," Matthew replied as he walked over to the coffee machine.

"Weird? How so?"

"Well, I was hungry last night, so I figured I would open a can of chicken noodle soup. So, I went and got the can out of the refrigerator."

"You keep soup in the fridge?"

"You know, that is exactly what I was thinking. Since when do I keep soup in the fridge? Anyway, I took the can out. Huh. Since when is soup in a twelve ounce can, I wondered. I popped the top. Well, at least some soup cans do have a pop top, you know. I emptied the can into a tumbler. Hmm. Since when do I pour soup into a Tervis tumbler? Wait a second! There are no noodles, I said to myself. There was no chicken either! Silly me. It was not a can of chicken noodle soup. It was a can of Elysian Space Dust IPA. Come to think of it, I have no cans of soup in my house. Oh well, I figured I would just have to drink the beer."

"Man, you are not right."

"Well, it's almost a true story."

"Almost a true story?"

"Well, I did drink a beer last night," Matthew replied with a smile.

"Yo, Matt, you are good with heights, right?"

"Yeah, I suppose so." He could not very well admit he did not like heights. Though not quite afraid of heights, they did make him nervous. "I prefer keeping my feet on the ground, but I do not have a problem getting high."

"Getting high," Ted said laughing. "We know you do not mind drinking, and smokin' a lil' somethin'-somethin', but that is not the getting high he is talking about."

"Funny boy, I replaced the flood lights up on the roof here a month or two ago. Do you not remember? No one else wanted to go up that high."

"Yeah, yeah," Alfonso said while slowly shaking his head. "You ever do any roofing?"

"Roofing?"

"Yeah, like putting on a roof." Alfonso explained that he wanted to replace the roof on his house within the next couple of weeks. This would involve getting up on the roof, removing the existing shingles and felt, and then installing new felt and shingles.

"Hey, Alf. Are you sure about this?" Ted asked Alfonso.

"Sure about what?"

"About asking Matthew to help with the roof," he said laughing. "After all, he does not know the difference between chicken noodle soup and beer. Heck, he might get confused and bring a cooler full of soup to drink."

"Okay, okay," Alfonso said, shaking his head and laughing, "Matthew does not bring the beer."

"See? There is method to my madness," Matthew exclaimed. "I just got out of buying the beer!"

"So, I take it you are in?"

"Sure, just let me know when and where and I will be there. I have never done any roofing, but how hard can it be? Count me in."

Chapter 4

"Lookie here, boy," Frank said to his son.

The 10-year-old boy obediently looked at his father. When the man said do something, the boy did it without question and without hesitation.

Frank picked up the fish from the white 5-gallon bucket that sat next to him at the end of the dock. Matthew had just caught the bluegill a few minutes earlier. Reaching into his pants pocket with his right hand, he produced a small firework. "This here thing, boy, is called an M80. It's the real McCoy. It ain't one of those wimpy things they sell nowadays. This here thing will blow ya hand clean off."

He placed the firework into the mouth of the 12-inch bream. "It has a waterproof fuse too." Taking the cigarette that dangled from his mouth, Frank touched the lighted end to the green fuse sticking out of the fish's mouth. "Down the hatch," he exclaimed as he pushed the explosive further into the fish and then tossed it into the water. The fish immediately swam down under the surface of the water and out of sight.

Matthew was both hurt and confused. "What did that do? Why did you throw my fish back?" he asked as tears slowly made their way down his cheeks.

"You just stop ya crying and watch, boy. This is going to be good," Frank said as he took a long swallow of beer from the longneck bottle that sat atop the handrail of the dock.

About that time there was a muffled "blahbloop" sound, and pieces of fish began to appear on the surface of the water.

"WhadITellYa?" he said, almost unable to control his laughter.

Matthew turned around and ran down the twenty-foot long dock and up across the sloping yard. He could hear his father calling to him, "Boy! Get back here boy!" Refusing to turn around, Matthew ran up the six wooden steps and into the mobile home to his mother.

"He blew up my fish. Daddy blew up my fish!" and the tears began to flow unabated. It took Katie a full minute to get Matthew's crying under control.

She heard the stomping across the deck and knew this could not be a good sign.

It did not matter to Frank that it was not their lake home as he violently kicked the black front door open.

Paul Jessup and his wife lived in Elgin, just over a hundred miles away from the lake home in Waterloo. Paul had bought the place at a steal in September for $97,000. With a lot of hard work rehabbing the home and clearing and beautifying the almost six tenths of an acre lot, the lake home with a new dock was listed for sale eight months later for almost $220,000. Of course, relying heavily on friends for help, Paul did not do all or even most of the work himself. Frank was one of those that pitched in. There were promises of a "big shindig" when everything was finished. All that went out the window when Paul was hospitalized in March.

Frank still could not understand that one. Paul was just fine, he seemed healthy as a horse. One day he walked the seventy feet to the end of his driveway to get the mail from the mailbox. About halfway back he noticed he was tired. Ten feet away from the front door he was so exhausted, he was not sure he was able to make it back inside. Fortunately, Edith was just coming out the front door to water the plants hanging on the front porch. Rather than help him inside, she helped him sit down, then immediately went inside and called 911.

Paul was admitted to the hospital and, after two days of testing, was diagnosed with leukemia, acute myeloid leukemia. He was released two days later and, two weeks after that, a week after chemo treatment had started,

Paul was more like a frail old man. Frank could not figure things like that out. Someone seemingly fine was suddenly diagnosed with a horrible disease and shortly thereafter they rapidly declined and, more often than not, died. Some survived, some fought and survived. What he could not understand was the rapid decline. Was it that the diagnosis sapped most peoples' will to live? Was it the treatment? Or was it simply coincidence, that the disease was that bad and, whether there was a diagnosis or not, the person was soon going to experience the full impact of the disease, and the treatment was too late to make much difference except to delay the inevitable?

Frank himself had been out here more than a few times to help. He and three other guys cut down about twenty trees over a weekend in late October. Frank did not know much about felling the trees, but he quickly learned how to use a chainsaw to remove the branches once the tree was on the ground.

The following weekend he learned how to use the heavy equipment Paul had rented to clear and grade the land. He had gotten pretty proficient at operating the Skid Steer, using the eighty-inch-wide bucket to clear the land and move dirt and debris, and using it to grade the land while driving the Cat 226D in reverse. In early November, Frank helped Paul and two others build the deck and porch, and they built the dock over Thanksgiving weekend.

Paul and Edith had an offer on the place and it looked like it was sold, but the deal fell through May 13th and the property was going back on the market for the same $219,900 price. Frank knew the Jessup's were selling their prized property only because of Paul's medical issues. He knew Paul was in no condition to travel anywhere and Edith certainly was not going to come out here by herself. Since the sale had fallen through, and the house was not quite back on the market yet, Frank figured there was no time like the present. He decided he would "borrow" the lake home for the weekend. He figured he was entitled to it because of the time and labor he invested in it. Of course, Katie did not know the Stockmores were uninvited guests. Katie also did not know the Jessups; she had never met nor spoken with either of them and knew Paul only as someone Frank knew.

The day before they arrived, Frank had been in Greenville and drove back to their home in Cayce via Waterloo. Before leaving Greenville, he stopped by Lowe's and bought a lockset. Once at the property in Waterloo, he drilled out the doorknob on the entry door, removed it, and replaced it with his own lockset. When they were finished with their weekend stay, Frank might leave the key under the door mat, or he might throw it in the lake, or he might take it with him. He really did not know, nor did he care. It would not be his problem.

"Where is that boy?" Frank bellowed as he walked through the door. "Woman, get me a beer. Now! Ok you," he said pointing at his son, "come here, boy."

Katie felt the baby kick, and she instinctively put her right hand on her stomach. The baby girl inside her seemed to get active, even agitated, whenever Frank went on a rampage. Oh God, how she hoped Frank would treat this little girl better than he had treated their son. Matthew, poor Matthew. Katie prayed Frank would never lay a hand on their daughter. Oh, she prayed, too, that Frank would stop hitting and beating Matthew but, somehow, she felt it was too late for that.

Sniffling, Matthew hesitantly walked towards his father.

"And stop that crying right now. If you want something to cry about, I'll give you something to cry about. Is that what you want?"

Matthew slowly shook his head.

"I said, is that what you want?"

"No."

"What was that, boy? No?"

"No, sir," as he sniffled again.

"I said stop that crying. No boy of mine is gonna stand there crying like a little sissy."

"Frank, please, he is not a sissy," Katie said gently as she handed him an opened beer. She smiled, trying to diffuse the situation.

"What? Why are you always taking his side?"

"He is ten years old, for cryin' out loud. He is just a boy, Frank."

"If I had ever cried like that, my old man would have beat the tar out of me."

Katie knew better than to say anything about Frank's father. "Well please, just let it go. Alright? Let's just enjoy the weekend. It was so nice of Paul, isn't that his name, Paul? It was so nice of Paul to let us use this place for the weekend to reward you for all your hard work here."

Taking a long pull from the longneck bottle, "Yeah, okay. Let's take a walk, boy."

Standing at the end of the dock, Frank tipped back the bottle and swallowed the remaining contents. Dropping the empty bottle on the dock, he reached down and picked up another one, removed the top, and took a swig.

"Okay, it is your turn now. Here is a fish I caught. I blew your fish up, so you can blow mine up and we'll call it even, okay?"

Unsure of what to do, Matthew simply nodded his head.

Frank pulled an M80 from his pocket and handed it to Matthew. "This thing here, this is an M80. They's illegal now. Leastways the real ones are." He took a long swallow of beer. "It is a very powerful firework. They were originally made by the military. They used them for training exercises to simulate artillery fire and explosives or something like that. So, they ain't toys. You understand me?"

"Yes, sir."

"Good, now get over here and let's have some fun."

One more swallow of beer and, setting the half-empty bottle on the deck, he lit a cigarette.

Frank reached down and pulled a ten-inch bluefin from the bucket, squeezing the fish to open its mouth. "Alright, Matt, now put that firecracker right inside here. Leave that green fuse sticking out, that's what you need to light."

Matthew slowly put the explosive into the fish's gulping mouth.

"Now take the cigarette from my mouth and light it."

Matthew did as his father instructed.

"Quick, now throw the fish in the water!"

Parts of fish floated to the top of the water.

"Hey, that was pretty cool, Dad! Can we do another one?"

"Sure, but you do this one all by yourself."

Being out of M80s after three more explosions, the remaining fish in the lake were safe.

Chapter 5

The heavy rain had ended about an hour ago, being replaced by a light mist. A dense fog now enveloped downtown Columbia, particularly along the waterways.

Fifteen minutes after the downpour ceased, he watched the fog rolling in. Convinced the rain was done, or at least hoping it was, he rolled up his blanket and stuffed it into a nook under the overpass. He instinctively rubbed the right side of his chest. It often flared up during rain or changes in barometric pressure. Then he briefly rubbed the back of his right hand. He could feel the plate and the screws. That hand just seemed to always be bothersome, but he did the best he could to ignore it, to block out the discomfort. Emerging from under the bridge, he went searching for food.

It had been raining for the past thirty-six hours, compliments of some type of front moving up from the Gulf.

Every shelter he went to was already closed. He did not fare much better at the soup kitchens. Without having found any food, and still hungry, he decided he would make his way down to the river. The Cayce or West Columbia side of the river might be better than the Columbia side. Who knows, he might even run into someone he knows. Maybe someone had some extra food they might share with him.

One month and two days after Samuel Harkins six-month probation period ended, the day started as any other day.

At two minutes past eleven that morning, Sam stood drinking coffee, looking through the plate glass window into the mall. Sunshine filtering in through the sky lights illuminated the mall's interior. Artificial lighting made evenings in the mall extraordinarily bright, and there was perhaps something to be said for that, especially in his line of work, but he definitely preferred the subdued natural light.

There were no customers in the jewelry store, so Sam lackadaisically watched the people stroll through the mall.

People watching is something he enjoyed. At Christmastime he enjoyed going to the mall and watching people, as he would say, "watching people that came out of the woodwork only once or twice a year." He would sit on a bench with a bucket of popcorn or a soft pretzel and some semblance of drink and simply watch the people go by while letting his imagination run wild.

Unbeknownst to these people, they were stars and bit players in intricate stories Sam would make up about them in his head. Sometimes he would weave but a small snippet, other times he would weave an entire elaborate story. Their lives would be intertwined with those of other mall dwellers in ways they could not even begin to imagine.

Sam and his wife, Holly, used to enjoy sitting in restaurants with a drink collaboratively spinning fanciful yarns about the people around them. That is until the unthinkable happened. One moment she was there, young, beautiful, vibrant. The next she was not.

His eyes moistened just a bit, even as a slight smile crossed his face. He thought wistfully about her sandy brown hair and piercing gray eyes, and the red lipstick. Oh, how that woman loved her red lipstick. She told Sam it made her happy. She said it was a sign of optimism. Holly had mentioned something one time about red lipstick sales and the economy, but he really paid no attention to that; he was simply lost in those gray eyes as she talked. All he knew was that her pouty lips made red lipstick look good.

For the first three years they were married, Holly continued working as a bartender. She had graduated from school with an art history degree, but she never found much use for that and wound up as a bartender. It was not really a career choice; it was more just biding time. She had dreams, aspirations. Holly and Sam had met through mutual friends and the sparks flew almost immediately. Six months later she was Holly Harkins. No hyphen for her; "We are Mr. and Mrs. Harkins," she would proudly proclaim.

Less than a year ago, Holly had graduated nursing school. Passing the NCLEX-R.N. licensing exam the next day, she immediately started working at Saint Barnabas Medical Center, an acute care hospital. Three years earlier she and Sam had talked about making her dreams of becoming a nurse come true. For the next year, she enrolled in Seton Hall and applied for financial aid, while he set about working two jobs. A year and a half later, Holly Harkins graduated from Seton Hall's accelerated B.S.N program. Armed with a Bachelor of Science in Nursing degree and just over fifty thousand dollars in student loan debt, Holly was now a nurse. The next day she started a new job in the cardiac unit at Saint Barnabas.

The world was theirs to conquer; and then it was not. Six months ago, they were sitting on the sofa watching a movie. It had been a toss-up between *Tower Heist*, *Contagion*, and *Puss in Boots*. They settled for the feline with a questionable clothing choice. "I have a question, a question for the ages. Why is it Puss wears boots but no pants," Holly had asked Sam. She was like that; always observant, and always asking funny little questions.

Halfway through the movie, Holly proclaimed she wanted popcorn and paused the DVD. "Whoa! I think I stood up too fast. My head is all wonky and wobbly," she said giggling, and pausing for just a moment. In less than five minutes she returned with the popcorn, stumbling once as she approached the sofa.

"What was that?"

"You know how clumsy I can be. I guess maybe I forgot to pick my foot up."

Resuming her spot on the sofa, she set the bowl between them. "The cloud, it tickles my nose," Puss said as the movie was restarted.

A few minutes later, Holly never heard Kitty Softpaws ask Puss, "What are you gonna do? Hit it in the head with a guitar?" Holly's head slumped toward the left as her left hand dropped into the bowl of popcorn. She would never see her twenty-eighth birthday.

They assured Sam Holly did not suffer, that she more than likely never even knew anything happened. The brain aneurism, they called it an intracranial aneurism, was both massive and instantaneous.

Wiping the tears from his eyes, Sam casually watched the patrons in the mall walking past as he stood unnoticed behind the jewelry store window. This is the closest he got to people watching at Short Hills. There was no sitting on a bench and people watching here. No, Short Hills Mall was a bit too upscale for that. The median home price in Short Hills was just recently reported to be one point seventy-five million dollars. In two short years later, in 2014, with seventy percent of the household annual incomes above one hundred fifty thousand dollars, *Time* magazine would name Short Hills the "Richest Town in America."

A month before the blood vessel ruptured in Holly's brain, Sam had started working as a security guard at the jewelry store. It had been a long journey, and they were both so excited when he landed this job. For the previous year he had worked in loss mitigation at a big box hardware store, and before that he spent two years at Walmart. With the position at the jewelry store, he was able to quit his second job as a picker at a fulfilment center for an on-line retailer.

He saw them pause in the center of the mall; two men and a woman. It was not so much that they stopped that had caught his attention, but they seemed to be slowly looking around. And, it appeared they were trying to be discreet about it.

The well-dressed woman left the group, and slowly looked around, and then up, as if looking for a video camera, she began walking towards the jewelry store. Dropping his unfinished cup of coffee into the trash can, he took his customary place in the corner, near the back of the long display case.

Walking into the store, the woman discretely shifted her gaze around the store, and then slowly walked to the display case and pretended to be looking at diamonds. Sam did not like this; something was off. She did indeed appear to be looking at diamonds, but she remained erect, never bending down to peer through the glass like most people tended to do.

Two minutes later the two men entered the store. Without saying a word, one went over towards the watches in the display case on the left, while the other made his way to the necklaces in the display case on the right. To the casual observer, it would appear these were just three random customers, complete strangers to each other. But Sam knew better.

Suspicious, he moved from behind the back display case and casually sauntered to a position closer to the front of the store. While Matthew Stockmore was doing battle with Dr. Jenkins in his Intermediate Microeconomic Theory class seven hundred miles away in Columbia, South Carolina, here in Short Hills, New Jersey, Samuel Harkins was about to engage in a different kind of battle.

The guy closest to Sam looked up, and slowly turning, asked, "Hey buddy, do you have the time?"

This struck Sam as particularly odd since the guy was standing in front of the watch display case, and Sam noticed the guy was indeed wearing a watch.

Glancing up at the clock on the back wall, before Sam could tell the guy it was eleven thirty-seven, the woman turned and opened fire. A bullet tore through Sam's right hand, and passed into his right thigh, with another bullet embedding into the right side of his chest. With his damaged hand, he managed to pull the gun from his holster and shift it to his left hand as he was falling to the polished floor. Three pulls of the trigger and the woman was on the ground, with a hole through her forehead. Firing four more shots in rapid succession, the watch guy dropped lifelessly to the ground. A shoe kicked violently into Sam's face. The guy from the necklace case had slipped unnoticed over to Sam. Stomping onto Sam's left wrist, Sam's grip on the gun loosened. Kicking Sam's gun across the floor, he stomped repeatedly on Sam's right hand, before running out of the store empty handed.

Having thwarted an attempted robbery at the jewelry store. Sam was hailed a hero. The mall declared they owed him a debt of gratitude, as did the high-end jewelry store. Two months later Sam was back at work, with a new holster which he wore on the left side. He had learned two months earlier he could indeed shoot with his left hand if pressed to do so.

There was much fanfare about his return and there was constant lauding of his heroic deeds. And, they even proclaimed that day to be Sam Harkins day.

Having earned a metal plate, two pins and six screws, his right hand was largely useless. Lacking flexibility, and being able to really only move the thumb to grasp things, his right hand more or less resembled a claw.

Nine months later, Sam was without a job. They told him they were going in a different direction, but he knew the real reason. Not only was his right hand essentially useless, but he sometimes suffered from migraine headaches due to the kicking he had received, he got emotional when talking about what happened during the robbery attempt, and he was extraordinarily suspicious of potential customers.

Two months after Holly's death, Sam sold their little two-bedroom house nine miles away in Irvington and moved into an apartment. With only one income, the loans for Holly's degree, and the funeral expenses, he simply could not afford to live there anymore. The one hundred- and eight-year-old house sold quickly at eighty thousand dollars. It was a break-even proposition, but it meant he was not saddled with the mortgage payments or the upkeep.

Six months later, with no job and unable to pay the rent, he was evicted from the apartment. For three months he slept in his car and scavenged food where he could. With no options, he called a friend in Columbia, SC. Fred told him to come on down to South Carolina, that he and Sheila had plenty of room. "Nothing like helping out an old army buddy," Fred had said. With no money for gasoline, Sam sold the car and bought a bus ticket southward to the Palmetto State.

Fifteen months after arriving in Columbia, Fred told Sam he and Sheila were moving, he had accepted a job elsewhere. Fred pre-paid a month at a local motel for Sam. After thirty nights, Sam was without a place to live.

Chapter 6

Matthew turned the white Jeep into the apartment complex about halfway between Knox Abbott Drive and Gervais Street. The parking lot was as good as any, and he figured there would be less chance of any security cameras. He had driven by here a few weeks ago and saw none on his initial reconnaissance of the area.

The Grand Cherokee Laredo did not belong to him. It was more or less borrowed without the owner's consent. A former neighbor had asked him to feed their cat while they were away on vacation for the week. They had gone to the Smokey mountains to enjoy the vibrant colors of the fall leaves. There were cooling temperatures in the mountains, a key ingredient in the changing colors of the dying leaves, but those temperatures had not yet made it to Columbia. The evenings were perhaps getting a bit milder, but not by much.

He parked the Jeep. Exiting the SUV, he grabbed the backpack and the small Styrofoam cooler from the back seat, closed the door and pressed the lock button only once. This locked the doors without chirping the horn. The less attention he drew to himself, the better off he was. He pocketed the key fob and walked towards building 300, situated along the back of the property.

He walked down the breezeway towards the right of the building. Passing apartment 305 on his left and the staircase on his right, he continued through the breezeway. He could just make out the river in the darkness beyond. Walking past apartment 307, he was at the end of breezeway. He quietly gazed into the night. The globe lights on the wall at the end of the hallway gave off enough light that he was able to easily see the grass hill sloping down towards the paved West Columbia Riverwalk trail that paralleled the Congaree River.

Stepping out of the breezeway and onto the grass plateau immediately behind building 300, Matthew took three steps and was at the edge of the steep grass hill. Quickly making his way down the hill, he walked across the grass landing to the edge of the decorative metal fence that separated the Riverwalk trail from the private property along the trail. Looking around and seeing no one, Matthew pulled a pair of blue latex gloves and a disposable mask from his pocket. He slipped them on and easily climbed over the black fence.

The haggard old man slowly turned to the sound of the voice. "Hey, excuse me," Matthew had called out to the man. As the man turned around and Matthew could see his face, he realized he was not as old as he first thought.

"Huh," sounding more like a grunt, was the man's response.

"How are you this evening?"

The man grunted again, and started turning away.

"Whoa, whoa. I do not want to hurt you," Matthew said to the man's back. "I want to help you. Are you hungry?"

The man stopped walking and looked back over his left shoulder towards Matthew. He had not eaten for almost a day and a half.

"I have food."

The transient turned around. "Food? I'm hungry," came the reply in such a low volume Matthew could barely hear it as he set the Styrofoam cooler on the ground.

Removing his backpack, he said, "Let's see what we have in here for you. How about a couple of sandwiches?"

"Really?" the man said with a smile beginning to form across his face. "For me?"

The man's missing front top tooth and another on the bottom right made him appear somewhat older. "Here you go, here is a roast beef sandwich," Matthew said, extending the sandwich. "Hey, if you don't mind me asking, how old are you?" he asked while the man tentatively reached out his hand. Matthew noticed the guy's extended right hand seemed almost deformed. It certainly did not seem to bend and resembled more of a claw. Noticing Matthew staring, he withdrew his right hand, extending his left hand instead for the sandwich.

"Oh, I don't know. Thirty-eight, or thirty-nine, I think. I lose track of those things out here." He quickly snatched the sandwich and held it against his chest, as if protecting it and making sure no one could take it from him.

"It's okay. Don't worry. I have another one for you." Late thirties? Matthew was genuinely stunned. Wow, life on the streets apparently really takes a toll, he thought. He initially thought the guy was very old when he saw him from a distance. That is partly what caused Matthew to select him. Of course, the fact that the guy was by himself and there was no one else in sight played into the decision as well. As the man had gotten closer, Matthew surmised the guy was perhaps in his early sixties. "How long have you been out here?" he asked, resisting the urge to add "old-timer" to the question.

Apparently convinced no one was going to take his sandwich, the guy began unwrapping it. "Five years, six years, something like that. A long time. I've seen things, you know. I've seen people come and go. I've seen lots of things," he added as bits of unchewed food fell from his mouth.

"I bet you have," Matthew said, a bit disgusted by the sight of this man devouring a sandwich like a wild animal. Still, he handed over the turkey sandwich too. "Have a sit, try to enjoy this one."

He could not help but think he would be doing the man a favor.

The guy started to sit down on the grass. "Hey, wait a second. Not here. How about over there," Matthew said, pointing to a spot about thirty feet away, at the edge of the tree line.

The man looked at him suspiciously. "What is wrong with here? I do not want to go over there."

"Well, I might just have a beer in here for you."

"Beer?"

"A nice ice-cold beer. Now, we would not want anyone to see your beer now, would we? Someone might try to take it away from you."

"Beer? For me?"

Yep, he would definitely be doing this guy a favor.

"Yes, sir. A beer just for you. I might even drink one with you, if you'll let me."

"I like you. You are my friend."

"Yes, we are friends. Now let's go sit down over there. You can eat your other sandwich and I will get the beers. I am John," he lied. "What is your name?"

"Sam," the man replied as he sat down.

At the edge of the trees, Matthew removed the cover of the cooler, which he had placed behind Sam. White smoke poured over the top edges of the cooler and flowed down to the ground. "Now then, let's see what we have in here for you, Sam." He removed a small glass bottle and nonchalantly set it in the grass. He quietly removed a small block of dry ice and tossed it into the trees. "I don't think we will need that anymore." Sam was not paying attention as he began to work on the turkey sandwich.

Matthew removed from the cooler a plastic grocery bag which had been sitting on top of another small block of dry ice. Reaching back into the cooler with the other hand, he removed and tossed that ice into the trees as well. Holding the plastic bag with his left hand, he reached into the bag and removed the icy knife.

Sam took another bite of the sandwich and did not notice Matthew step behind him. Holding the frozen knife in his right hand, he reached around in front of Sam and swiftly dragged the knife across the man's throat. The sandwich dropped from his hands as he feebly grabbed at this throat. Matthew took a few steps backwards, dropping the knife on the ground.

He stood watching, mesmerized by the dying man in front of him, and rather enjoying the spectacle. He was actually quite proud of what he had done. In his mind he had just put the poor guy, a pathetic guy, out of his misery. The guy was living a miserable life, he told himself, he won't have to live it anymore. And, let's be honest, he had some fun while doing it. "Well, that is enough of that," Matthew said aloud, as he set about preparing for his departure.

Reaching down and picking up the small glass jar, he carefully opened it. He doused the outside of the cooler and its lid with the gasoline in the jar. The liquid began immediately melting the Styrofoam. Without wasting time, Matthew carried the cooler and lid across the dark sidewalk and towards the river bank. With the gasoline breaking down the Styrofoam and releasing the trapped air, the cooler was already turning into a white gooey mess of polystyrene. There was absolutely no way anyone would ever be able to get finger prints off of this, he thought, before tossing the blob into the river.

He made his way back towards Sam. Sam was lying on his right side, motionless. "Sam, Sam, Sam the man," Matthew said softly in a singsong voice while kicking Sam's foot. Nothing. Another kick. Still nothing.

He picked up the plastic grocery bag and the small glass bottle. After walking a full minute, he made his way to the edge of the river. Removing the cap from the bottle, he tossed both into the river. Removing the blue disposable gloves, he placed them in the grocery bag and stuffed the bag into his right front pocket.

Matthew turned away from the river bank, and slowly looked around. Still no one. He made his way back to the Jeep.

He was amazed it worked so well. Oh, sure, he had tested it when he first made one. But, testing at home and performing in the field were two different things. He had made a form in the shape of a knife, filled it with water and then stuck it in the freezer. After a couple of days, he removed the knife from the form. The edge was a bit dull, so he honed it a bit and put a crude edge on it. He had to be careful of course because every minute it was out of the freezer was a minute it was melting. Playing around with his knife, he found it would indeed cut.

The thawing was definitely both a blessing and curse. Curse? It was a major problem. The blessing was that the knife would quickly melt, leaving absolutely no traces except a small puddle of water that would quickly evaporate. And even if it did not, even if someone saw the water, so what? Who would possibly think that water used to be a knife? But how to transport the knife without it melting was the problem. Until the dry ice solution occurred to him. He had once ordered some steaks on-line and he remembered they came packed in dry ice. If meat could be packed in dry ice, then why couldn't he pack ice in dry ice? Using the plastic bag to separate the two different forms of ice was, he thought, sheer genius. It would prevent his ice knife from sticking to the solid carbon dioxide. And both his knife and the dry ice would simply disappear. Poof! Just like that, they would be gone without a trace.

It occurred to Matthew that he was hungry. "Who knew a good kill could," he laughed, "pardon the pun, awaken a killer appetite." He wanted something to eat. He needed something to eat. He could not help but laugh at the fact he had given Sam two sandwiches and not did think about anything for himself. Then again, he was just a little preoccupied with something else, thank you very much. Besides, he had not expected to be this hungry. He did not recall being this hungry after the train tracks. Then again, that was late at night.

A sandwich did not interest him, especially not a roast beef or turkey sandwich. Oddly, a frozen pizza sounded appealing. "What the heck," he thought, "I might as well drop the grocery bag with the gloves in the trash can at the store." How ironic. Matthew would be returning that bag to the same grocery store he had acquired it from.

He returned the key to its proper place on the counter. They would never know their Jeep had been borrowed.

Walking past the Jeep, Matthew continued to his motorcycle at the edge of the parking lot. After putting the pizza and the six pack of beer into the right saddle bag, he climbed onto his motorcycle and pulled out of the driveway.

Chapter 7

The frozen pizza he had heated and removed from the oven over an hour ago sat on the counter. It was sliced but not a single slice was yet eaten. An open beer sat on the counter next to it. The pizza was already cooling off, and the beer was already warming up; they were both approaching room temperature.

Matthew was too excited to eat. He was really amped up. Neither returning the Jeep nor riding the motorcycle home was a problem. He had a purpose with those activities. He had a task. He was focused.

But back here, back inside his apartment, it was a different story. He was restless. He was anxious. He was fidgeting.

"Wow!" Matthew said aloud. "Wow, wow, wow!" He stood up from the sofa where he had been sitting for the last several minutes. "That was intense." Reaching down, he picked up the rocks glass sitting on the coffee table. He had poured three fingers of bourbon into the glass within a minute or so of opening the beer that was still sitting untouched on the kitchen counter, next to the uneaten pizza. The beer had sounded like a good idea as he was removing the pizza from the oven, but as soon as he opened the IPA, he decided he wanted something with a little more bite. He opened the bourbon bottle and took a nice long swig. "Now that's what I'm talking about," he said aloud before pouring the three fingers of bourbon that now sat in the glass he had just picked up from the coffee table.

He felt like his insides were vibrating. Raising the glass to his mouth, he paused, "Outstanding!" and then promptly drained the contents of the glass. There was a hummin' and a buzzin' and his head felt fine, except the three ounces of bourbon had done very little to dilute the feeling of electricity coursing through Matthew's body.

Making his way to the kitchen, he set the tumbler on the counter and picked up the bourbon bottle. Tipping the bottle, he poured another two ounces down his throat. Frank had taught his son well.

"Wow, every bit as good as the first one," Matthew said as he thought about the guy down by the river. That was cool, that was intense. What was the line from that song, a country song, maybe by Tim McGraw he thought, something like "I like it, I love it, I want some more of it." I am going to have to do that again, he decided. Hmm, but how am I going to do it? It has to be fun; it has to be unique.

"Whoa! What the heck?" he exclaimed to the empty room. An argument began inside his head, a stream of consciousness leaving him utterly confused and mentally distorted as the thoughts muddled together. *What am I thinking? Seriously? God, please help me. Why am I doing this? Because it is fun. Satan, be gone from me. Leave me alone. God, please give me the strength to fight this. Why am I killing people? God, please help me! You are killing people because you enjoy it. Satan, stay away from me. But it is fun. And, you are good at it. No! God, please help me. Give me strength. But it is fun, oh so much fun. No! I don't want to do this anymore.* Raising the bottle, he took two long gulps. The warm feeling down the back of his throat was comforting, but did little to allay the inner-turmoil. *Yes, you do. You want to do it again. You need to do it again. You want the feeling. You like the feeling. You are good at it. No! I don't want to do this. Please God, HELP ME! Where are you? I need you. God is not here right now. In fact, God is nowhere. God? Please help me. God is not going to help you. What you need is to figure out how to keep this feeling going. You are good at this. When is the last time you were ever good at anything? Never! You never have been any good at anything. You have never fit in. Now is your chance.*

Please God, this is not me. Help me, PLEASE help me. He is not listening to you. You are just having doubts is all. You are good at it. If you are careful, you can have fun and not get caught. This is wrong, so wrong. Satan, be gone. Leave me alone. Please God. Help me. Give me the strength to fight this. Please, please, please help me God. God is not going to help you.

He raised the bottle to his mouth one more time, but stopped. "I don't need this," he said, turning and walking towards the kitchen. He began praying. "Our Father, who art in Heaven, hallowed be thy name. Thy kingdom come, thy will be done. Thy kingdom come, thy will be done. Thy will be done. I am sorry, God, but I do not remember the rest of the words. But please, do not hold that against me, please just help me. Amen."

Feeling a sense of calmness wash over him, he put the cork back into the top of the half empty bottle, the bottle that had been full less than an hour earlier. Sitting the bottle on the counter, he placed the slices of pizza into a plastic bag and placed it in the refrigerator.

"Thank you, thank you, thank you God, for giving me strength. Please forgive me for what I have already done. Please guide me. Please strengthen me. Please let me kill no more. Thank you so much for this warm feeling of peace that has descended upon me. Amen."

Opening his laptop, Matthew checked for email. He had not sent a resume to anyone in over six months, so he had really not expected a job offer, but he could always hope. He could hope his resume was still on file, and he could hope someone would go through those resumes on file. And, he could hope someone would read his resume and see his potential and contact him. But who was he kidding? This was not a fairy tale and hoping these things would happen was about as useful as believing in a ten-day weather forecast. He did not need hope, he needed action.

According to his sister, Matthew was the one who needed to take action. According to her, *he* needed to continue applying for jobs, *he* needed to continue sending resumes, and *he* needed to be building contacts. "That is just the way the game is played," she told him. As much as he loved his sister and valued her input, in this case she was simply wrong, and this was most definitely not a game. *He* was not the one who needed to take action. It was the companies he had already applied to that needed to take action. After all, they were the ones that had done nothing. They had sat on his resume and applications for months and months. It was not his fault. The people reviewing his resume were to blame. The HR people should be held accountable by these companies, they should be fired. They were the ones who were not letting his resume get through. And the managers who did see his resume did not seem capable of realizing his potential. The companies should fire those managers too because of their incompetence in recognizing valuable people like him.

His sister had suggested Matthew go back to school, but what was the point, really? He tried that before, but they did not recognize how smart he really was. He attended the university downtown for a few years —majoring in biology— but he eventually quit. He was smarter than the professors and they just did not seem to appreciate it. One acted like he did, but he was just being sarcastic.

In an economics class, *Intermediate Microeconomic Theory* if he recalled correctly, Matthew had made several comments. The professor, Dr. Jenkins, said, "If you think you know so much, then why don't you just come down here and teach the class." So, Matthew got out of his seat halfway up in the auditorium and made his way down to the dais. As he walked towards the lectern, Dr. Jenkins stepped aside, sarcastically saying, "Have at it, sport." For the next five minutes Matthew lectured, and answered two students' questions. The more Matthew spoke, the clearer it was to Roger Jenkins that Matthew was completely clueless. "Alright, that's enough. You've had your fun, now please return to your seat." Matthew was dumbfounded. He was smarter than the professor and the professor could not stand it. It did not matter that the professor told Matthew he did not know what he was talking about and, turning to the class, Dr. Jenkins told them it would be wise if they disregarded everything Matthew had said. Matthew protested and Dr. Jenkins asked him to please leave the classroom. To Matthew, that was just further justification that he was smarter than the professor, and the professor was jealous. Matthew was expelled from the class and was ultimately given an F for the class. Yep, he was convinced it was just another case of him being so much smarter and, instead of it being appreciated, he was penalized for it.

Matthew was so discombobulated by the professor's treatment and attitude, he did not even bother returning to his seat. Instead, he simply walked out the door, leaving his backpack and books at the desk up on the seventh row of the auditorium. Walking out the door of the classroom, Matthew kept right on walking, walking across the campus to the commuter student lot on Pickens Street. The old 1974 MG MGB belched a cloud of white smoke as he started it up. He had been planning on fixing that someday. The difference between tomorrow and someday is that someday never becomes yesterday.

Pulling out of the parking spot, he and the yellow convertible left nothing behind except for the fresh saucer-sized oil spot and bad memories. He never did return to the campus.

Stirred from his reverie, Matthew mused, "Now there is someone I would like to kill. Dr. Jenkins should be killed. He deserves to die for what he did to me, and I am just the guy to take care of that."

The voice inside his head stirred from its years-long slumber. *Matthew. What? What do we think we are doing? What do you mean? We are talking about killing a professor? Yes, he deserves to die.* The voice is fully awake now. *But Matthew, that is about vengeance, it is not about fun. So? He deserves to die. We do not do retaliation; we do fun. But he deserves it for what he did to me! I never had the guts or the ability to do anything about it before, but I do now. Matthew, that was nine years ago, we should forget about it. I will not forget about it. It is payback time. We do not like that, Matthew; we do not care about payback. But I do. Matthew, we are doing this for fun. Okay, I will make it fun. Trust me, killing that guy will be fun. We are worried Matthew. I am not. Please, just listen to us. We are deviating from the plan. If we start changing things up, if we start killing for revenge, we are bound to make mistakes. I won't make mistakes; I know what I am doing. We are not so sure about that. Revenge makes us personally, even emotionally, tied to the victim. We do not like it. Don't worry, I've got this, it will be fine. Matthew, picking a victim to settle a grudge, this is not randomization.* Paraphrasing Rufus Sewell as Count Adhemar in *A Knight's Tale*, Matthew replied, "You have been heard, you have been measured, and you have been found wanting."

Chapter 8

The light of the early morning sun coming through the window awakened Matthew. Looking at the clock, he saw it was almost seven. Sitting up, he yawned and stretched. What a night, what a night. Wow, that was fun. This first time was great, but last night was so much better. Making contact with the guy, actually talking to the guy, interacting with him was so much better. At the train tracks, I did not even know if it was a male or a female until I happened to see something about it on the news a day or two later.

Not that he was looking for information about it, he just happened to stumble across it. He really was not doing this for the attention. This was all about the excitement, the thrill. In the future he may follow the media coverage just to make sure none of them are linked together.

To make sure none of them are linked together? Certainly! I mean I already have two. The next one needs to be different.

Already gone and forgotten was the prayer to God last night. Already gone was the notion that the sense of peace and contentment may have come from God.

"This next one, it has to be good, it has to be different," he said to the empty room. "I've got to make sure they cannot possibly link this to either of the other two. The first was in Irmo, in Richland County. The guy at the river was in Cayce, in Lexington County. So far, so good. There is no linkage. The same group of cops will not be investigating, and there is no reason for them to think they are related."

The voice inside his head was once again awake. *So, what is it going to be Matthew? Are you a man or a mouse? I am not a mouse! I need to make a statement; I need to do something that will make a statement. Make a statement?* The voice was fully engaged now. *That is neither man nor mouse, Matthew; it is just plain stupid. I am not stupid! Since when did this become about making a statement? I thought we were doing this just for the thrill of it, doing it just to have some fun. Well, we are, I mean I am. But, making a statement is not a bad thing either, is it? People will finally know who I am. People will finally know Matthew Stockmore, they will know Matthew Alan Stockmore is somebody. Is that what we really want? I am not a nobody. Do we really want anyone to know who we are? I can finally be somebody. All my life I have been a nobody. I have failed at pretty much everything, except this. I am good at this. Just stop, just stop and think. If they know who we are, then we will be caught. If they catch us, then we are either going to jail for a very long time, or we are going to get the death penalty. Jail might not be so bad. At least I would fit in, and I would be somebody. I would have respect. Do we understand what they do to people in jail? Yeah, but I would have respect. No one would mess with me because they know I would kill them. Are we out of our mind? We can't get caught. We do not want to get caught. We do not want to go to jail. Did we miss the part about the death penalty? Death penalty, what death penalty? You know, the one where they kill us for killing other people? It is called an execution for a reason; we end up dead. The death penalty is a joke. They rarely execute anyone. And the appeals process drags it out by ten years, maybe more, and then there are stays and appeals. It will never happen Even so, we really do not want to go to jail. Why would we want to go to jail? Look, it is not like I want to go, it is just that I am not afraid to go. Well, we need to be afraid to go. We do not want to get caught. We need to remember this is about having fun. We need to remember that. This is not about making a name for ourself. We do not want people knowing who we are. We are happy with that. I am tired of being a nobody. In this case, we are happy to be a nobody. I am twenty-nine years old, and what do I have to show for it? I have a lousy job, I live in an apartment. I have no house and probably never will have, I have no girlfriend and have not dated anyone seriously for several years, heck,*

I can't even get women to give me the time of day. Is that what this is about? We are not afraid to go to jail because we do not have a girlfriend? Well, no, not really. I was just sayin'. We want to make a name for us because we don't fit in? Yes. Exactly! Well, we better suck it up. We need to get our head screwed on straight. We do not want to get caught. We do not want attention. We are doing this for fun. Yeah, but. There is no yeah but. We need to focus. Remember, the person at the train tracks was just to find out what it was like to kill a person. The guy at the river was just to see if the feeling would be the same. It was better. If we want to keep experiencing that, if we want to build on that, we cannot be caught. We will not be caught. If we are in jail, we will not be able to get that rush, will not be able to feel the excitement. If we killed someone in prison to scratch that itch, we would immediately be thrown in solitary. Then where would we be? No more rush, no more thrill is where we would be. Oh, and by the way, it is not like we would have that opportunity anyway. Have we happened to stop and consider that if given the death penalty we will probably end up on death row? We won't exactly have a lot of interaction with people. Well, there is that; you may have a point. We are glad we are starting to understand. We will keep a low profile. No attention. No making a name for ourself. Okay, have it your way. Great, we are on the same page. We need to focus. When we lose focus, that is when we will make mistakes. No mistakes. Okay, I'm in.

It was nine thirty by the time Matthew finally got out of bed. In the kitchen, taking a pod from the drawer, he made a cup of coffee. While the coffee was brewing, he took the plastic bag of pizza from the refrigerator, removed two slices, and returned the bag to the fridge. Seeing the container of orange juice, he removed the lid and took two large gulps directly from the plastic bottle. He dropped the empty bottle in the trash can. Picking up the cup of hot hazelnut flavored coffee and the slices of cold pizza, Matthew made his way to the sofa. Sitting down, he began to ponder what was next.

After an hour Matthew was still no closer. At first, every idea he came up with he quickly shot down for one reason or another. It was too similar to the other two. It was too close to the other two. It could be linked to the other two. It might look like a pattern. After that, he could not seem to focus and his mind kept drifting. His mind seemed to be blocked. He knew he would not come up with the answer immediately, that it was going to take a bit of time. And, he also knew he could not really force it. Forcing it would mean it did not come naturally, it would mean less than complete focus, and that would increase the possibility of making mistakes.

A semblance of an idea began swirling about in his head. Nothing was clear yet, there was nothing he could mentally grab hold of. It was like a song he could not think of, one where he could softly hear the tune in his head but not yet make out the lyrics. When the words did finally make themselves known, the song title did not. There was something, maybe just an unrelated feeling, but something was stirring.

Matthew was not quite sure what to do with the nascent idea, but he was not just going to sit around waiting. Pulling a pair of hiking boots from the closet, he put them on and walked down the stairs to his motorcycle. Something would materialize.

Chapter 9

He saw the signage indicating camping and alcohol are prohibited. Matthew could not help but laugh. Fortunately, he saw no sign indicating a prohibition against killing someone here, so he was good. Oh sure, there was that little detail of it being illegal to kill someone, but that was, in his mind, more of just a minor inconvenience.

He had driven around Big Rock Lake to the main parking area to get an idea of the number of visitors based on the number of cars in the parking lot. Three parked cars logically indicated there were at least three visitors, but most likely a few more. It was certainly manageable.

"But what if there is no one climbing, what if it is a wasted trip?" he wondered out loud. "Don't' worry, it will be fine."

He had been to Nine Times Forest a few years ago to hike, but he had almost forgotten about it. This past weekend he had gone hiking with a friend at Table Rock State Park. Kayla had sent him a text message Friday evening saying she was going there Saturday with her dog and wanted to know if he wanted to go. What that really meant was she wanted someone to keep her dog occupied while she took pictures. She was like that. It seemed there was always an ulterior motive with her. Having nothing better to do, he agreed. He thought a bit of exercise in the outdoors and the clean fresh air would do him some good. It might even get his mind unstuck and help him figure out what, rather who, to do next.

"It's a date," Matthew texted back.

"To be perfectly clear, this is NOT a date. We are NOT dating. This is just a hike."

Oh good grief. Not this again. "It is just an expression."

"As long as you understand."

She went out of her way to make sure nothing was ever construed as a date. She would call, and be playful. When they were together, she was often smiling, and even flirtatious. People noticed that, and sometimes even commented on her happiness. Her family and friends would tell Matthew how much Kayla thought of him, and of how frequently she talked about him. They all wondered why she would not give him a chance. She apparently had her reasons, reasons unbeknownst to anyone except herself. She was always interested in the bigger better deal; she did not want to sell herself short.

What if she chose to settle down with someone and, in doing so, missed out on someone or something better that was just around the corner? That thought seem to drive Kayla, even at a subconscious level. She wanted kids, wanted a family, more than anything else, but she just could not shake the fear she might get that with the wrong guy. She simply refused to be unhappy and miserable and, ironically, her philosophy often left her unhappy and miserable—and quite lonely.

Traveling north on Moorefield Memorial Highway, generally referred to as Highway 178, they passed a sign for Nine Times Preserve and Big Rock Trail just before the junction of E Preston McDaniel Road on the left. He found that interesting: the sign referred to Nine Times Preserve, but he had thought it was Nine Times Forest. The sign, and seeing the turn off, had jogged his memory and, by the time they reached Cherokee Foothills Highways less than four miles later, he was lost in thought of that long ago hike.

"Hey! Toby!"

"I do not particularly like being called Toby."

"I know, but you did not answer when I call you Matt."

"I do not much care for Matt either."

"Well, you did not respond to Matthew either, so I had to do something to get your attention. We are here."

He looked around and sure enough they were parked. He had not noticed they had turned onto Cherokee Foothills and traveled the four minutes to Table Rock. He was not even aware they had gone through the entrance gate and paid the fee.

"Where have you been? Whatcha thinking about?"

"Oh, nothing really. Just some stuff. Sorry about that. Let's get this show on the road." Matthew, of course, could not tell Kayla what he was really thinking of.

As much as he had wanted to pull out his smart phone and search for Nine Times and Big Rock, he knew he could not do that. He knew he had to be careful, very careful indeed. And that of course meant speaking to no one about anything. He could not begin to count the number of times he had seen in real life crime investigation television shows where someone was arrested and convicted because of something they had said to someone. That would not be his downfall. He was telling absolutely no one anything. After all, he had already decided he was doing this, was killing people, for fun, for sport, not for notoriety and attention. And, part of that fun was just about finding a different way without getting caught. *That* was the thrill, not necessarily the kill. Proving he could outsmart the police, proving he was smarter than them, now *that* was the ultimate goal.

Leaving the main parking lot and continuing on Big Rock Lake Road he drove the three tenths of a mile back down to the alternate grass and gravel parking area along E Preston McDaniel Road. He considered parking his motorcycle behind the clump of trees near the back edge of the parking lot, but he decided that might seem a bit suspicious if someone happened to see it. Suspicion equals attention and that is something he did not need. The whole "see something say something" thing could bite him. If someone saw a motorcycle behind a clump of trees, a call by some well-intentioned busybody to the police to report it might not be too far behind.

Walking back across E Preston McDaniel, he followed the gravel road for about a tenth of a mile and crossed under the high-tension power lines running high overhead. Seeing the trail sign, he took the path on the right and began the one and a quarter mile trek along the Big Rock Mtn Summit trail, following the signs with green blazes along the way.

Approaching the inversion wall, he counted five people in the distance. They were all climbing rock faces. As he got closer, he noticed three were using ropes, while the other two were free-climbing.

Situated at the juncture of the Southern Blue Ridge Mountains and the Piedmont, the almost 1650-acre recreation area encompasses five mountains and caters to enthusiasts of hiking, bouldering and climbing. The crown jewel is Big Rock, which offers year-round crag climbing. Nine Times derives its name from the fact that once upon a time there were nine bridges crossing some creek somewhere. Matthew couldn't recall ever seeing a creek. But he accepted there either is a creek he simply had not seen, or there used to be a creek but no longer is. His thinking drifted to a road he once went down, a road called Five Mile Road. The only thing was the road was eleven miles long. Either roads were joined together over time, the road was lengthened, or someone simply grossly mismeasured it ages ago. He figured a mismeasurement, especially by that amount, was highly unlikely. There was of course another possibility, he thought: someone with an offbeat sense of humor thought naming an eleven-mile-long road Five Mile Road would be hilarious and a great way to mess with people. He once knew someone who named his dog Cat, and his cat Dog. Matthew appreciated off-beat things such as that.

"Don't overthink it, Matthew, don't overthink it. Just focus. Just do it. Focus, Matthew, just focus," he told himself. "Be clean. Be efficient. But most of all, have fun."

Circumventing the climbers, he made his way to the top of Big Rock. He tried to make sure they did not see him, which, considering they were focused on other things, was not too difficult.

The climbers on rope were using a face slightly to the west. The free climbers were on a north facing crag.

Walking to the edge, Matthew carefully peered over. The two free climbers were nearing the top; one was about ten feet from the top, and the other about fifteen feet below.

Glancing to his right, he could not see the climbers with ropes that were around the corner climbing a different face. That, of course, also meant they could not see him.

Hearing a sound, he looked down and saw a hand settle on the rock about three feet from where he was standing. It was the hand of the first free climber as he was reaching the top of Big Rock and beginning to pull himself up.

Matthew's "Hey" seemed to startle the climber.

Raising his head to look up, he saw the bottom of Matthew's hiking boot a foot away from his face.

Laughing as he stomped his foot downward, his boot landed squarely in the climber's face, knocking him back over the edge and into the female climber five feet below him. Losing her grip due to the impact, both climbers fell almost eighty feet to the ground, landing on the rocky ground below. There was not much time for them to really yell in the roughly two and a quarter second free-fall, but they did each make a considerable thump when they landed.

Since they had landed at the base, Matthew was unable to see the actual impact. Grabbing ahold of a small pine, was it a juniper, maybe it was, he held on tightly and nervously dared to quickly glance over the edge. Their bodies lay motionless on the ground.

"Hey, that was pretty cool," Matthew whispered, "two for the price of one."

Still, he could not help but wonder why they never yelled or screamed when they were falling. "Focus. Worry about that later," he told himself. He was actually glad they did not scream on the way down because otherwise the rope climbers around the corner would have heard. The thump. Did they hear the thump? Did they hear the impact? Surely, they did because he could certainly hear it up here where he was standing. But did they know what it was? Were they curious? Matthew did not know and he was not going to wait around to find out.

His initial inclination was to run, but he knew he should not. It might look suspicious if someone saw him running away. On the other hand, he could always say he was running for help if he encountered anyone. He nixed that idea and simply made his way surreptitiously back to the parking lot. With going down considerably easier than going up, he covered the mile and a quarter in less than seventeen minutes.

Feeling restless and anxious, Matthew made his way down Highway 178 into downtown Pickens. He needed something to eat and wanted something to drink. Perhaps he had that backwards, he thought. He needed something to drink and wanted something to eat. Rolling into downtown, 178 changed names to Ann Street. Coming to West Main Street, he decided to take a right for no particular reason other than he felt like it.

One minute later he saw something appealing, the Fiesta Mexican Grill tucked behind the Burgess & Taylor General Store. A margarita suddenly sounded good to him.

Parking his motorcycle in the front row, he casually strolled to the portico, above which hung the establishment's rectangular sign featuring three equally sized vertical pales of green, white, and red. Matthew wondered why a Mexican restaurant would have a sign in the colors of Italy. Had this originally been an Italian restaurant which was repurposed as a Mexican eatery?

The confusion was easily understandable. The flag of both countries are indeed tricolor flags consisting of the same colors and in the same order. The key difference is that the Mexican flag bears in the center of the white center panel the national coat of arms of Mexico. The sign on the front of the portico had no coat of arms, thus the confusion with the Italian flag. The sign was instead emblazoned with Fiesta Grill Mexican Restaurant.

Sitting at the table in the booth eating the complimentary chips and salsa, he was still astonished by all the brilliant colors around him. From the bright green walls to the colors on the booth, Matthew could not help thinking that it looked like a box of crayons had exploded in here.

Picking up the margarita glass, he took a nice long sip through the straw. He actually wanted it on the rocks, but he knew if he had it that way, he would drink far too many of them. He still had an hour and a half to ride to get back home so he thought it best to not drink too much.

He leaned back in the padded booth and pondered. They did not make a sound, not even a sound. Well, except for when they hit the ground. That part was pretty cool. I had not expected that. Then again, I did not expect two for the price of one. A smile crossed his face and he took another drink of the margarita. Why did they not scream? Surely, they had time. How long did they have? "Hmm. I should calculate that," he mumbled.

After a moment of thought, Matthew remembered an equation, or at least thought he did, that stated velocity was equal to the acceleration due to gravity times the duration of time in free-fall.

"Let's see if I remember correctly," he muttered. But was it even the correct equation? He pulled out his smart phone and did a quick search for velocity of free-falling bodies. Without reading everything on the web page he opened, he focused on *"the rate of acceleration due to gravity is thirty-two feet per second per second, or thirty-two feet per second squared"* He did not know the duration of the fall, heck, that is what he was trying to calculate. Well, that was a dead end.

Matthew could sometimes be a bit obsessive. If he set his mind on something, he usually stuck with it and even became obsessed with it. He generally would not quit, would not let it ago, until he either achieved his goal or something else popped up that captured his attention and laser-like focus.

"Hmm. I need a different equation," he said without realizing he was speaking aloud. "For an exact answer do I need calculus? Heck, I don't know. All I really need is an approximation. How about the tried–and–true distance equals rate times time?"

Absentmindedly reaching into the basket for another chip, his fingers found nothing. He barely noticed. Another drink of the margarita and the glass was empty.

"Hmm. Rate times time. A little crude. Perhaps a variation of that equation? Something involving velocity rather than simply rate. What is that velocity equation?" The answer was there somewhere. It was on the tip of his tongue. Like a song title he could not remember while listening to the song. "Something like velocity is distance divided by time. Ugh. What I really need is calculus for an exact answer. Velocity is actually the rate of change of an object's position with respect to a frame of reference and time. That means differentiation. I need speed and a direction vector. Wait a second! I don't need to be exact; I just need a good rough estimate. Rough, but pretty close. Let's keep this simple."

He pulled up another web page, https://www.omnicalculator.com/physics/free-fall. Again, he did not bother reading the entire page. He stopped scrolling though the page when he saw the free fall equation. "Hmm. This might work. Distance is equal to one half the product of the acceleration due to gravity and time squared." Matthew was not sure if that was the correct equation. He thought it might be, but if it wasn't, considering the short distance it would probably be good enough. "Knowing about how far the climbers fell, or at least making an educated guess, I can simply solve that equation for time."

Matthew again leaned back into the booth and noticed the couple at the table across from his looking at him. Oops! He gave them a polite smile, a quick nod, and a half-wave of his hand, and decided he needed to keep his thoughts to himself. If Big Rock is eighty feet high, or thereabouts, then if the guy was, say, six feet tall and his hand was extended to reach to top, that means his feet are about seventy-four feet high off the ground and his torso is about seventy-eight feet high. Maybe his feet are seventy-two feet above the ground? But would he really be standing straight up? I don't think so. Not if he is climbing. So, let's stick with the seventy-four feet. The woman was about five feet below him, and when he collided into her his momentum would have been altered. That is where calculus and differentiation would be handy, but I don't need that precision, this doesn't have to be exact. Heck, let's just say they fell from about seventy-two feet. Per the equation, simply dividing seventy-two by thirty-two yields two and one quarter seconds. A fall from the full eighty feet would yield a time of two and a half seconds. Great, I know they fell for between two and two and a half seconds. Two to two and a half seconds? Hmm. It seemed like a lot longer. I am not sure if the math is correct, but it should be close enough.

Matthew thought it was pretty cool watching them fall and trying to grab at nothing. The expression on their faces was priceless. A smile crossed his face as he thought about a line from an old commercial "There are some things money can't buy, for everything else there is Mastercard."

Reaching into the basket, he retrieved and slowly ate two tortilla chips. He was not aware someone had replaced the empty basket.

Still, why did they not scream? The thought gnawed at him. Were they simply too shocked to scream? Were they too scared to scream? Did they figure it would do no good? Or were they too busy praying? "I do not understand, I just do not understand," he mumbled. Picking up the glass, he pulled another drink of the frozen margarita through the straw.

Realizing the empty glass had been replaced by a full glass, he supposed he had obviously, at some point, consented to another drink. He also noticed the plate of food sitting in front of him. Looking at his watch, Matthew realized he had been sitting here for almost forty-five minutes. Oops! Where did the time go?

Ordinarily he might have gotten the fish tacos or fish burrito. But not today. Today, all he wanted was a good old-fashioned burrito, either chicken or beef would do.

The number forty-two, the Baja Burrito. The description of the menu described it as *"Rolled flour tortilla filled with rice, whole pinto beans, lettuce, pico de gallo and sour cream, steak or grilled chicken with a blend of white cheese."* He asked if they could make it combination of steak and chicken and they consented for two dollars more.

"Really? You do not have to do any extra work. I do not want extra meat. I want the same amount of meat; I just want half steak and half chicken. Why can't you just do that?"

"We can, but it will just be two dollars more. That is our policy."

"Well, my policy is not to be a sucker. I'll just go elsewhere."

"Is there a problem?" came the voice from someone else.

"No, not really, I was just leaving."

"What seems to be the problem?"

"No problem really. I wanted a burrito with half steak and half chicken. He told me it would cost two dollars extra. I decided to go elsewhere."

"We do have to charge for extra meat. We cannot just give food away. You can understand that."

"I did not want you to give me anything. I wanted the same amount of meat, I just wanted half of it to be chicken and half of it to be steak. It would be the same amount of meat. Surely you can understand *that*."

"Please, sir, sit back down. I am terribly sorry for the misunderstanding. We can certainly do that. What would you like to drink? We will give you a drink on the house, no? A beer? A margarita, maybe?"

As Matthew sat back down, he could not help but wonder momentarily if perhaps he should have just ordered the shrimp fajitas. He was then lost in thought wondering again about the lack of screams.

Taking a bite of the Baja Burrito, he was happy with his choice. The food was excellent. It was a bit cold, but he supposed he could not really complain about that. He had no idea how long it had been sitting in front of him.

Something was off. Something was not quite right, he thought while taking the last bite of burrito. It was like something was sitting in the back of his mind and he just now allowed the thought to come out front.

With a smile crossing his face, Matthew said, "Hello Mr. Thought. Welcome to the frontal cortex. We hope you had a great trip from the subconscious."

With the smile fading, he briefly thought about the climbers. Oh, sure it was great fun, and it was pretty cool watching them fall, but where was the excitement? Where was the thrill? Maybe he just missed that part because of being fixated on the lack of a scream.

Drinking that last bit of water in the glass, he shrugged it off. Looking at the bill, he dropped some cash on the table and made his way towards the door.

Chapter 10

The metamorphosis had begun. He was not quite sure when that happened. Was it a gradual thing? Was there a defining point? A tipping point where things clicked, or snapped? He wasn't sure, he simply wasn't sure.

It was more of an evolution, a movement from point A to point B, and there was no turning back. Was not unidirectional change the whole point of evolving? There was no real defining point, it was more of an awakening really. It was a point where Matthew suddenly realized the change, but only because he thought about it for a moment. He was not sure if he should be excited about it or not.

For better or worse, Matthew realized he was acting more or less like a serial killer. Oh sure, after the first kill he did casually wonder what it would take to be classified as a serial killer, and had even joked he would not be allowed to join their club. But now, now he was wondering if he was not indeed becoming a member of the serial killer club without even realizing it.

What started as killing for the thrill of it, killing mainly to see if he could get away with it, had now become a need to kill. It was no longer just about getting a thrill, just having some fun, it was now about fulfilling a need. With that came a change in attitude more so than a change in behavior.

Um, Matthew, we are concerned. About what? About the way things are changing. What do you mean? This is not just about fun anymore. The first one was just to see what it felt like. The second was to see if we had the same feeling afterwards. Yeah, and we did. It was great, wasn't it? We certainly agree it was great. We think it was great fun and a great feeling. So, what is the problem? We think that rush, that thrill is gone. What are you talking about? The climbers; we do not remember a thrill. Yes, it was cool, but we do not remember a rush. What does it matter? You just said it was cool. Well, the girl, that was about us scratching an itch. We are not so sure that was about a thrill. That was hardly planned. That was an impulse. Do I have to do this now? Matthew, we are just concerned that we are not killing for fun anymore, that we are now killing to satisfy a need. Remember, part of the fun in all of this was finding a different way without getting caught. THAT is the thrill, not necessarily the kill. What difference does it make? I mean, I, or we, can have some fun along the way. We need to be careful. If this is becoming an obsession, we think there might be mistakes. We think a pattern might develop. Look, I will be careful. I know what I am doing. Each one will be different. I have told you that before. I will be creative in the approach. There will be no pattern. Just let me have some fun. Matthew, we are just wondering, are we a serial killer or not? Yeah, I guess maybe I am.

"Here's to me!" Matthew exclaimed as he swallowed a shot of bourbon straight from the bottle. "I am officially a serial killer," he exclaimed, taking another swallow of bourbon. He had come into the kitchen to get another beer, his third one, when the milestone occurred to him so, of course, he had to celebrate. Recorking the bottle and setting it on the counter, he reached into the refrigerator and grabbed a bottle of IPA.

"Note to self, I need to get more beer," he said aloud upon realizing there were only four more beers. Well, only four more IPAs.

It was just after seven thirty. He had returned home from Pickens roughly four hours ago. Walking up the stairs to his apartment over the garage, he had come inside and, after turning on the television, he sat down in the recliner and immediately drifted off to sleep for the next two hours. The two large margaritas he drank at the Mexican restaurant had a definite impact on him, more so than he had realized during the two-hour ride back home.

Fully awake now, Matthew walked back into the small living room and sat down on the sofa with his opened beer and a bag of potato chips. He reminded himself not to eat too many chips, as he was having dinner in West Columbia in about two hours.

Sitting back, he stretched his legs out in front of him. Resting his heels on the coffee table, his excitement quickly built as he began reminiscing about the events earlier in the day at Big Rock.

"Now that was cool, way cool," Matthew said aloud, taking a slow swallow of IPA.

He remembered laughing as he stomped his boot into the dude's face. He could not quite remember the exact feeling though. He thought he felt resistance as his foot made contact, but did he really feel that, or was it just a Smokey, a Smokey Robinson as he called it? "Was is just my imagination?"

Thinking, thinking, trying to recall the exact sensation. Another swallow of beer. It was so hard to tell. "I remember him looking up. Boy was he sure surprised when he saw my boot. If I was him, I would not let go immediately. I would try to hold on, hold on for dear life. I guess he would have done the same thing. But did he have time? Surely his instincts would have kicked in and he would have tried to hold on. I just don't know. Still, there would have had to be some resistance when my boot hit his face, right? There just had to be." Try as he might, he simply could not remember. He yearned to recall. He really wanted to know if his foot met initial resistance as the guy hung on, and then if his foot sped up as the guy began to fall. He wanted to recall that feeling, the feeling of his boot, of his foot, driving the climber to his death. Alas, so far, no such luck.

Another swallow of beer, a long swallow. Ah, but one thing he surely remembered was the fall. That, in itself, convinced Matthew the guy must have tried to hang on, there must have been some resistance, whether or not he could recall his foot slowing down.

"Man, when that cat was flailing his arms, his arms were all over the place! I am telling you, man, that dude, his arms were flailing all *over* the place. He was trying to grab anything and everything, except there was nothing to grab. And that chick. Wow, he just grabbed that chick on the way down! Was he hoping grabbing her would save him? What a shmuck. Of course he was not grabbing. Instead of grabbing her, his arm clearly hit her and knocked her off the rock. I had not planned on her, but hey, I'll take the nice bonus. Two for the price of one!"

The funny thing was the guy stopped flailing after that. And, she never did flail, at least for the brief moment he could see her. Both of their arms were extended towards him, as if they were asking him for help.

After that, he really could not see them. When he peered over the edge, while holding on to the tree, (Matthew did not like heights, heights always made him nervous) the next thing he saw was the two bodies lying on the ground on their backs.

He would have liked to have seen the actual impact. Now that would have been cool.

Still, he could not help but wonder why they never yelled or screamed. He still had no explanation for that and expected that he probably never would, and that was a bit frustrating for Matthew. So many things he had read on the internet indicated people screamed when falling, seemingly to almost assert it was guaranteed to happened, and those articles even offered psychological and physiological explanations for it. Then again, that was the internet. He recalled a commercial, he thought maybe it was a car insurance commercial, where a young woman and man are speaking.

"Where did you hear that?"

"The internet."

"And you believe it?"

"Yeah. They can't put anything on the internet that isn't true."

"And where did you her that?"

Both responding in unison, "The internet."

"Oh, look. Here comes my date. I met him on the internet. He's a French model."

The bespectacled and bearded sloppily-dressed guy wearing a fanny pack, who was certainly not French model material, or any other model for that matter, uttered with no European accent, "Bon Jour."

He had read somewhere that something like fifty or sixty percent of the stuff on the internet is either fake or simply wrong. That car insurance commercial was certainly making fun of the credibility of the internet.

Regardless of what the articles and opinions on the internet proclaimed, whether or not they more or less asserted someone falling was guaranteed to scream, he had seen first-hand two people fall and not scream. Still, he could not quite understand why they did not utter a sound.

After another swig of beer, which emptied the bottle, Matthew stood up from the couch and nonchalantly began whistling *Zip-A-Dee-Doo-Dah* off key as he made his way to the trash can in the kitchen. He remembered whistling that same tune as he approached his motorcycle during the walk down from Big Rock.

Emerging from the bathroom after brushing his teeth, he began whistling again, still as off key as before. Picking up his wallet, keys, and cell phone from the counter, he made his way to the front door. It was time he headed to his sister's house.

Picking up the phone, he sent her a quick text. "On the way. Leaving now."

Chapter 11

"Great dinner, sis," Matthew said while helping Todd and Alex clear the dishes from the table. "Great lasagna."

"Why, thank you. And thanks, Matt, for the wine. Great choice. We've never had Chianti before."

"Yeah, it was a good wine. Thanks for helping clean the table too," Todd said as he put the leftover lasagna into the fridge.

"Sure, no problem."

"We've got dessert too, but that will have to wait a bit. Todd has this thing he has to do."

"Yeah, a work thing. It will only take about an hour. You two can go sit on the patio and have another glass of wine or something."

"What is wrong, Matt? You seem distracted. Unhappy. Maybe even lost."

"I'm fine, I guess. I don't know. I am bored. I'm restless. I don't know what to do."

"Let God guide you. God has a plan. Let His plan for you unfold."

"Yeah. What a crock. My job is lousy, I live in a rented room over someone's garage or workshop or whatever you want to call it, I have very few friends, and I have no girlfriend and no prospect of finding one anytime soon. Oh yeah. Life is just a barrel of monkeys. Everything goes to hell in a handbasket and you want me to turn to God?"

"Fear not, Matt. God is there with you."

"Really? Where has God been in all of this?"

"God is there, He is here," Alex replied. "God is everywhere."

"God is nowhere. He has never been there for me."

"Have you tried praying? Have you tried praying to God?"

"Yeah, right." Matthew could not very well tell Alex, his own sister, that he had tried praying to God to help him stop killing people.

"Prayer works. You should try it. Scripture tells us to pray to God and He will give us whatever we ask in his name." While cleaning up from dinner, a light drizzle had begun outside and they had settled in the den. Picking up the Bible next to her, Alex continued, "According to the gospel of Mark, Mark 11:24, Christ

94

says, `Therefore I tell you, whatever you ask in prayer, believe that you have received it, and it will be yours.'"

"To quote Jim Morrison, `You cannot petition the Lord with prayer.'"

"Jim who?"

"Jim. Jim Morrison. Of the Doors. Just one of the greatest rock bands of all time."

"My source is the Bible, the word of God, and your source of infinite wisdom is some song lyrics?"

"Jim had it right. You cannot petition the Lord with prayer."

"You are wrong. I have already given you scripture that proves you can. Jesus Christ himself told us to pray to God and He will give us whatever we ask in His name." Flipping through pages, "John 4:13, Jesus also tells us, `Whatever you ask in my name, this I will do, that the Father may be glorified in the Son.'"

"That is pretty convenient, but if I recall, sometimes the answer is yes, no, or not right now."

"Well yes, but—"

"No buts." Referring to his smart phone Matthew continued, "I give to you, `And this is the confidence that we have toward Him, that if we ask anything according to his will, He hears us.'"

"True."

"And you have no problem with that? It shoots a hole in your argument to simply ask God in prayer and He will give it to you. What John tells us is that God will give it to us if that is what God wants. That we should really pray to God and ask Him to give us what He wants, not what we want. That whole thy will be done thing. So, the idea of petitioning the Lord in prayer for something we want is fundamentally flawed. It apparently does not work that way."

"But scripture tells us we are to pray with faith and God will hear and grant our prayers. Jesus says so in Matthew 21:22. I give you, to use your expression, `And whatever you ask in prayer, you will receive, if you have faith.'"

Reading again from his smart phone, "And James 4:43, `You ask and do not receive, because you ask wrongly.'"

"True, you have to ask with faith."

"Ah, so now there are catches, caveats, and disclaimers. You started off by quoting scripture that simply said ask God for something in prayer and he will grant it. Then we find out that we are supposed to pray to God to give us what He wants and not what we want. Then, there is the added catch we must pray with faith in order for the prayer to be answered. But, if we refer back to the passage from Matthew that you previously quoted, `whatever you ask in prayer, believe that you have received it, and it will be yours.` According to that, I only have to believe I have received it in order to get what I prayed for. A bit of circular convoluted logic, don't you think?"

"You are making this confusing. You are confusing me. You only need to have faith. Believe in Our Lord, in Jesus Christ our Savior."

"I have no faith."

"You need to have faith. You need to believe in Jesus Christ. You need to have faith in God. God is about love."

"Love? Really? Not always. Your Jesus had a bit of a temper, did he not?"

"Jesus was kind and compassionate. Jesus was all about love."

"You are mistaken."

"Perhaps you should read scripture."

"I have. Once upon a time I read your book of fairy tales."

"They are not fairy tales. They are the inspired words of God."

"So, it is all true?"

"Yes, it is. You can count on it. You can bet your life on it, and perhaps you should consider doing just that."

"But you will concede there are errors and omissions due to translations. Plus, there are inaccuracies due to mans' limited ability to express himself."

"There are no inaccuracies in the Bible."

"The confusing part about prayer, where there are apparently a lot of restrictions in the fine print, we'll ignore that. Let us also ignore the flaws in Genesis."

"Genesis is accurate. There are no flaws in the Bible. The Bible is truth."

"The Bible is flawed. It was written by man."

"The words in the Bible are divinely inspired. They are truth."

"Then explain this to me. From Genesis, specifically Genesis 1:3." Matthew said, referencing the website he had pulled up on his smart phone.

"Which version is that? Which translation? King James is the authoritative version. You confused me with the version you were using earlier. It was not King James."

"This is from the NIV version, if you want to play along. But, since you assert there are no flaws, differences, or discrepancies due to translation, it really should not matter which version we use.

"But King James is—"

"But Kings James nothing. You said there are no errors due to translation, and that the Bible is all inspired by God, so any version should be fine. NIV it is."

Matthew began reading Genesis from his smart phone. "'And God said, Let there be light, and there was light. God saw that the light was good, and he separated the light from the darkness. God called the light "day," and the darkness he called "night." And there was evening, and there was morning—the first day.` So, on the first day God created light and dark. Indeed, on the second day God even refers to evening and morning."

"Correct. God created light and dark on the first day."

"Then riddle me this. Why then if light and dark are created on the first day, but the sources of light are not created until the fourth day? I give you Genesis 1:14, 'And God said, "Let there be lights in the vault of the sky to separate the day from the night, and let them serve as signs to mark sacred times, and days and years, and let them be lights in the vault of the sky to give light on the earth. And it was so. God made two great lights—the greater light to govern the day and the lesser light to govern the night. He also made the stars. God set them in the vault of the sky to give light on the earth, to govern the day and the night, and to separate light from darkness. And God saw that it was good. And there was evening, and there was morning—the fourth day.' Weird also since there was now morning and evening created on the fourth day, yet God refers to morning and evening on the second day. A bit of a logic problem and a timing problem. Hmm. God refers to light that exists on the first day, yet the sources of light are not created until the fourth day, and God refers to the existence of evening and morning on the second day, yet he does not create them until the fourth day."

"No, that is not a problem at all. God is all knowing. Time is infinite with God. In fact, there is no time with God. Everything is instantaneous with God. There is no notion of space and time."

"Pretty convenient, don't you think? Well, try this one on for size. Genesis tells us God created two great sources of light; one to light the day and the other to light the night. Well, the Sun is a source of light, but the Moon, the Moon is a rock. It is a reflector. It reflects the light of the Sun. The Moon is not a great source of light. It is a reflector."

"But that depends on what God meant."

"So, God could have had it wrong? Surely God, if He exists and is all knowing, did not get it wrong about the Moon."

"Man may not have understood God. Or, God explained it in terms man could understand. The words of the Bible are, after all, divinely inspired. It is *not* wrong."

"Man may not have understood God? What, and wrote down the wrong thing, and God let him do it? Regardless, it is wrong. The Moon is not a source of light. And your excuse is that God explained it to man in terms man could understand? So, God knowingly gave man incorrect information?"

"No, not at all. It is just that maybe man could not comprehend it. That God did not want it to be confusing."

"Oh, yeah, like the whole trinity thing. Christianity has no problem with simply saying there are some things we cannot comprehend and leave it at that."

"You need to have faith. You need to just believe the words of God. The Bible is real. The Bible is the truth. The Bible is the living word."

"You need to quit believing in fairy tales. If your God is real, then you would be better served learning the concepts of the Bible. Focus on the principles. In that way, flaws and inaccuracies in the words written by man would not really matter."

"Again, there are no flaws in the Bible. The Bible is truth. You find flaws because you lack faith."

"Wow, what blinders. So, I should take everything in the Bible as truth, correct? And focus on the words as written?"

"Absolutely."

"In that case, back to my point about Christ having a temper."

"That simply is not true. That is heresy. Jesus Christ had no temper. He was perfect in every way."

"Ah, then we should ignore that little bit about turning over the tables in the temple? Wasn't that done out of anger?"

"Well, yes, but it was only because they were disrespecting His Father's house."

"Ah, so justified anger? Okay, but what did the poor little fig tree ever do to Jesus? Absolutely nothing."

"Excuse me? I don't follow you."

"I give you Matthew 11:12." Matthew again began reading from his smart phone, "'On the following day, when they came from Bethany, he was hungry. And seeing in the distance a fig tree in leaf, he went to see if he could find anything on it. When he came to it, he found nothing but leaves, for it was not the season for figs. And he said to it, "May no one ever eat fruit from you again." And his disciples heard it.' So, let me get this right, Jesus is hungry, and he wants figs but it is not yet fig season so he curses the tree for not producing fruit out of season? As the Son of God, if not God Himself, should he have not known when fig season was? Yet, he cursed the poor innocent fig tree for doing what fig trees, fig trees He created by the way, for doing what fig trees are supposed to do."

Alex stood up. "You are hopeless."

"Isn't that rich? Someone supposedly a Christian telling another human being they are hopeless."

"You need only believe. According to Romans 10:9-10, 'Because, if you confess with your mouth that Jesus is Lord and believe in your heart that God raised him from the dead, you will be saved. For with the heart one believes and is justified, and with the mouth one confesses and is saved.' Again, you need only believe and have faith."

"Well, then, I guess I am just out of luck. I have no faith and I don't believe in God."

"Then surely you will burn in Hell for all eternity."

"Not really."

"Surely you will, for it is so. This you will find out at your time of judgment."

"Ah, but if I do not believe in God, then surely I do not believe in final judgment. When I die, I am, well, dead. I do not believe in the concept of heaven, which means therefore, by extension, I do not believe in Hell. You can believe in your fairy tales all you want to, but they do not apply to me."

"Matthew, you are going to be in for one heck of a surprise when you die and stand before God in judgment."

"Well then, your God is going to be in for one heck of a surprise when I do not show up."

"Matthew, Matthew, you have no choice. It is going to happen. Just because you do not believe something exists does not make it so, no more than believing in something that does not exist will make it exist. Some kids believe in Unicorns, but no matter how much they believe that, Unicorns do not exist. Old lore asserts that it takes seven years to digest gum, which of course is not true. And, there is a supposed fact that if you drop a penny from the top of the Empire State building it will kill a person on the ground if it hits them. No matter how many times people repeat it and no matter how many people believe it, it simply does not make it true. Just because you do not believe in God, do not believe in Heaven and Hell and final judgement, just because you do not believe these things does not make them not exist."

"And, no matter how many of you people believe in God, a God you can neither see, touch, nor feel, will make Him exist."

"It is a matter of faith."

"I have no faith."

"May God have mercy on your soul when you die. I will pray for you, Matt."

"Back to petitioning the Lord with prayer? No thank you. I will be just fine."

"Believe that if you will. But that does not change the fact you *will* stand before God in judgement when you die. You have up until your last breath on this earth to choose God. He is compassionate. He will give you every chance. God loves you."

Matthew stood up. "Yeah, whatever." He turned around and began walking away.

"Matt, wait."

Stopping, Matthew said with his back still to Alex, "You know, your Bible, the King James version by the way, mentions Unicorns a half dozen times, if not more."

"What are you talking about?"

"You said earlier that believing in Unicorns would not make them exist."

"Yeah, so it is true."

"But you also said the Bible is unerring, that every word in it is true. I am just pointing out that the Bible mentions unicorns several times. You say they do not exist, we know they do not exist, but the Bible says they do exist."

"It does not quite say that. It does not state they exist."

"Well, the Bible does reference unicorns, and references the horn of a unicorn. It seems weird they would reference something that does not exist."

"Well, they must have meant something like an ox then, it was probably a translation thing."

"Ah ha!" He turned to face Alex. "When I said earlier there were errors or discrepancies due to translations, you rejected that. You said there were no inaccuracies in the Bible. Now you say there are in reference to unicorns."

"Look, this is not about the Bible. Let us not get bogged down in that."

"That is about par for the course. Whenever a Bible-thumper gets cornered, they suddenly want to talk about something else."

"Matt, please. You know me better than that. I am not a Bible-thumper, as you call it, and you know it. I am just concerned about you."

"Yeah, you want to save me," Matthew exclaimed, while exaggeratedly flailing his hands in front of him.

"You are not funny."

"I thought it was hilarious."

"I am sure you did. Now seriously, Matt, I am concerned about you. I love you."

"I love you too, sis. I'll be fine. I do not need any saving."

"Come on, Matt. Let's sit back down. We can at least drink our wine," Alex said while pointing to the glasses of red wine. "You have not even touched it. Neither of us have."

Sitting back down, he picked up the glass and took a sip of the dark red wine.

Cradling the glass in her hands, Alex spoke softly, "What happened to you? Why are you so anti-God? That is not the way we were raised."

"You know, I've tried the whole God thing. I tried believing in God, but God certainly did not seem to believe in me."

"That is not true, Matt. God believes in you. God loves you."

"No, no that's not true. God does *not* love me. I don't know if I would say that God hates me, but God does not exist."

"Why do you say that? That is not true! God loves you, Matthew. God does exist!"

"Well, He has a funny way of showing it. It seems like everything in life works against me, like everyone is against me."

"Everyone is not against you. No one is against you."

"Whenever I start to make progress, someone gets in the way. It is not my fault. It is God's fault. He has the ability to change things, has the ability to put the right people in my life, has the ability to open people's eyes and let them see my true potential. But no! No one sees my potential. Heck, most people do not even know I exist."

"Matt, listen to me. That is not God's fault. God is not doing that. You cannot blame God."

"You know, you are right. I would say I can and do blame God. But it is a lot easier to say He does not exist.

That way I am not blaming Him. It is kind of hard to blame Him if He does not exist."

"Do not say that! It is not true. God does exist. God does love you."

"No, He does not. If anything, He hates me."

"Matthew! That is not true! I will not have you saying that."

"Fair enough. If God existed, He would hate me. But since He does not exist, He cannot hate me. He is kind of like those unicorns."

"Matthew Alan Stockmore! I will not have any more of that, certainly not in this house. You listen to me, and you listen well. God does exist. God is there for you; God is always there for you. All you need to do is ask. And, believe it or not, God does love you."

"Well, he has a funny way of showing it. You know, sis, you were not there. You were not there for a bunch of stuff. All that stuff with Dad."

"I know, I know, but Mom told me about some of it."

"It is not the same. You never had Dad beat the crap out of you. I did. You never had Dad break your arm. I did. I missed two days of school because of that. I was only eight years old!" Tears began welling up in Matthew's eyes, as he added in a much softer voice, "all because I ate a goldfish at a party."

"I am so sorry, Matt. I did not know."

"How could you know? You were not there. You were not even born yet." Tears were slowly streaming down Matthew's cheeks. "You never had to deal with Dad. The old man could be pretty mean." Looking over, he saw tears welling up in Alex's eyes. "Oh gee. Hey, look, I am sorry. I did not mean to upset you." Slowly standing up, he added, "I think maybe I should leave."

"No, stop. Do not apologize, Matt. Don't you dare apologize. I am so sorry. You are right, I did not have to deal with him or go through anything you went through. He was gone by the time I was two. I do not remember anything about him, except for the few things Mom told me. She did not like to talk about him, and you would hardly ever talk about him, understandably so. Heck, I don't even know what Dad looked like because Mom did not keep any pictures of him."

"There were not that many pictures of him to start with. The man was not much into the whole family photo thing. But trust me, I remember what he looked like. Every time the man beat me, it is like his image was etched deeper in my mind."

Through her now almost uncontrollable sobbing, all Alex could manage was, "Matt, oh Matt, I am so sorry. I am sorry, Matt."

Matthew walked over to Alex. She stood up and immediately threw her arms around her brother. "Matt. Matt." And with that, the flood gates opened up even more. When the sobbing subsided, Alex spoke again. "Matthew, because of what happened, that is all the more reason to rely on God. He was surely there to protect you from him."

It was not his fault, and it was not intentional, but Matthew simply could not suppress the guffaw as he took two steps backward. "Yeah, right! God was there to protect me? Where was he during all the beatings? Where was he during the broken ribs? That broken arm? That was mine. The old man broke my arm, not God's arm. And God did nothing but stand by and let it happen."

"But Matt—"

Without pausing, Matthew continued, "Oh, I prayed, oh boy how I prayed. The number of times I prayed. After every beating, I prayed. And you know what happened? You know what that got me? Just more beatings down the road, with each one more severe than the last one. I swear, the old man enjoyed hurting me. And you know what? I am pretty convinced God enjoyed watching it."

"Okay, Matthew, I understand now why you might feel that way. But listen for a moment. Try to be a little bit open minded. For me, okay? God was there. You may not see it, and you may not feel like he was there for you."

"Really?"

"Please. Just listen. God does not stop bad things from happening, but that does not mean God lets them happen or enjoys seeing them happen. He does not encourage them or condone them. He simply does not interfere. There is such a thing as free will. But God was there for you. Can you imagine how much worse it would have been if God had not been there?"

"Yeah, right. First you tell me I am supposed to pray to God to change things, but that will apparently only happen if it is His will. You know, I prayed, I prayed and prayed to please make it stop. It did not. I prayed and prayed for Dad to die. That did not happen either. I prayed and prayed for Mom to just take us and run away, and that did not happen either, at least not until the end. If God was answering that prayer, he certainly took his sweet time about it. So, I prayed again, over and over and over for God to please just make it stop. It never did. The abuse became more frequent and more severe. It was a never-ending cycle. The more the old man drank, the more he beat me. The more he beat me, the more he drank so he would not have to deal with what he had done to me. What a coward. I see that now. Beat on the poor helpless kid and then hide from the shame behind booze. What a loser. But where was God in all of this? You say it could have been worse if God was not there? But what difference did it make if He was there? You also said God does not interfere. So, I am supposed to pray for God to change an outcome, but that will happen only if God wants it too. What is the phrase? If it is His will, right? Thy will be done. So, apparently God's will was for me and Mom to be used as punching bags? Gee, I sure am glad God was there to sit and watch."

Making no attempt to placate him, Alex said, "I do understand the cynicism. I mean, I can understand why.

I might even say you are entitled to it. But it could have been so much worse without God there."

"Really? How so? If God does not interfere, then God being there did not lessen anything. Did it?"

"Think about this, Matt. God was there for you. And for Mom too. He gave you, gave both of you, the strength to endure, the strength to survive. And He gave Mom the strength to finally get us out of there. Can you imagine how hard it would have been without that, without God? You have a point that God being there did not stop the beatings, did not stop the abuse. But God being there helped you survive it. Maybe He did not change what was happening, did not change the events, but He changed *you* by giving *you* the strength to survive it. You may not appreciate that, but I do. I love you more than you will ever know and I, for one, am grateful that God was there for you."

"Maybe. But we have no way to test that theory, and I certainly am not going to go through that again. You know, I have tried praying about some stuff recently. I have prayed and asked God to help me through some stuff."

"Great!"

"No, not really, so far, the result is the same as it has always been. Absolutely nothing. God has ignored me completely. He ignores me now like He did way back when. You say He gave me and Mom the strength to endure. Maybe, maybe not. But now, I can tell you there is nothing. I have prayed to God to change some stuff, to help me change, and there has been no response. Nothing. Nothing has changed. God is not there. God does not care. God does not exist."

Alex started to tell her brother that things happen on God's time, not ours. But thought better of it. "I am so sorry, Matthew."

"It is all good. I think I will head home now."

"Hey, where are you going?" Todd said entering the den. "It's time for dessert."

"Thanks, but I might go ahead and head out."

"Nonsense. Alex made a chocolate cake. And we have ice cream too. She got it just for you."

"Please, Matt. Stay for dessert," Alex added.

"Well, if you have ice cream, how could I say no?"

With Todd leading the way, Matthew followed him into the kitchen.

Alex sat for a few moments longer, and quietly prayed for Matthew, prayed for God to have mercy on Matthew's soul, to give Matthew another chance.

Chapter 12

On the way home from dinner with Alex and Todd, Matthew could not help but think about the old man.

During dessert, Alex had inquired about their father.

"So," she started slowly, "whatever happened to Dad?"

"What do you mean?"

"I mean, like, where is he buried?"

"Honestly, sis, I have no idea."

"I was only three when it happened and, well, Mom would never talk about it."

"Well, I was only thirteen."

Alex had tried asking her mom several times over the years whatever happened to her father, but her mother would never talk about it.

All Matthew knew was one day in 2005, when he was only twelve years old, he came home from school and the old man was not there. His mother would only cry and say that his father would not hurt him anymore. He did not like seeing his mother cry, he saw enough of that when his dad had been around, so he did not ask. He simply accepted the fact that his father was gone.

Matthew did not really care what happened to the old man but, mainly for Alex's benefit, he did ask Katie last year, when she was dying from pancreatic cancer, what happened to Frank. The day before she died, she spoke with them. She finally told them the story of Frank.

Frank had been drinking as usual and he beat Katie pretty badly because she had meatloaf for dinner and he had already eaten meatloaf for lunch at Lizard's Thicket restaurant. How was she supposed to know what he had eaten for lunch? That only enraged him further, and he punched her in the head.

Matthew tried to intervene, tried to protect his mother.

"Oh, you want some of this too?" In a drunken rage he turned his attention to Matthew and beat him mercilessly.

Katie was certainly no match for Frank. With no real options, she picked up the pot of boiling water that was intended for the macaroni and cheese.

"Hey loser, yeah you, you are a real man beating on a kid."

As Frank turned, she threw the boiling water into his face. Letting out a yell, his hands left Matthew and went to his face. Picking up a cast iron skillet from the stove, she swung it at his head as hard as she could. Frank dropped to the floor, stunned and in pain.

Katie told Matthew to run, to grab her purse and run to the car. Matthew turned and ran from the kitchen. Swinging the black skillet at Frank's head one more time, she made direct contact. Dropping the heavy skillet on the floor, she ran into the other room, grabbed her two-year-old daughter from the play pen and bolted from the house.

Matthew was already in the car. She quickly started the engine and took off down the road. Katie was not really sure where to go, she knew if she went to her sister's, Frank would surely track her down. In fact, that might be the first place he would look. Not knowing what to do, she made her way to the Catholic Church in downtown Columbia. On the way, she called her sister.

Claire found Katie and the kids inside a conference room at the church.

With the encouragement of her sister, and the help of a priest and nun, she finally called the police.

After the police had left the church, Claire insisted her sister and the kids come stay the night at her house. After all, they did not even know where Frank was.

"That is just the point," Katie said, "I do not want him coming to your house looking for us. If he sees my car parked there, there is no telling what he will do."

"That is not a problem. We will just leave your car here, and I will take you in my car. Frank will not know you are there, and if he does drive by, he will not see your car because your car will not be there, it will be here."

Katie told Matthew and Alex that Frank was arrested at work the next day. Frank was convicted and went to prison. She never once visited him. The following year, she received a phone call one day informing her Frank had died. She did not care.

She began crying and apologizing. Katie said when she got the phone call she was still hurting, was still traumatized. "I did not care what they did with his body, I just did not care." She explained that two months after Frank went to jail, when she was finally convinced he would be there for several years, she began divorce proceedings.

"Mom, shh, stop, it is okay. You do not need to apologize," Alex said, while holding her mother's hand.

"Sure, Mom, there is nothing to apologize for," Matthew added.

Katie was fading fast; this was clearly taking a toll on her. "Yes, but I do not know what happened to him. I do not know where he is buried. I am so sorry. That was selfish of me. I was not thinking of you two."

"Mom, it is okay, really. We love you."

Alex leaned down and kissed her mother's forehead. "Mom, like Matt said, it is okay. We love you. You did what you needed to do."

"I love you too, both of you. Thank you for understanding," she whispered. A slight smile, a comfortable smile, formed across her lips, across her face, as her eyes closed and she drifted off to sleep. Katie would not awaken the next morning, or ever again.

Chapter 13

With the air rapidly forced from his lungs as the toe of the shoe slammed into his ribs, Frank could do little more than utter a feeble, "Ugh." Laying on the ground, almost in a fetal position, he was unsure whether to grasp his ribs, to protect his abdomen, or to protect his head. The toe of a slip-on deck shoe slammed into his face. Frank saw the white rubber band encircling the beige canvas shoe just before it crashed into his mouth, causing a spray of blood as his top lip split open. Coughing, he spit a tooth out onto the floor.

He refused to beg. He simply refused. Frank had tried that during the first "education session" with this group, and it did not end very well. In fact, it caused the beating to intensify. He remembered that first time, several months ago. At first everyone left him alone and he seemed to get along, at least for the first few weeks. But one day, one day he apparently did the wrong thing by trying to do the right thing.

Prior to Frank's incarceration, his attorney had told him there were rules that needed to be followed and there were consequences for not following the rules. Felix Hooperman, Attorney at Law, had handed Frank a printed list of rules he had compiled and the consequences for failure to follow the rules. These included both rules for the detention center itself, and the rules and suggestions for surviving in the inmate population.

Igor had asked Frank to keep a carton of cigarettes in his own storage unit. Inmates are allowed one prison issued bin to store personal items. Items that do not fit into the bin are considered contraband and are disposed of. Frank replied that he was not supposed to do that, he was not supposed to keep items belonging to someone else and he would be in trouble if the guards found out. Igor told Frank Trog was not going to be very happy.

Frank did not know who Igor was, and he certainly had never heard of Trog. "Well, I am sorry," Frank told Igor, "I cannot help you; I do not even know you. Besides, all tobacco products are banned and are considered contraband. I am not going to get busted, especially not for someone else."

"Wise up, man. Trog is not going to be happy."

"Well. I guess he will just have to get over it. I do not know who or what a Trog is." Oh sure, when Frank first arrived, he had been told a guy named Trog sort of ran things, but he really gave it no thought. He was certainly very capable of taking care of himself. After all, he was ex-infantry.

The next day, Igor introduced Frank to Trog and Donk.

During that half hour long introduction, it was made abundantly clear to Frank that Trog indeed pretty much ran the prison, and Donk was essentially the enforcer. Igor was pretty much Trog's lieutenant and mouthpiece. When Trog issued an order, it was generally through Igor, and the order was expected to be followed. Likewise, anyone wanting to confer with Trog did so via Igor. Even the guards respected this hierarchy.

They repeatedly punched Frank in the abdomen trying to educate him about who really ran this joint. When he begged them to stop, they became annoyed, telling Frank to take it like a man, and telling him that beating his wife and kid, he was nothing better than a chomo. If he was such a big man for beating on a defenseless kid, then he should be man enough to take what he had coming to him. Trog shifted to pummeling Frank's right ear while Igor and Donk continued abusing Frank's gut.

Whether or not Frank respected the inmates control structure, he certainly understood it as he made his way to the infirmary to have his broken left forearm set in a cast. He told them he fell down the stairs, which the orderlies initially questioned, upon seeing the blood on Frank's face and his swollen ear, at least until they saw Igor lingering outside the door.

While Frank may not have been a child molester, the other inmates still had issue with him. Sure, some of the other inmates knew Frank had been given three to five years for assault and child abuse. Naturally Trog knew exactly why Frank was in the pen; Trog knew why everyone was in the joint. With Frank's refusal of Igor's request, Trog spread the word that the inmate population was free to extract their own form of vengeance upon Frank. He had beaten his own wife and kid. Oh, sure, abuse of the wife could have been tolerated, but the abuse of the defenseless boy simply was not acceptable. After all, they had families too. They may be incarcerated for a variety of crimes, most of them violent crimes, but they still had families and abuse of a kid simply was not condoned. For the next few months Frank was a pariah.

Another shoe crashed into his ribs. He was not sure if he actually heard it, but he certainly felt the searing pain as two ribs broke. Frank relented, breaking the vow to himself to not beg. "Stop, please stop," he mumbled.

"What was that, punk?"

Gasping for breath, "Stop. For the" –a short breath– "love of" –another labored breath– "God," a brief pause and a gasp for air, "please stop."

"Funny guy."

"Yeah, Trog, he is a real comedian."

Trog's shoe slammed into Frank's face. Blood exploded from his shattered nose.

"Yo, punk, you got blood all over Trog's shoes," Donk said, letting a foot fly into Frank's abdomen.

Barely audible, another plea, "Stop."

"And Trog don't like that," Bugs added to the exchange as his foot landed in Frank's lower back. Frank felt a tingling sensation course through his legs.

"And you got blood on my pants too," Trog said with a smile. Frank's head jerked back as Trog's foot slammed into Frank's forehead.

"Big guy, yeah, real big guy. Beating on your wife and a defenseless little kid. You ain't nothing but a punk." A shoe slammed into his left shin.

"God, please stop," he gasped. "Please, God, make them stop."

"You praying to God? You catch that, Trog? Little big man here is asking God for help."

"Yeah, Donk, you think his wife and kid prayed like that? You think this punk here paid attention to them?"

"Yeah, Bugs, makes you wonder. So, big man, did your wife and kid ask you to stop?" Trog asked the crumpled man on the floor.

Frank lay on the floor, barely coherent. A single cough, blood spewing from his mouth, and a groan his only reply.

"When they prayed to God for you to stop, did you?"

"What, yes." A labored breath. "Oh God." Cough. "I am sorry." Groan. "Stop. Please stop."

"Still praying to God? I gotta tell you, little big man, God don't much come around here. The closest thing you got to God in here is Trog."

"Please," cough, "stop." Labored breath, "Help me."

"What is it going to be, Trog? How do you judge this piece of work?"

Saying nothing, Trog, like Commodus in Ridley Scott's movie *Gladiator*, extended his right arm and gave a thumbs down. It did not matter Scott's movie had it wrong; the thumb down gesture meaning the gladiator died and the thumbs up meaning the gladiator lived was actually the opposite. In reality, the thumb down gesture meant "swords down" and the gladiator was allowed to live to fight another day.

Nodding, Bug's foot slammed into the back of Frank's neck. Final judgement had been rendered; Frank was no more.

At the age of thirteen, Matthew was fatherless, and Alex never would know her father. Katie Stockmore, who had never visited Frank in prison, did not claim Frank's body. When notified of Frank's death and asked about her desires, she told the representative from the South Carolina Department of Corrections that she did not care what happened to Frank's body, to do with him what they will as long as it did not involve her and she promptly hung up the phone with no regrets. There was no point in going through with the rest of the divorce; Katie was now a widow. Frank listed no next of kin.

Chapter 14

In mid sip of his coffee Matthew suddenly froze. "Holy cow. The gun, the gun. I have got to get rid of the gun." It occurred to Matthew he had never disposed of the gun he used at the train tracks.

Wrapping a cloth around the barrel, he clamped the gun into the vice. Matthew did not want to leave any vice marks on the gun. Forensics examiners could identify those types of marks.

Picking up one drill bit after another, he continued until finding one that was slightly larger than the inside diameter of the barrel. Securing the bit into the drill, he began slowly drilling the barrel. Once finished, he began running the drill bit in and out of the barrel.

"There, that should take care of that." Matthew was convinced there was absolutely no way a ballistics match could ever be made with this gun. Nonetheless, he still needed to get rid of it.

He had purchased the gun from someone in Georgia he found on-line. He traveled the hundred and fifty miles or so to the parking lot of a Baptist church near a finger of Lake Oconee, five miles west of Greensboro. He always thought that choice of meetings spots was a little odd. Did they find some sense of security in conducting such a transaction in a church parking lot? What did God think, if there really was a God, about people selling guns in the church parking lot? Jesus went berserk, flipping over tables and stuff when people were selling animals at the temple. "He would probably go ballistic, pardon the pun," Matthew could not help but laugh, "if he knew people were selling guns at ye old church house." What did the pastor think? Then again, Matthew wondered if perhaps it was the pastor that was selling the gun.

He had no idea who was selling the gun or why. The person selling the gun had no idea who was buying it or why. They exchanged no personal information and they exchanged no real pleasantries. The only thing exchanged was cash for a gun. Less than two minutes. No IDs, no paperwork.

If the gun had been registered at all, perhaps it was registered in GA by the person who sold him the gun.

Matthew did not know about that; he did not really care and he never asked. But he figured the guy was from GA, as he had glimpsed the license tag on the seller's Toyota Tacoma. From Georgia the gun came, to Georgia the gun would return.

But first, there was one other small task. Matthew needed to make the serial number disappear. Not that the gun was ever registered by him, nor was it traceable to him, but one could never be too careful.

Acid is one of the best ways to remove a serial number from a gun. Unfortunately, Matthew had no acid at his disposal. Coincidentally, acid is often also used to recover serial numbers.

When a serial number is stamped onto a gun, the impact causes compression in the underlying metal. Grinding the serial number off leaves the compressed metal below. Though the serial number is no longer visible, some parts of it may still be recoverable through acid etching. This technique involves applying acid to the surface of the gun to dissolve the uncompressed metal in an attempt to discover the serial number on the compressed part. Sometimes entire serial numbers are recovered, sometimes only a partial number is recovered, and on rare occasions nothing is recovered. Matthew was going to make sure he was one of those rare occasions. In fact, he was going to guarantee it.

Opening a beer, he got to work. His plan was simple: do not just grind the serial number away, grind all the metal away. Taking a grinding bit from the pack sitting on the workbench, he placed it into the rotary tool, powered the tool on, and began moving the rotating bit back and forth, across and around the serial number.

Two hours and four beers later, the grinding bit emerged on the other side of the gun. Holding the gun up in front of him, Matthew peered through the slot he had just ground completely through the gun. "Where there is no metal, there is no serial number. I will drink to that," he said, reaching for the last beer sitting on the workbench. "A job well done, if I do say so myself."

After donning a pair of latex gloves, Matthew opened the bottle of isopropyl alcohol. He poured alcohol on the piece of old t-shirt and thoroughly wiped the gun. With how he was planning on disposing of the gun, he did not expect any fingerprints could survive. Still, wiping the gun down would just make sure there were no fingerprints to start with.

After crossing the South Carolina state line into Georgia, Matthew exited from I-20 onto River Watch Parkway. Turning left and passing underneath the interstate, he continued driving, passing Eisenhower Park on the right. Slowing down, he glanced to the left and decided the river was still too far away. Matthew was not quite sure where he was going, he just knew he wanted to get closer to the river.

Several miles later River Watch turned into Reynolds, and shortly thereafter he turned left onto the 13th Street bridge and crossed back over the river. He pondered for a brief moment about just stopping on the bridge, but with all the traffic he knew that would be too risky. "Someone throwing a gun from the bridge into the river below might be just a *little* bit suspicious," he said with a slight chuckle.

Halfway across the river, the road changed names to Georgia Avenue above the logical state line in the center of the river below. On the other side of the river, he saw a walkway which ran along it. "Perfect, absolutely perfect." Now the trick was to get to it. Watching the walkway on the left, he missed the sign on the right indicating he was back in South Carolina.

Turning off Georgia Avenue, he made his way to the North Augusta Greenway. "Can life get any better than this?" Matthew asked as he saw a building. "I know where I am having lunch. But, business first."

After parking, he walked across the grass to the greenway. Though there did not seem to be many people on the path, he continued walking for several minutes. Stopping, he looked around for a few seconds. He was alone. Matthew could hear the sound of the river. He left the greenway and walked to the river bank.

Looking in both directions, he saw no one. He pulled a latex glove from his front pocket and slipped it on his right hand. Reaching behind himself, he pulled the gun from the waistband of his pants. One more quick scan. Still no one. As he was pulling the gun back to throw it,

Matthew suddenly paused as a thought occurred to him. "Wait a second. If I was in Georgia, and the Georgia and South Carolina border is in the middle of the river, that means I entered South Carolina when I crossed the bridge. I am not in Georgia anymore." Feeling marginally deflated, "Oh well, I guess the South Carolina side will just have to do."

He unceremoniously tossed the gun into the river and muttered, "At least the deed is done."

Walking back to the greenway, a rock caught Matthew's attention. The relatively clean oval-shaped rock looked decidedly out of place. Curious, he picked it up. Turning the rock over, he saw the words painted in bright blue on the bottom. The words took a moment to register, and then he burst out laughing. "Oh, that is good. I *like* that," he said out loud.

A line from the song *One Tin Soldier* popped into his head. "Turned the stone and looked beneath it, `Peace on Earth` was all it said," Matthew laughed again. "They got peace on earth; I got a pretty good joke. I think I got the better deal."

He set the rock back in its place so that others might enjoy it, and continued back to the parking lot via the greenway. He could already see the Green Jacket Stadium where he would be eating lunch.

The Lake Olmstead Stadium built in 1994 in Augusta, GA, served as the home of the Augusta Green Jackets from 1995 thru 2017. The Minor League Baseball team moved in 2018 to the newly built SRP Park in North Augusta, SC. Both Ballpark Digest and Baseballparks. com named SRP ballpark of the year in 2018.

At the Southbound Smokehouse, located on the perimeter of the SRP Park, Matthew ordered a half rack of ribs, collard greens, Cajun slaw, and a Sweet Water 420.

While waiting for the food to arrive, he began trying to figure out what to do next. He took a long drink of beer, and then set the glass down on the table front of him.

Leaning against the cushioned back of the booth, Matthew folded his arms across his chest, casually scanned the room and began pondering. What to do, what to do. He had four already, why stop now? He needed a number five. Maybe that would be the last one, maybe not. Regardless, the next one needed to be fun. It needed to be epic. It needed to be special. He needed to step up his game. Game? He needed to step up *the* game. Sure, the cops had no way to tie the others together, of that Matthew was pretty certain. He picked up the glass from the table and emptied it in one long gulp.

It was now time to really have fun. Oh sure, the killing part still needed to be fun, but it was now time to really mess with the cops. "I need to confuse them, make them really scratch their heads," Matthew mumbled. He would show them just how smart he is, and the beauty of it is they would not even know it.

"Would you like another beer?" the young woman asked as she set the food on the table in front of him. "Wow, it looks great, and wow, it smells incredible." And yes, Matthew would like another beer.

"Now that was a good lunch. I deserve some good food every now and then," he said as he dropped the napkin on the empty plate.

"Now then, what am I going to do?" he said as he took another drink of beer. As noisy as it was in the restaurant, he had no concerns about anyone hearing him. Matthew decided there needed to be deception, there needed to be misdirection. "I need to make it look like one thing happened, when in reality something else happened. I need to make it look like someone else did it. Hmm. Maybe even make it look like several someones did it. I like that."

Matthew took another drink of beer, and continued pondering. First of all, he needed to make it look like something happened, and it needed to be convincing. Hmm. Thoughts swirling inside his head began to take shape. He could make it look like someone was lying in wait outside, perhaps under a tree close to the house. He could trample around the grass under the tree and make it look like someone had been there for a while. To add to the illusion, to make it more convincing, he could even drop a few cigarette butts under the tree. And maybe, just maybe, a beer bottle or two. "Oh, this is good," Matthew proclaimed, and then took another swallow of beer, of what he often called *thinking juice.*

"What would be better, is if someone else's fingerprints and DNA were on the beer bottles and the cigarette butts." But how was he going to do that? The answer was apparent almost before the question was fully formed. Simple, he just needed to go to a bar somewhere, find a table where someone was drinking beer from a bottle, and smoking cigarettes.

Another swallow of thinking juice. The glass was now empty. After a few moments, a location occurred to him. He thought of a place on Two-Notch Road outside of Columbia, a low-key biker bar type of place in Elgin. Something else occurred to Matthew: he might as well get multiple beer bottles and multiple cigarette butts and make it look like several people were waiting under the tree. That would change the cops' perception of the crime; instead of him, just one person, killing someone for fun, the cops would think several people were involved, were waiting, and indeed had a very specific reason for killing that particular victim.

Matthew was quite pleased with the rough plan that was taking shape in his head. "Oh, I like it, I really, really like it."

As he was starting to get up from the table, a thought, taking priority over all other thoughts, popped into Matthew's head. He started laughing as he stood up. He thought about the joke written on the bottom of the rock by the greenway: "Two guys walked into a bar. The third guy ducked."

Chapter 15

He pulled into the gravel parking lot of the little hole in the wall local bar just off of Two Notch Road in Elgin. He had first thought of this place, thought it might be a possibility, while sitting in the Smokehouse. Parking his motorcycle, he casually strolled into the bar through the front door.

Most of the dozen or so patrons turned and looked in his direction. He did not know if they were looking at him because of him, or if they were looking towards the bright light that momentarily invaded their dimly lit sanctuary.

With the door closed behind him, he noticed people were still watching him as he made his way to the bar.

When the bartender asked, "Yeah, what do you want?" he was pretty sure he was not welcomed here. Sure, he knew it was a biker bar from all the motorcycles in the parking lot, which is why he stopped here, but for some reason he expected it to be a bit friendlier, seeing as how he had a motorcycle too. Of course, they could not see his bike from inside here so they did not know if he rode a bike or drove a Kia. And wearing jeans and a flannel shirt with a pair of tennis shoes, he was not exactly dressed to fit the environment. The majority of the other patrons were in jeans or leathers and tee shirts. "Oh yeah, you blend," he could hear in his head the soundbite of Marisa Tomei saying with a thick New York accent in the movie *My Cousin Vinny.*

"Give me a beer," he said to the 40-something bartender wearing a tube top that was barely able to contain her. The butterfly tattoo on the top of her right breast was clearly visible and caught his attention.

"What, you see something you like, slick?"

"Um, no, I was just —"

"Staring is what you was just doing."

"No, not that at all. I was just admiring the ink is all."

"What kind of beer, city slicker?"

Matthew knew better than to order on IPA in a place such as this. He started to reply with "Give me a Bud." He knew rule number one in an establishment such as this was to make friends with the bartender, or at least do not get on her bad side. He was not off to a very good start. "A Bud will be fine, thank you." She gave a slight smile. "Wow. No woman, no sweet stuff, no hot thang, and a thank you too." She handed him a long neck bottle. "Here you go, darlin'."

"What's a clean-cut fella like you doing in here?"

"Just out for a ride. Wanted to wet my whistle, so stopped in."

"Just like that, out for a ride," the guy to his right interjected.

He was glad he had not worn his leather jacket, it was still too new looking. They would have labeled him a Weekend Warrior, or worst yet, as a waxer. As it was right now, he was just some guy that stopped in. "Yes, sir, just like that. Needed a break from the saddle. And, I was thirsty."

"So, you ride, sweetie?"

"Yes, ma'am. Vulcan; it is right outside. Sure, it is not a hog or anything, but it is a good bike. Reliable. Easy to work on." He knew that even if you did not ride the *right* kind of bike, these guys respected someone that would and could turn wrenches.

"That's cool. I can dig it," came the reply from his right.

As he took a swig of beer, he managed to steal a glance around the bar. No one was really staring at him anymore, so he figured he was safe. The juke box in the corner was idle. He knew that was a pretty important rule too in a biker bar, probably had to be rule number two or number three: never play the juke box without permission. He had no intention of playing the juke box, and even if he wanted to, he had no idea whom would grant or deny that request. He did not know who the lead dog was and he really had no desire to find out.

Matthew also noticed ten patrons were spread amongst three tables, and two more at the bar. This was not a good place for what he needed; it simply would not do. There were only four cigarette smokers in the place, not counting the bartender, or at least only four were currently smoking. On top of that, the bartender periodically cleared the table of dead soldiers. Nope, this would not do at all. He would need to find someplace else.

Finishing the beer, he set the empty bottle and a ten spot on the bar and casually strolled out the front door into the bright sunny afternoon. He figured those inside were staring at the door, not knowing, or really caring, if they were staring at him leaving or if they were staring at the invasive light.

Mounting his bike, he drove towards his apartment. He needed a better place. This trip was not a complete waste; at least he drank a beer. He really wanted another one, but he figured it was best to just get out of there. About halfway through his beer, there had been some type of an argument, disagreement, altercation; he was not sure what it was. Maybe it was just posturing. Whatever it was, he was surprised by the childish and immature behavior of the grown men. He only caught snippets; he was trying to mind his own business. When he heard one guy say another had disrespected him, well, he knew it was best to leave. While they were busy getting their feelings hurt and acting like second grade schoolkids, he drained his beer and made his exit unnoticed. Unnoticed, until the invading sunlight gave him away.

Chapter 16

Walking down the wooden staircase that ran down the side of the building from his apartment over the garage, he felt a light drizzle. His thoughts drifted to earlier in the day when he had watched two grown men in a biker bar act like children, with one complaining and almost throwing a temper tantrum because one man had eaten that last pretzel from the basket on the table, a pretzel the other man apparently wanted to eat.

"You took that."

"So?"

"Give it to me. I was going to eat that."

"There is popcorn." Popping the pretzel into his mouth, "Eat the popcorn."

"I cannot believe you just did that! I wanted to eat that!"

"Chill, dude. Eat the popcorn."

"I do not want popcorn! I wanted a pretzel. I did not get any pretzels."

Another rider tried to diffuse the situation. "Hey barkeep. We need some pretzels over here."

The gesture was apparently in vain. "I do not want another pretzel. I want *that* one! He took the pretzel I was going to eat. He disrespected me!"

Grown men arguing over who ate the last pretzel. Matthew had not waited around to hear the rest.

It had been sunny when he left the drama behind him. After returning home and taking a nap, the weather had apparently changed; it was now overcast and dreary. Standing in the light rain, he eyed the faded blue pickup truck sitting all alone in the driveway. Deciding to take the truck, he finished his descent down the stairs and ambled towards Kevin's old Ford F150.

The exterior lights were trying to keep the approaching darkness away from the house across the driveway, but they were failing miserably. The house was dark, it was quiet, it was lonely. It had been that way for the last several weeks. Margie had been staying at her sister's home for the last few weeks, ever since her husband's incident.

The man had a stroke, yet it was being counted as a COVID-19 case. Kevin had been in the hospital for three weeks. He was checked for COVID-19 when he was admitted, and three times after that. Each time he was negative. Ah, but the fifth time he was tested, wouldn't you know, he tested positive for COVID-19. "Now where do you imagine he might have gotten that?" Matthew would often say.

The number of flu cases and flu deaths in 2021 were extremely low. The talking heads on TV would proudly proclaim the sharp decrease was due to people wearing masks and social distancing. Really? Then why, Matthew would ask, the sharp spike in COVID-19 cases from Thanksgiving 2020 and into early to mid-January? The so-called experts and the politicians who just wanted to brainwash everyone proclaimed the sharp rise in COVID-19 cases during that period was due to a breakdown in social distancing and lax mask wearing as families gathered together for the holidays, ignoring the so-called experts' advice not to. If that was the case, then why did flu cases not also spike? They were wanting to have their cake and eat it too. Money is why, money and control. There is no money in the flu, Matthew regularly ranted. Institutions, hospitals, doctors, people all get money from the federal government for a COVID-19 case, but they don't get anything for a flu case. To Matthew's way of thinking, of course they are going to classify everything as COVID-19. But then, then they would use those same numbers next year to try to tell everyone to wear masks and social distance and close businesses because masks are "proven" to stop the flu. Matthew Stockmore was not buying into it. This was not about some illness. No, this was about control. The only herd immunity Matthew could see in all of this was the herds of people that were immune to rational thought.

The Delatorios had told him just a few months ago that he could use the truck whenever he wanted to. Matthew reached under the left rail of the truck bed. Sliding his cupped finger along the rail, he found the magnetic key box towards the front of the bed.

Extracting the key, he opened the driver side door and climbed into the cab of the truck, and dropped the key box into the cup holder. "Note to self," he said aloud, "I need to get a key made."

Backing out of the driveway, Matthew wondered how much longer he would be living here. He supposed that would depend on whether or not Kevin and Margie came back. Would Kevin even be able to live here? Or would he need to be in an assisted living facility? Surely Margie would not stay here without Kevin. Admittedly, he did not exactly know Kevin's condition. Exactly? Who was he kidding? He had absolutely no idea how Kevin was doing, except the man had suffered a stroke, was diagnosed with COVID-19, and had been in the hospital for three weeks. Other than that, he knew nothing about the condition of the man he had been renting an apartment from for the last two years. Matthew decided he should probably make some effort to find out how the old man was doing. If nothing else, he needed to know what the future might hold. He figured, in the worst case, he was probably good for several months. After all, if the Delatorios never returned back here and decided instead to sell the home, it would take a little bit of time for them to move all their stuff out of the house, a bit of time to make a few repairs and otherwise ready the house for the market, and a bit of time for it to sell. In Matthew's mind, he was probably okay for the next four to six months. Then again, maybe the new owners would like the idea of a monthly revenue stream and allow Matthew to stay. He did not really think they would go for it, but then again, it could happen. Deciding he would worry about that when the time came, he pushed the thoughts of his future living arrangements aside.

Turning off of Piney Grove Road, Matthew drove down the driveway, passing the Waffle House, until he arrived at the cigar and taproom.

As soon as he pulled into the parking lot, and before he even parked the truck, he knew this was the place.

On the concrete porch were, he guessed, about seven or eight tables. Every chair was occupied, and a dozen more people were leaning against the wrought iron railing around the patio. There were easily forty people on the patio which was a stark contrast to just a month ago when COVID-19 induced social distancing was in full effect. Back then, a maximum of two people were allowed per table, and only every other table was utilized. He had thought that was a bit extreme. After all, the tables were outside and there was easily eight feet between tables. In his mind, the whole thing was a bit silly and accomplished absolutely nothing. He thought most of the reaction to COVID-19 was ludicrous and illogical, and wholly ineffective. Last year he had gone to one of the big box home improvement stores, the orange one if he recalled correctly. They were only allowing about two dozen people in the store at a time. In a store the size of warehouse, heck it essentially was a warehouse, and only allowing twenty-something people inside? That made no sense to him. Worse yet, they had ten red Xs spaced six feet apart on the concrete in front of the store. The part he found hilarious was there was a queue of people wrapped halfway around the parking lot. The people were standing front to back just a few inches apart, waiting for up to an hour for their turn to take their spot on the red X and be magically socially distanced and instantly protected from COVID-19. It was abundantly clear to him these people were just going through the motions and making it look like they were trying to do something even though what they were doing was largely illogical.

Opening the tinted glass door, Matthew walked inside.

The lighting was dim, except for the rectangular fluorescent light hanging over each of the eight billiard tables in the area to his right. This place was really hopping. All of the tables appeared to be occupied.

Cigar afficionados filled most of the leather chairs set around the dozen or so small round tables to the left.

His gaze shifted to the bar at the end of the room. He began walking towards one of the few unoccupied seats.

His mind kicked into overdrive.

Focus, Matthew. Focus.

As much as he would like a beer, he really could not be seen sitting down and drinking one. It might send the wrong signal. He needed to be invisible. The closest thing to that was being unmemorable; blending into the background by appearing to be an employee. And, an employee would not be seen sitting at the bar drinking a beer.

Continuing to scan his surroundings, in the left corner he saw a lonely pinball machine, not far from the waiter's station, often referred to as the bus station.

At the bus station were two rectangular bus tubs, the gray plastic tubs the staff used to transport dirty dishes from the tables.

And several stacks of clean ash trays.

Pulling a pair of blue latex gloves from his pocket he pulled them on. It occurred to him that once upon a time this might have looked a bit odd. But somewhere, somewhere a few years ago, he started seeing people wearing disposable gloves. The last year, goof grief, the world went crazy with the whole COVID-19 thing and it seem like most employees in stores and restaurants were wearing gloves. That did not make a lot of sense to him. Oh sure, he wore them every now and then when working on his motorcycle or when painting or staining or something like that. But that was to keep his hands clean. These other people, the people that put a pair of latex gloves on and wore them all day, *that* he did not understand. Ugh! Surely, they did not think they were protecting other people. They could not really think that, could they? He noticed that nonsense at the height of the COVID-19 drive-thru craze. People working the drive-thru window wearing gloves. Even more weird was a fast-food chicken chain where an employee in gloves would deliver food to as many as three different cars, all while wearing the same pair of gloves. "Should they not have been changing them after every contact?" Matthew often asked.

Picking up a blue face mask from the box sitting on the shelf above the ash trays, Matthew put it on. The mask hid the smile that formed as he briefly wondered, "Should I have put that on before or after putting the gloves on? Oh dear me. I hope I do not violate Fauci's COVID protocol."

At least with the mask and gloves he fit in, and he was both unmemorable and somewhat unrecognizable. More importantly, the gloves would ensure he left no fingerprints.

Picking up one of the bus tubs and a couple of clean ash trays, Matthew wandered over towards the billiard tables.

As with the tables outside, those inside were littered with an assortment of beer bottles and ash trays.

Stopping at a high-top table near one of billiard tables, Matthew said to no one in particular, "Here, let me swap that ash tray out for you."

The four guys engaged in a game of eight ball barely noticed him. picking up two dirty ash trays he replaced each of them with a clean one.

"Looks like you guys could use another round," he said as cleared the empty beer bottles from the table.

"Sure, that would be great," the guy leaning over the cue ball replied without looking up. "Three ball. Corner pocket."

"Hey, those guys over there, that group of four, they could use another round," he said to the waitress as he was walking towards the front door.

Walking out the front door still carrying the bus tub, Matthew walked off the porch and across the parking lot to the truck.

Opening the door, he climbed into the truck with the gray plastic bus tub. It occurred to him taking the tub was risky, it might even be a little bit sloppy, but it certainly was convenient. He decided it was not that big of a deal, he would just dispose of it in the woods somewhere.

Still wearing the latex gloves. he transferred the empty bottles from the tub to a large resealable bag and zipped the bag shut. Retrieving two smaller bags, he placed each ash tray into a separate bag and sealed them shut. He placed the empty tub onto the floor board on the passenger side. Pressing the clutch and turning the key, the old truck roared to life.

Chapter 17

Matthew was anxious. He was restless. He had an itch and he needed to scratch it. It was still early. It was only seven thirty. The night was still young, so many opportunities. What to do, what to do, he wondered.

Leaning over, he put the bags containing the ash trays into the glove compartment. He stuffed the bag with the bottles under the passenger side of the bench seat. He had an idea.

Down the driveway from the taproom, Matthew turned right and made his way through the adjoining parking lot, past Green's Discount Beverages, and out onto Fernandina Road. The orange big box home improvement store would be his next stop.

A two by four might work. Matthew thought. Gee, would that break on impact? Yeah, it probably would. With a slight chuckle, he mumbled, "the wood would. I just made a funny."

Two inches thick would not do. He needed something thicker. Strolling eighty feet down the aisle, he stopped at the pressure treated lumber. He thought he might have found something that would work.

An eight foot four-by-four post was only eight and a half bucks. Whoa! There was another one for eighteen bucks and some change. What the heck? Why was one more than twice the price of the other?

"Excuse me," he called out to an employee walking past the end of the aisle, "Do you work in this department? I have a question."

"Sorry, no, I do not. Let me get an associate who does." Removing the radio clipped to his right front pocket, he announced, "Customer needs assistance in aisle fourteen. Need an associate from lumber to aisle fourteen." Without another word to Matthew, he secured the radio and continued on his way.

Matthew started comparing. For eight dollars and forty-eight cents, according to the sign he could get a piece of "Ground Contact Pressure-Treated Southern Yellow Pine." For eighteen dollars and thirty-five cents he could get a piece of "4 in. x 4 in. x 8 ft. #2 Better Kiln Dried Douglas Fir Lumber."

"Um, are you the customer that needs assistance?"

Turning around, he said, "Yeah, I am. Can you tell me the difference between these two?"

Glancing at the signs, the tall lanky young guy responded, "Well, one is more expensive than the other."

"Yeah, I figured that one out for myself. What is the difference? Why is one more than twice the cost of the other?"

"Well, that is just the way they price them."

"No kidding. What is the difference?"

Again reading the signs, the ever-so-helpful twenty-five-year-old store associate provided Matthew the answer, "Um, well, one of them is ground contact and the other is kiln dried."

"Great. What does that mean? Is the kiln dried pressure treated?"

"Um, I don't know. I just work here. Maybe you want to look it up online. Anything else I can help you with?"

"No, I'm good," Matthew said with just a touch of sarcasm.

He surmised the kiln dried lumber was not pressure treated. In the end, it did not really matter. For what he needed it for, the less expensive post would suffice.

"Excuse me," Matthew called out.

The associate turned around.

"Actually, you can help me with something else. This is a bit long. I only need something about six feet or so. Can you cut it for me?"

"Yeah, well, here is the thing. I am not qualified to cut lumber."

"Not qualified? How hard can it be? It's a saw."

"Well, I am not checked out on that piece of equipment, am not certified to use it yet."

"What equipment are you certified to use?"

"Well, none actually. I have only been working here for about a month."

"Oh, great. Is there anyone here who can cut it for me?"

"No, I am the only one in this department tonight."

"Just my luck. Well, is there *anyone* in the store that can cut it for me? A manager maybe? Can you call and check?"

"Sorry, no can do. I don't have a radio."

Exasperated, Matthew replied, "Let me guess, you are not checked out on that piece of equipment."

"Sometimes you just have to do things yourself. Sometimes you just have to get creative," Matthew said to himself as he picked up the treated post.

On aisle twelve, he stopped at the first bay. Picking up a Milwaukee tape measure, he bent down and picked up an indelible marker. Measuring out six feet, he scribed a red line, and returned the marker and tape to their proper places.

Stopping at bay seven on the same aisle, he reached out and removed a hand saw from the peg on the wall while balancing the vertical post in the crook of his right arm.

Turning around, he cleared a space a few inches wide on the second shelf. Placing the wood perpendicular on the shelf, he slipped the protective cardboard cover from the saw blade and began cutting along the red line.

With the saw hanging back on the wall, Matthew picked up the shorter piece and set it on the shelf. He had no use for that piece. They could figure out what to do with it. After all, it was their fault. If they had someone that could have cut the wood for him, he would not have had to resort to this. They got what they deserved.

With no remorse or guilt, Matthew picked up the six-foot post and began making his way to the register.

Whoa! Matthew stopped abruptly. *Wait just a second! This is wood. Wood splinters. Wood will leave a trace. It will be evidence. Do I really care?* he asked himself.

The voice in his heard weighed in.

Sloppy, Matthew. We are getting sloppy. No, we are not. Yes, we are. Splinters? Really? Hey, at least I thought about it. At the last minute. And you are still asking if you care. You may not care but we do. We thought we made it clear that we do not want to go to jail. Okay, okay. Let's just be careful. Let's not get sloppy. Give me a break. That was not sloppy. Yes, just like the bus tub sitting in the truck. Taking that was sloppy. That was not sloppy. It was convenient. It was a convenient way to get the stuff out of the bar. We think it was sloppy. It was clean and efficient. It is not what we agreed to, it was not our plan. Hey, I improvised. That little improv could get us in trouble. There is nothing to worry about, everything is good. We do not like it. We are concerned. Did you happen to think they might have video cameras? That they might have pictures of us? Stop being so paranoid. I admit I did not think about the cameras. Sloppy, Matthew, sloppy. Stop saying that. So what if there is a video of me walking out with the tub? They cannot tie it to anything. It is no big deal really. I will dump it in the woods some place. What if I take it to Gaston? We guess that will work. We just want to be careful. Perhaps I should rethink the wood. Maybe I should use something else? Metal perhaps? We think that would be wise.

He preferred the 3/8-inch think angle iron, unfortunately it was only four feet long. That simply would not do. Reluctantly, he selected something six feet long and an inch and a half wide.

At a quarter of an inch thinner and a half inch narrower than his first choice, he just hoped it would do. The fact that it was angle iron should give it sufficient strength, as least for what he had in mind.

At twenty-two bucks and some change, it was more expensive than either of the posts, but it seemed to be a better option.

A metal rod in the next bin over caught his attention. "I wonder," Matthew said aloud. He set the angle iron on the floor.

Pulling the smart phone from his pocket, he spoke into it. "Convert nine millimeters to inches."

"It is zero point three five inches," came the response from the phone.

Well, that was not very useful. Matthew tried again. "Convert nine millimeters to a fraction."

"Here is what I found," as a list of websites appeared on the screen.

Selecting the `Conversion Chart for Millimeters, Decimals and Fractions` entry, a table from cableorganizer.com appeared on the screen. This was helpful, very helpful.

Leaning against the shelf he began reading and calculating, not realizing he was mumbling out loud. "Nine millimeters is 0.3543 inches in diameter, which is slightly less than 23/64 of an inch. That is what, just under 3/8 of an inch? I need a hole about three eights of an inch diameter. Hmm. That could work. So, I need something about a half inch diameter."

Referring back to the chart on the phone, he looked up a few more sizes and performed a few more rough calculations. Matthew decided thirty-eight one-hundredths of an inch was pretty close to the nine millimeters. "A half inch diameter rod will work for that one too. Hmm. But for forty-five one-hundredths? A half an inch is fifty one-hundredths. That will not leave much room on the side walls. Let's see. That would leave five one-hundredths, which is what, one twentieth of an inch? Hmm. Guess I need something bigger for that one."

He thought the three quarter of an inch rod might do nicely. Back to the phone to check one more diameter.

"Hmm. Yep, it will work for that one too. Actually, for either of them."

Matthew surmised he would only need six inches, but it might not hurt to have twelve. Regardless, the pipe was sold in four-foot lengths, so he would have plenty. Heck, he could even afford to make a mistake or two. Grabbing a piece of half-inch diameter pipe and a three-quarter inch diameter pipe, he picked up the angle iron when another thought occurred to him.

Picking up the phone, Matthew asked, "What are the dimensions for a quarter inch PVC pipe?"

"Here is what I found," came the electronic voice of the phone's virtual assistant.

Looking at the information on the screen, Matthew wondered if it could be correct.

"Excuse me."

"What can I do for you?" replied the store associate in the plumbing section.

"Quick question. What are the dimensions of a quarter inch schedule 40 PVC pipe? I checked on-line and they gave me a crazy answer."

"You mean lengths?"

"Uh, no. Diameter. Inside diameter specifically. The stuff I saw online did not make a lot of sense. I asked my phone but she was clueless."

Tom, at least that was the name on the badge, chuckled. "Yeah, I have problems getting my phone to tell me anything useful. It will usually tell me everything except what I am asking about."

"I hear you, man. Anyway, the table I saw online makes no sense." Holding the phone cut to Tom, "Heck, let's look at an easy one. Two-inch pipe. The OD is two point eight seven five. The wall thickness is point two zero three. If I subtract the wall thickness from the outside diameter, I get two point two two one. That is not two inches. Heck, that is closer to two and a quarter inches."

"Yeah, that can get a little confusing. Here is the thing, you need to subtract double the wall thickness. You only subtracted it once. There are two walls." He picked up a piece of PVC pipe. "See," as he ran his finger around the outside edge of the opening, "this is the OD. But see, there is a wall here and directly across from it is this wall. So, logically there are two walls."

Pulling up the calculator on the phone and subtracting the thickness of the wall indeed yielded two point zero six seven. "Yeah, I guess I did not think about that." Matthew rechecked the calculations on the quarter inch pipe. "That seems to work on the larger pipe, but not on the smaller pipe. But the eighth inch and quarter in pipes are way off. Look at this. A quarter of an inch is point two five, right?"

"Yeah."

"Well, the OD of a quarter inch pipe is point five four, that is over a half an inch. The ID, if I subtract two times the wall thickness is point three six four. Heck, both the OD and the ID are greater than a quarter of an inch, yet they call it quarter inch pipe. Why is that?"

"It has to do with the extrusion process."

"Really? The extrusion process makes the internal diameter of a pipe greater than the size of the pipe? That does not make a lot of sense. That is kind of like stopping something before it begins, or my arriving here before I ever got in the truck to come here."

"Well, what can I tell you. It is just the way it is, just one of those things."

"Wow, look at the eighth inch pipe! The ID of that is zero point two six nine!" Heck, the ID of the eighth inch pipe is greater than a quarter of an inch. Why did they not call *that* a quarter inch pipe? It would have made a lot more sense."

"Hey, that is just the way they do it."

"Well, it's a bit confusing. I need to put something a little over two tenths of an inch diameter through the pipe, without too much slop. So, I am logically thinking a quarter inch pipe. But now it looks like the eighth inch pipe will work better."

"Well, I guess it would, but we do not sell either one. You might try a plumbing supply house. The smallest we sell here is half inch."

Consulting his phone, he said, "Crap, that ID is over six tenths of an inch. That will not work."

"What exactly are you trying to do? Maybe we can come up with something that will work."

"Um, well, I just need something a little less than a quarter of an inch diameter. I need to have something pass through it. Oh, I do not know. I am still working out the kinks. For now, let us just say a marble."

"A marble? In a pipe? How long is this pipe?"

"I am not sure, maybe about six inches, maybe a bit longer, but no longer than twelve."

"Does the marble just sit in the pipe, or does it roll through it?"

"Hmm. It will roll, or maybe slide."

"Any liquid?"

"Nope."

"Lubrication?"

"Nah. Do not think any is needed."

"So, a very short cylinder, no liquid, no grease or oil, about a quarter inch diameter? Have you thought about just taking a wood dowl, like a wooden rod, and drilling a quarter inch hole in it?"

"Wow. Great idea. I never thought about that."

"Aisle 17. We have half inch and three quarter over there. Other sizes too, but one of those sizes should work for you."

"Thanks!"

Chapter 18

S he wiped her mouth and dropped the napkin into the empty bowl. There was no trace of Shepherd's Pie left behind. Lizzie pushed the bowl off to the side. Johnathan Edward Baxter, Jeb as he was commonly known, had already finished his plate of Bangers and Mash and was nursing a glass of water.

She noticed him looking around; he tended to do that. She was not quite sure if she would classify him as a womanizer, but he definitely had a wandering eye. And yes, on occasion it did seem like he would talk too much to other women, like he was flirting with them. She took consolation in knowing that she had him, regardless of whom he was looking at or talking to, she and he were together. So he liked to look and liked to flirt, but none of those women had Jeb and *she* did. That meant she was better than them, at least she hoped so. But this was different, tonight was different; he seemed nervous. Was he looking for someone? Was he looking at someone? Lizzie noticed Jeb periodically glancing over towards the bartender.

"Would you like another drink? Let's have another drink."

Jeb was still looking around. Maybe he was just looking for the waiter, she thought, but still he looked nervous. Or maybe he had a reason to be nervous. Was he trying to discretely check out the bartender? Or did he perhaps already know the bartender?

The waiter poured each of them a glass of wine, set the bottle on the table, and walked away. They each picked up a shot glass of Jagermeister the waiter had left with the wine. They clinked the glasses together, "Down the hatch."

Setting the empty glasses on the table, Jeb said, "Hey, Liz, we need to, um, talk."

Lizzie picked up the wine glass and drained it in one gulp. "So you are breaking up with me?"

"Well, just more of a break really."

"The keyword there is *break*. You are *breaking* up with me," Lizzie said quite loudly, as she poured herself another glass of wine.

"Just calm down," Jeb implored her.

"I.WILL.NOT.CALM.DOWN," she roared back emphatically. "You have me come out here and get me good and drunk so you can break up with me?"

"It is not like that."

"It sure looks like that to me. I guess I should have been suspicious when you asked me to meet you here instead of you picking me up. I suppose that is so you would not have to ride home with me after you dumped me. You really are a class act."

"Liz—"

"What, is it another woman? Is it that bartender over there? I have seen you looking over there all night." Her glass of wine was emptied in a single gulp.

"There is not another woman, not really."

"Not *really*?"

"Look, there is not anyone else. It is just—"

"It is just *what*? It is just *me*, is that what you are saying", she screamed.

He leaned towards her and hissed through clenched teeth, "Lizzie, people are looking."

She poured the rest of the bottle into her glass. "Well, as long as they are looking, we should really give them something to look at." Standing up and sliding the chair back, Lizzie picked up the half-filled glass and flung its contents at Jeb.

She turned and walked away from the table, leaving behind a dark red wine-covered Jeb, humiliated as the surrounding tables erupted into applause.

Without another word, Lizzie made her way alone through the restaurant and stumbled out the front door.

Driving northwest on East Main Street, Matthew was just passing the Irish pub when he caught a glimpse of her stumble alone out of Ohara's Public House. Stealing glances in the sideview mirror and hoping she did not get away, he travelled about two hundred feet further, past the center divider in the median, and made a U-turn.

The itch. He had to scratch the itch. Still seeing her in the distance, he accelerated. The adrenaline was pumping. There was no plan.

Coming up on the coffee house less than ninety feet from Ohara's, he let off of the gas pedal and began to coast.

"Careful. Careful, Matthew," he said out loud in the cab of the truck.

Now only forty feet from her, it was time to act. Still staggering, and still alone, she turned onto a little side road, more of an alley, staggering in the darkness.

Rolling down the passenger side window, he slid the angle iron through the open window, extending only about a foot of it for now to make sure he did not hit a sign or a pole.

Making the turn, he quickly scanned the surroundings and noticed no one else around. She was alone, isolated.

Slamming the gas pedal to the floor, the truck rapidly accelerated while Matthew thrust another three feet of the steel through the open window.

Five. Four. Three. Two. One.

Matthew barely had time to see her head snapping violently backwards as the angle iron made contact with the back of her neck.

The sound was deafening. Not the sound of her screaming; she never made a sound. Not the impact of the steel with her body. The force of the impact viciously ripped the steel from his right hand, driving the angle iron into the windshield. He had not counted on that. After all, it was unlike anything he had ever done before. The steel impacting the windshield was indeed the dominating sound.

He had been looking out the passenger window at the point of impact. It was all so surreal. She was there one minute, all five foot three of her, and then she was gone in an instant. Sort of.

Checking the rearview mirror, she was a lifeless heap laying on the ground. Of course she was.

Slowing, he started to pull into the parking lot on the left when he realized it was the back side of the Lexington Traffic Court and the Magistrates Office. Oops. It may be ten thirty at night, but if any place had security cameras, he guessed it would probably be them.

He wanted to get out of the truck and take a look. He wanted to verify he saw what he thought he saw. But he really could not take the chance. Whether or not he saw what he thought he saw, he knew he really should get going.

Making his way to South Lake Drive, he turned right and continued briefly before turning right into the parking lot of a pain specialist.

"Wow, what a mess," Matthew thought without much feeling while standing outside the passenger side of the truck. The end of the metal still sticking out the window was covered in blood. He did not expect this. Then again, he did not expect anything. Actually, he did not even know what to expect. Reaching through the open window, he held onto the angle iron and yanked it out of the windshield. Holding the bar, he looked around. He knew he could not put it into the cab of the truck, at least not in its current state; he might have a hard time explaining blood in Kevin's truck. Or at the very least, it meant he would have to clean it up.

Seeing a hose spigot on the side of the building, he casually sauntered over to it. Looking around, he was convinced there were no cameras. Quickly, very quickly, he turned on the water and numbly rinsed the woman's blood from the angle iron.

Chapter 19

S topping outside the white side door to the garage, Matthew stood and slowly looked around. His gaze shifted from the Delatorios small house across the driveway to the narrow stairway running up the outside of the garage to his small apartment above.

He was invigorated, excited, and hyper-alert. His senses were alive, on overdrive. Last night was just what he needed.

For the first time, he noticed the staircase that had once been white was in desperate need of a fresh coat of paint. He made a note to tell Kevin and Margie that he would paint it. Of course, he never would. Oh sure, he would tell them, and they would be grateful and thank him but, somehow, he would just never get around to it. Matthew did not realize it, but he seemed to do that a lot.

Lowering his gaze, he glimpsed the wildly overgrown grass in the yard. He absentmindedly leaned the metal rods and wooden dowel against the cinder block garage wall. About a month ago, about a week before Kevin went to the hospital, Matthew had told the Delatorios that he would take care of the yard. Standing here now, he thought it needed to be cut soon; he needed to either break down and cut it himself or pay someone else to cut it. That should probably be done before Margie returned home. His thoughts took an abrupt turn. Why did *he* have to do it? Oh sure, he said he would, but that was only because they probably expected him to. People always quietly expected *him* to do things, they always expected *him* to volunteer to do things. No, they did not come right out and say it, but he could tell, he could tell by the way people looked at him they expected *him* to bow down to them and do their work for them. People were always taking advantage of him. But today, today did not matter. He was refreshed, he was energized! His mind was firing on all cylinders. The yard would just have to wait.

One day Matthew would be out of this apartment. One day he would have his own house, and a nice brick house, too, with a nice big yard and a concrete patio where he could set chairs and a firepit. Maybe not right now, but one day. He was not exactly sure how this was going to happen. Okay, he had absolutely no idea how this was going to happen but, mark his words, it would happen. He just knew it would, somehow it just had to.

Sometimes life just seemed so hard for him. Things were not always easy for Matthew. He had to pretty much fight for everything. Oh sure, sometimes a piece or two of the puzzle of life would fall into place, but that was certainly more the exception than the norm. Usually when it seemed like things might start to work out in his favor, things would suddenly go South. It was not his fault, mind you. Someone just seemed to always get in his way. At times it felt like a conspiracy. It felt like the world was somehow against him, like the universe was conspiring against him. He could not even begin to count the number of times he had lashed out at God. The number of times he had yelled at God, yelled at the top of his lungs, "Why? Why God? Why are you doing this to me? Why do you hate me so much? What did I ever do to you? Is this some kind of a game for you? What, you just want to see how much Matthew can endure? I am not Job. I cannot endure anymore! I am done! Leave me alone! Please, just leave me alone."

One day his ship was going to come in. People could not stand in his way forever. At some point, and some point soon, they were going to have to step aside. And when they did, his star was going to shine. And oh, how it was going to shine!

Sooner or later, he was going to land a decent job. One day someone would see his potential and ask him to work for them. Matthew had not sent out any resumes, nor had he applied for any jobs. He did not need to, at

171

least not to his way of thinking. Once upon a time he used to play that game, but no more. He used to send resumes, he used to take the phone calls of recruiters, he even did the interviews. He played their game, he humored them. What a complete waste of time that was. None of it ever panned out. It was not his fault; it was theirs. He could not help it if they could not see his true value. He could not help it if he was smarter than them. They were just so blind, so stupid.

Sooner or later, someone would see his real worth, someone would see his intelligence, and they would reach out to him and offer him a job. It is bound to happen; it is just a matter of time, he told himself.

Walking through the doorway, Matthew instinctively reached out his left hand and found the switch. The garage was suddenly awash with light. The intensity settled down as his eyes adjusted to the whitish light emitted from the set of fluorescent lights hanging in the center of the garage.

Wandering towards the workbench, he found another switch and the bank of LED lights over the work area sprang to life. Ah, much better. He much preferred the bright white of the LEDs to the fluorescents. It was a funny thing really. He used to think fluorescents were the brightest light, certainly compared to incandescent lights. He had even replaced all his lights bulbs with those curly little compact fluorescent thingies. What were they called? Ah, yes, CFLs. But once he discovered LEDs, he immediately made the switch.

CFLs really did not seem to be around all that long. Incandescent bulbs were around, for what, like forever? Well, they had been around for over a hundred years, of that he was quite sure. But it seemed the CFLs were here one day and everyone was extolling the virtue of this great little green bulb, this little energy saver that would last for years. The next thing he knew here were LEDs, the bulbs that used way less energy than any other bulb, emitted a freakish amount of bright light, and would last for many years. Heck, they would probably outlast him! And just like that, CFL bulbs were evil; they consumed too much energy, well at least more than LEDs, they had a short life span, they never did last as long as the so-called experts predicted they would last, and they apparently contained some dangerous chemical or something, was it mercury, he thought maybe it was mercury, that was reportedly bad for the environment. He seemed to recall on top of all of that, CFL bulbs also emitted some high levels of radiation. As quickly as they appeared, they were gone. It was kind of like the all-wheel steering that Honda was hawking many years ago. When was that? He was not sure, it could have been the late eighties or early nineties. Whenever it was, it was only around a couple of years and then was seemingly gone.

Laying the rods on the workbench, he sat on the black vinyl covered stool and opened the beer he had brought from upstairs.

Swig was an understatement. Matthew took a large gulp of beer. "Ah! Just what the doctor ordered."

He had to reach out and set the beer on the workbench because he spontaneously began laughing so hard.

"Too bad a doctor can't help her!" he said aloud, beginning the laughing anew.

He was still having trouble completely comprehending, or perhaps processing was a better word, the events from last evening. "Wow, wow, wow," he said while slowly moving his head in a diagonal after each word.

Matthew was still in utter disbelief that something like that could happen. He never expected that to happen. The truth is, he did not quite know what to expect. Okay, so perhaps he had no expectations, except maybe that she was going to die. He had not really planned it out, it was just sort of one of those last-minute things. Still, he never expected *that* to happen. Barely above a whisper, he said, "Whoa. That was intense. Insane."

She had made no attempt to move. It was like she was oblivious to the sound of the rapidly accelerating truck approaching from behind her.

At thirty miles per hour, the angle iron hit the back of her neck, just below the base of the skull.

Through the open passenger-side window, he saw her head snap back. In an instant she was gone.

Looking into the passenger-side mirror, he saw her body standing there, her knees buckle, and her body drop to the ground.

Shifting his gaze to the rearview mirror as he let off the accelerator, he saw her lifeless body on the ground. Something was odd, very odd. It took a moment to register. There was no head. Where was the—As if on cue, he saw a head drop onto the pavement behind the truck, bounce slightly, and roll off to the side.

Did he just see that? Whoa! He did see that. At least he thought he saw that. Surely that did not happen, surely that could not happen. True, he was looking through the small rearview mirror. Still, in utter disbelief, he thought he just saw that happen. He had wanted to stop to confirm it, and had started to slow, but he decided stopping was not wise considering he was next to the back parking lot of the Lexington Traffic Court and the Magistrates Office.

Matthew was beginning to convince himself that last night actually happened, even though it still seemed like a dream. What he did know is that on the news this morning there was mention of a "gruesome death in Lexington" where a twenty-three-year-old female, identified as Elizabeth Hawkins, was apparently decapitated. Naturally, "police are investigating." So, it apparently was not a dream and he apparently did indeed see what he thought he saw. Still, somehow it did not quite seem real.

Just thinking about it, he was now restless. Standing up, he began pacing back and forth in front of the workbench. "I mean, her head, wow. Decapitated. And her head bounced. I. Saw. Her. Head. Bounce. As sure as I am standing here, her head bounced. I did not know heads bounced. I guess I never thought about it. But it bounced maybe three times. It hit the ground the first time and then bounced what, maybe six inches or so. Then it hit and bounced about half that height, and then only slightly the last time. And it rolled too. Rolled right to the edge of the road. Wow. What a rush! What a thrill!"

Abruptly stopping, a staccato guffaw filled the room. "Well judges, how do you score her? Well Ted, I only give her about a six point two. She had nice form, but she simply did not stick the landing."

After another bout of laughter, Matthew decided it was time to focus. "Come on, let's get it together. We have work to do."

Referencing his notes on the paper in front of him, he selected an eight-inch-long auger and placed it in the drill press. This morning while drinking a cup of coffee, Matthew again referenced the conversion table he was looking at last evening. He calculated the size drill bits he would need and wrote them on a scrap of paper.

Clamping the wooden rod in the drill press, he bored a hole the full length of the drill bit. Removing the rod from the press, he clamped it in the vise mounted on the workbench and cut off a six-inch piece from the bored end.

The metals rods would be a little more complicated. Those he would need to cut to length first, about six inches would do nicely, and then drill them. He obviously could not use the wood boring auger; he would need to use twist bits. Unfortunately, Kevin did not seem to have any long drill bits capable of drilling the metal rods, so Matthew would need to use an extension. And, drilling metal would take considerably longer than drilling the wood, and he would need to use oil.

Looking around the garage, he did not see any tapping oil or cutting oil. Heck, he did not see any oil at all, not even motor oil. He recalled seeing a machinist several years ago using bacon grease while drilling a hole in a thick piece of metal, and also using it to tap threads. But he did not happen to have any bacon grease either. Heck, he did not even have any bacon he could cook. Seeing a can of red spray paint on the shelf gave him an idea.

Pulling the cap off the can, Matthew walked over to the lawn mower sitting in the corner of the garage. Removing the oil filler cap, he tipped the lawn mower sideways until he had black oil about an inch deep in the red plastic cap. Heck, it was not like he was going to use the mower any way.

Chapter 20

With the hollow rods attached to the rectangular piece of plywood, all he needed was some type of firing mechanism. He had a couple of ideas, but the most practical one was the actuators for electric door locks for a car. He still needed to get those, and then figure out the electrical power source. But that was for another day. For now, he had a board with six homemade guns. Six barrels, three different diameters, three different calibers, two barrels of each caliber.

Taking a couple of steps back from the workbench, Matthew admired his handiwork. All great inventions need a name, and so did his. Tipping the bottle in his hand towards his mouth, he took a swallow of beer and pondered. Staring at the contraption, at the board with the six improvised guns, he was quite proud of the gun board he had made. That was it. The gun board, the GB. The gun board with six guns. The GB6. The electrically actuated GB6. The EAGB6.

"I should patent this. I really should. There is nothing else like it," he said aloud to the empty garage. Tipping his head back for the final swig of beer, Matthew returned to the workbench and set the bottle down. Picking up a pencil, he sketched out EAGB6 in the center of the board, near the top.

Picking up the quart sized can of black enamel paint, he vigorously shook the can for a full minute.

After opening the can, he took a small paint brush from the pack he had purchased at the arts and crafts store last week. Matthew slowly and methodically painted inside the block letters he had drawn.

"Now that looks good. I did a pretty good job, if I say so myself. Not that I'd want to make a career doing this. Still, I do quality work."

How many jobs has he had? Matthew thought for a few moments, mentally tallying his employers. By his count, he had had seven different jobs in the last eight years. In his mind he is a good worker, and he might actually be, but so far no one has really appreciated it; in Matthew's opinion, they simply have not seen his value. Sure, he does things differently, but he does them better. "How can they not see that?" he often wonders aloud, particularly when asked by family and friends about his job situation. Of course, being supportive they politely agree all the while wondering if perhaps Matthew needs a reality check. He asserts that every place he has ever worked things have been a mess, they have been so inefficient. He has recognized that and tried to show them a better way. And for what? His bosses certainly have not appreciated it. Oh sure, after they fired him, they probably took credit for everything he did. That is what usually happened to him. They took credit for his great work but fired him to cover up their own incompetence. They could not stand having someone smarter than them working for them. He would show them. He would show all of them! One day opportunity was going to come knocking, and he was certainly going to open the door. He would get a job, a great job, a management job so he could really show people how things are supposed to be done. Matthew always seemed to ignore the simple fact he had no leadership or management experience whatsoever.

His current job was certainly not ideal, it was certainly not the job he deserved, he deserved so much better, at least in his mind, but this job did provide him some flexibility so for now it happened to suit his needs rather nicely.

Matthew got this job unloading trucks some ten months ago, in October of last year, in fact.

Thanks to COVID-19 when companies were having problems attracting and retaining employees, he landed this job even though he had no experience. Matthew received a $2,000 hiring bonus, and they provided training and forklift operator certification.

The hours were not consistent, but the job was stable. It took on average three to four hours to unload a fully packed fifty-three-foot trailer and to move the contents to the proper place in the warehouse. The trailers could easily haul over thirty-four thousand pounds. With a volume of just over thirty-eight hundred cubic inches, the trailer could hold up to twenty-six pallets. Of course, all this was dependent on the cargo. Due to the irregular shape of many items being shipped, there were often voids and air pockets, meaning a trailer was often not completely filled.

He had to travel to the warehouse on Shop Road in Columbia to check-in in person at eight thirty every weekday morning. If there were no trucks to unload, as was the case about once a week, Matthew was still paid for an hour at his regular twenty-eight dollars per hour rate. Usually there were two to three trucks to unload, and they all had to be unloaded on that day. So, sometimes the work day was short, very short, only an hour, while other days were up to thirteen or fourteen hours when factoring in breaks and lunch. All in all, Matthew usually worked fifty to fifty-five hours per week, and no weekends.

The freedom and the lack of a regular, structured schedule suited Matthew. Oh sure, there was something to be said for a fixed and predictable work schedule:

show up every day, work from eight to noon, take an hour lunch break, then work four more hours. That was great for some people, but it really was not his thing. Oh sure, he, himself, used to embrace such structure, but perhaps that was because his father had such tight control over him. The old man had done a couple of years in the military, the infantry.

Frank had deployed during the Persian Gulf War in January of 1991. The ground campaign began on February 24th of that same year and lasted all of a hundred hours. But a hundred hours was enough for the damage to be done to Frank.

His unit had helped liberate Kuwait and had advanced into Iraqi territory when the Bradley IFV he was riding in hit an IED and was simultaneously hit by enemy RPGs. The vehicle was ripped to shreds. Frank saw both his commander and the gunner were in pieces. The gunner had died instantly, and Frank watched the commander suffer and die over the course of three minutes, three minutes which seemed like a lifetime. He tried talking to Petey, but there was no response. He tried to tell Peter Gambrell he was sorry, but he was not sure if he heard it. Frank watched his commander's chest slowly move up and down with each breath, until it did not.

The six soldiers they were transporting, the six grunts, he had no idea what happened to them. There was no movement, no sound. After the explosions it was eerily quiet, except for the ringing in his ears. He tried calling out, but there was no response. He was not sure he could even hear anyway. From where he was, encased in twisted metal, he could not see much around him.

Frank lay trapped in the rubble for the next thirty minutes, blaming himself, and wishing he could hurry up and die. He replayed the events over and over in his mind, trying to figure out just what had happened. What went wrong? What did he do wrong? For twenty minutes he waited for the soldiers in a trailing Bradley to cautiously approach—they of course had to check for other buried improvised explosive devices—and another ten minutes to free him from the wreckage.

Frank never saw the IED, and the RPGs just seemed to come out of nowhere. Things were happening so fast and, inside the Bradley, his view was somewhat limited. Still, being the driver, he blamed himself, he felt responsible for the crew. The commander may have officially been responsible for the crew and vehicle, but the commander, the gunner, and the driver, the three-person crew, they were a team. And as the driver, he felt personally responsible for the vehicle and keeping everyone inside safe. He felt he somehow failed them; he must have. Eight good soldiers were now dead because of him.

After two months of recovery, having earned a purple heart for his injuries, Frank walked out of the hospital carrying nothing but a duffle bag full of guilt and regret and was discharged from the service shortly thereafter.

Once home, he and the bottle became quick friends. Many times he could not sleep because of dreams of the event, dreams of seeing the captain dying, dreams of seeing body parts of other soldiers laying on the ground as he was unceremoniously pulled from the wreckage. Alcohol helped. Many times during the day random thoughts of the event flooded his mind. Alcohol was there. Sometimes he was on the verge of breaking down and crying. Alcohol comforted him. There was the constant struggle with guilt. The alcohol forgave him. The one thing the alcohol could not help with was the anger and rage he felt inside, anger and rage he usually took out on others. But alcohol did help squash the guilt he felt afterwards.

Frank's year and a half military career itself is not what instilled structure in Matthew. At least he did not think so. The old man would never talk about his military days, and would often fly into a rage when asked about them. Matthew had learned that the hard way when he was only nine years old. The lesson was quickly learned, though it took the broken nose a bit longer to heal.

Actually, Matthew thought, perhaps quite the opposite. Come to think of it, the old man was not one for the rules. He pretty much did things his own way, but everyone else better darn well do things Frank's way too or misery would not be far behind. Matthew and his mom had learned that the hard way.

Matthew looked down at the screen of his ringing phone. Heather.

"Hiya, Matt," came her reply to his mumbled "Hello."

First came the small talk, what she referred to as "chit-chat." Chit-chat; to Matthew that sounded like something little old ladies did, and probably while getting their hair done.

Heather finally got to the point. Could Matthew come over to look at her garbage disposal real quick? It was not working. "Well, I thought you said your boyfriend did not want me over there?"

She countered with she had never said any such thing, that he must have her confused with some other woman.

"Nope. You told me just two months ago. Hang on just a second." Scrolling through text messages, he found what he was looking for. "Here you go," he said as he read the message.

"Well, that must have been a different guy I was dating."

"It is not my job to keep up with who you are dating."

"Well, I am not dating him any more either anyway. I broke up with him about two weeks ago. You know, you really should delete old messages from your phone. People don't like it when you go back and pull stuff from them."

"Ah, you mean you don't like it when I go back and use your own words?"

"Exactly! People change their minds. Women change their minds all the time. You should know that by now. You can't always hold women to what they say."

Matthew said he did not get it; he just did not understand it. Sure, some things might change. Someone might like watching a TV show or something and something happens to cause them to not like it anymore. Or, someone may say or do something so offensive it ends a relationship. But if someone said today they like apples, well he should be able to reasonably presume they would like apples a few weeks from now. Consistency, that is all he was expecting.

"Yeah, women are not always consistent," she told him. "About that disposal."

"Sure, I guess I could stop by sometime and look at it. As long as he is going to be okay with it. I do not want to get shot, and certainly not over a disposal."

"No one is going to shoot you. And I already told you, I am not dating him anymore. I am not dating anyone at the moment."

They agreed on six o'clock. She offered to pay him, he declined. "Well, I will at least buy you dinner." He agreed.

"Okay, there are a few things going on here. First and foremost, do not put a banana peel in the disposal." Matthew explained that banana peels are tough and fibrous, and the disposal has a difficult time breaking them down.

"Don't disposals have blades? Won't the blades just chop them up?"

Yes, the disposals have blades, very sharp rapidly rotating blades, but banana peels are tough. After all, they protect the bananas inside. The disposal tends to kind of shred the peels, and the fibers of the peel kind of get stuck around the blades. And on top of that, the banana peels, or what is left of them after going through the disposal, can clog pipes.

"And that is what you had going on. You had banana peel fibers wrapped around the blades, well actually they are cutters, and there was a hunk of peel wedged in the cutters. That caused the breaker to trip."

"But I checked the circuit breaker like you taught me."

He was not talking about the circuit breaker, at least not the one in breaker box downstairs in the garage. Matthew explained there was a small circuit breaker, a reset button, on the bottom of the disposal.

"Now that you mentioned the breaker, why don't you go ahead and kill the breaker in the box in the garage? I am going to be putting my hand in there to untangle this mess, and it would probably be best to make sure the disposal cannot come on."

With the disposal unclogged, and the breaker downstairs back on, Matthew opened the tap and let water begin flowing into the disposal. Reaching over, he flipped the switch. An immediate click. Flipping the switch to the off position, he reached under the disposal and pressed the reset button. Flipping the power switch, the reset button immediately clicked again.

"What does that mean? Does it mean I need a new disposal?" Heather asked.

"Not so fast. A reset button clicking that fast a lot of times just means the disposal is stuck or clogged. The button trips, or resets, to keep the motor from burning up. You got a broom?"

Reaching up and turning the power switch off, Matthew stuck the end of the broom handle into the disposal, and wedged it up against the cutters. At first the cutters refused to rotate. But after a bit more pressure, they finally freed up and rotated freely.

With the button on the bottom reset, and water again running into the sink, he turned on the power switch. The disposal roared to life, with the entire sink vibrating violently for a few seconds before settling down, leaving the disposal quietly humming.

Turning off the power, Matthew proclaimed, "My job here is done. The disposal demons have been exorcised. Disposal demons be gone!"

Without warning, she kissed him awkwardly. Caught off guard, he was not quite sure what to do. He kissed back. Her arms wrapped around him, his wrapped around her, and the kissing was no longer awkward.

Just as quickly and unexpectedly as the kiss had started, it ended. Heather suddenly pushed Matthew away. "What was that?" she demanded. "What do you think you are doing?"

Matthew was totally confused. He was not quite sure what to say. "Um, well, um," he stammered, "you sort of started it."

"I was just giving you a quick kiss to say thank you. You did not have to kiss me back."

Still completely flummoxed, he managed to mumble, "I'm sorry."

"What would my boyfriend think? I cannot be doing this."

Now Matthew's head was really spinning. "I thought you said you did not have a boyfriend?"

"I never said any such thing."

"You said you broke up with him two weeks ago."

"We did. It is just that I am still his girlfriend but he just does not know it. We are going to get back together but he does not know it yet."

Matthew was rendered speechless, until Heather said, "Hey, let's go get something to eat." All Matthew could manage was a simple, "Okay."

After eating Mexican food and drinking two margaritas each, they were in Heather's car starting back towards her house.

"Hey, you mind if we stop off someplace?"

"I guess not," Matthew replied.

Good, because Heather wanted to drop off some clothes. *And there it is,* he thought. When Heather wanted to take her car to dinner, he knew there was an ulterior motive. She normally liked riding on the back of his bike, but tonight she said they should take her car if they were going to have a drink, something about it being safer. Ordinarily he might buy her argument, except not tonight; at least not after he found out the place there were going for dinner was only four blocks away. It was not raining and the temperature was pleasant. There really was no reason not to be walking, other than her saying she would prefer not to walk. When he heard that, he knew something was up, because that woman was borderline-obsessed about counting her steps.

"You want to do what?"

"Drop off clothes. See all those clothes in the back seat? I want to drop those off for other people," she said as Matthew was turning around to look behind him.

"Other people. What other people?"

"You know, poor people, homeless people."

"Why in God's name would you do that?" Matthew asked.

"Exactly."

"Exactly what?"

"In God's name."

"I'm lost."

"You asked me why in God's name I would give clothes to needy people."

"So?"

"I am giving the clothes to other people in God's name. You know, that whole feed the hungry and clothe the naked thing. I am just trying to help clothe them."

"Yeah, well, let them fend for themselves. Let them go naked. Nobody ever gave me anything when I was hungry. Nobody ever gave me clothes. I had to buy all of my clothes. I did not even have an older brother or any cousins where I could get hand-me-downs. I had to buy everything."

"But they do not have any money to buy clothes."

"Then let them get a job."

"God asks us all to help, to help each other."

"Yeah, well, I am not much into the whole God thing."

"I don't get that, Matt. It's really not about whether or not you're into the whole God thing. It's about doing what's right. It's about being compassionate."

"What about that whole thing about give a man a fish, and you feed him for a day; teach a man to fish, and you feed him for a lifetime? I am compassionate. Give the bums a job and let them buy their own clothes. Teach them to fend for themselves. Now that is true compassion. By giving them free clothes, aren't you just enabling them?"

"You know, I don't want to talk about this anymore. You're making my head hurt. You were always so nice; what happened to you? Never mind; don't answer that. Let me just drop these clothes off and then we will go get another drink."

Arriving back at Heather's house, they had already had two more drinks at a local bar. She opened a bottle of wine and they wandered out into the back yard. Sitting in Adirondack chairs under the stars, they finished the bottle. She suggested he probably should not ride his motorcycle after drinking as much as they did, that perhaps he should stay the night.

His helmet greeted the sunrise sitting on her kitchen counter.

Chapter 21

Reaching under the bed, his hand moved around blindly until it found what Matthew was looking for. His fingers closed on the edge, and he slid the gray plastic bus tub from underneath his bed. The three plastic bags were right where he had left them. He slid the box across the carpeted floor towards the closet.

From the closet, he pulled out one of the three brown cardboard boxes. Opening the box, he saw it was only half full, containing a yoyo, his old baseball glove, and various other miscellaneous items.

Removing the two small plastic bags from the bus tub, he placed them gently into the box. He likewise transferred the three-gallon plastic bag containing the empty beer bottles.

Closing the box, he slid it back into the closet. He picked up the bus tub and, carrying it down the stairs, got into Kevin's old truck.

Unfastening the seat belt, he held the steering wheel with his left hand while he leaned over to roll down the passenger side window.

Sitting back up straight, his gaze shifted from window to window and to the rearview mirror and saw no cars around him. Picking up the gray tub, he was ready to toss it out the window, when he realized that was not a very good plan. Instead, he pulled off the right edge of Highway 321 a few hundred yards before the dog food plant.

Getting out of the truck, he walked to the passenger side and opened the door. Glancing around, he saw a single car approaching from the opposite direction. He patiently waited for the car to pass and disappear down the road. Removing the tub from the truck, he walked to the edge of the trees and nonchalantly tossed it into the woods. Getting back into the truck, he continued further into Gaston.

Ten minutes after disposing of the bus tub, Matthew was slowly driving down Fallow Road looking for the address Alfonso had given him.

Seeing the blue sign with white numbers, Matthew turned left into the driveway. The gate was open, so he drove on in, and proceeded down the dirt road. A quarter of a mile later, he was starting to wonder if this was the correct place. Then he saw the roof of a house.

"Wow," that's a long driveway you have, Matthew said getting out of the truck.

"Yeah, it's about a third of a mile," Alfonso told him. "We like our privacy."

Following the introduction of the other three guys, Alfonso asked if he would like coffee or pastries. Matthew politely declined until Al told him, "Maria, my wife, she will be so disappointed. She made them herself from scratch."

"In that case, sure, I will most definitely eat a pastry."

After Alfonso had gone inside, Ted leaned in towards Matthew and told him not to believe Al, that his wife did not make them, that they actually came from a bakery in Cayce.

Ricardo contended that Ted is the one that could not be believed, that he was a practical joker. Ted did not refute the claim; he simply held up his coffee cup with a wink and a smile, and took a sip of coffee.

Within thirty minutes, the ladders were set up and they were on top of the one-story house with assorted shovels, spades, and scrapers.

Three hours later they were standing on the ground, each holding a beer, and surveying the mess they had made. Tattered roof shingles littered the ground. A blue rented dump trailer sat fifteen feet away; only a few of the shingles had managed to land in the trailer, and that was only by luck. The goal was to get the shingles and paper off the roof quickly. With any luck at all, the five of them might be able to have the new roof on this afternoon. The mess could be cleaned up later. The next order of business would be going over the roof and removing any stray roofing nails.

"Look guys, it is eleven thirty. What do you say we get some lunch?" Alfonso asked them.

After finishing their beers, they climbed into Alfonso's GMC Yukon.

At the junction of Fallow Road and SC Highway 6, heavy equipment was busy working in a field.

"What are they doing there?" Ricardo asked.

Alfonso explained the landowner decided it was time to sell the trees, making several hundred thousand dollars in the process. Just last week this had all been woodlands. Now it was being converted to farmland. In the last several days the trees had been harvested, and the ground cleared. They were grading it now to make it smooth, and to remove all the rocks, stumps, and roots. It would be plowed soon, and the landowner would plant corn to try to capitalize on the booming moonshine market.

While Ted was commenting that he would like to get into the shine business, Matthew was viewing things a bit differently.

Wow, what a great place to bury a body, he thought. The field is going to be plowed. And then they are going to plant corn. Hmm, that could work. Imagine, if someone was to plant a body out there. Sneak out there late at night after all the grading was done. Traipse out to the middle of the field. Dig a hole six or eight feet deep; need to make sure a plow could not possibly disturb the body. Plant the body and, Matthew could not quite suppress the laugh, and just hope it does not grow.

Ricardo turned and looked at him quizzically.

"Oh, it is nothing, I was just thinking how these people are making moonshine legally, but ten years ago it would have been illegal. Funny how times change."

Ricardo seemed satisfied as he smiled and nodded.

Matthew's thoughts returned to the field. The body would to be six or eight feet deep. Drop it in the hole and fill the hole back in. Corn would eventually be planted and— "Hey, Siri, how long does it take corn to grow?"

Other conversations stopped while they all awaited the response. Corn apparently takes sixty to ninety days to grow.

"See? See how profitable that could be?" Alfonso said. "This guy will have a corn crop in two to three months."

"Yeah, from seed to harvest," Ted added. "Al, maybe you should see about clearing out a little bit of that land you have—what do you have, fifty or sixty acres—and see about growing some corn yourself."

Matthew was not concerned about the profit potential; he was pondering a different potential.

So, if a body was planted in the field, and then seeds were planted, in sixty to ninety days the corn would be ready for harvest. So, that meant there should be corn starting to grow in a few days, and would be real plants in a few weeks. Perfect, absolutely perfect, Matthew thought. So, if a body was planted, within a week or two there should be corn plants growing, and within a month there should be some reasonably well-developed corn plants. If that buried person was reported missing, an investigation would eventually start. How long would it take? Who knows? "But I know one thing, there is no way anyone would ever think to look here," he said to himself. He simply could not imagine law enforcement deciding they needed to tear up every field of crops so they could look for a body. Brilliant, absolutely brilliant, he thought. What a perfect place to bury a body. Now, he just needed a body.

They had eaten lunch at a little hibachi restaurant in Red Bank, fifteen miles northwest of Gaston. It was the strangest thing; it was the only hibachi place he had ever been to that did not load the food down with onions. In fact, there were no onions at all.

On the drive back to Gaston, Matthew was struck by the number of people he saw walking alone on the side of the road.

"Yeah," Alfonso replied, "there are a lot of poor people out here. There are a lot of homeless people here too. But some of these people you see walking, some of them do drugs too. A lot of drugs, a lot of meth. If you are not careful, sometimes one of them will just stumble off the side of the road, right into the roadway."

"No, really?" Ricardo asked.

"Yep, it is true. Especially late at night. Just last week I had a meth-head stumble into the middle of the road, right in front of me. I almost hit him, and would have if my wife had not screamed."

"That is pretty sad," Chuck added from the other side of Ricardo.

"Yep. And the hookers too, the prostitutes. A lot of that going on."

"I never knew all of that was going on out here. I never really thought about it. I guess it makes sense though; there is not exactly a lot of industry out here, and most of the jobs that do exist are retail and fast food. Still, it is just so sad," Ricardo said dejectedly.

Matthew, on the other hand, was seeing opportunity. People wasted out of their mind? Wandering aimlessly into the road, perhaps oblivious to approaching traffic? And late at night? With very little traffic? Hot diggity dog! He could not ask for a better setup. "Me thinks I have found me self a body," he said, wondering if he had actually said that out load as he tried to suppress the smile that struggled to be set free.

While Alfonso and Ted snapped chalk lines, the other three guys walked the roof, removing roofing nails as they went.

After hoisting rolls of roofing felt up the ladder, the five of them managed to paper the roof of the fourteen hundred and eighty-two square foot ranch in less than an hour. They worked so fast, Matthew barely had time to think.

"Beer break," Ted announced. "But only one, boys; remember, we are on a roof. Oh, and that's chicken noodle soup for Matthew."

For the next twenty minutes, while nursing a beer and eating a bag of potato chips, Matthew's mind drifted back to the field at the end of the road, less than a mile away from where he was currently sitting. He was getting restless. He was getting antsy. His thoughts shifted to Red Bank. In his mind he began to form a rough plan. He was going to need Kevin's truck, of course. He could not very well run someone over using his motorcycle, at least not and survive it himself. Plus, if he managed to successfully run someone over without wrecking, he would still need to transport the body. Yep, he would definitely need the truck.

He was going to need a shovel, a garden rake, and a tarp. Definitely no flashlight; it would only draw attention. In fact, a moonless night would be best. The darker the better.

"Break time is over, boys," Ted proclaimed. "Back to the roof. Grab a bundle on your way up."

They each hoisted a sixty-pound bundle of shingles up the ladder, with some of them doing it more gracefully than others.

"I will tell you what, guys," Ted said. "Why don't me and Ricardo get the rest of the shingles up on the roof and you guys start putting them down." No one argued with that approach.

"How many bundles you need, Alf?"

Alfonso explained there are three bundles in a square, and a square covers one hundred square feet. So, for fourteen and eighty-two square feet, he is going to need fourteen point eight squares, so make that fifteen squares. With three squares per bundle, that is forty-five bundles. Though he would love to do the entire roof this afternoon, he did not really think that was possible and he would settle for getting about half of it done today. So, twenty-two or twenty-three bundles, minus the five they had all just brought up. "How about seventeen or eighteen more bundles," Alfonso replied. "That should be fine for today."

Chapter 22

"Really? Wow," Matthew said into the cell phone. "Sure, I can stop by. I have to work late tonight; we have three trucks to unload today. Is tomorrow okay?"

Disconnecting the call, Matthew was still surprised. It looked like he would be visiting his sister tomorrow evening.

After their mother had died last year, the few belongings Katie had in her rented mobile home wound up at Alex's house.

The landlord certainly wasted no time. The day after Katie died, the landlord had called Matthew.

He did not recognize the number and started not to answer the phone. Nowadays, what was the point? Most of the unknown numbers were usually a telemarketer or a scamster. Just in the last few days, Matthew had received three calls about his car warranty expiring. That was very considerate of them, to be that concerned about his car warranty—for a car he did not even own. He had also received two voice messages in the last week informing him there is a "warrant taken out in your name." He simply deleted the messages, figuring no one was actually going to come take him away.

Being a local number that was calling, Matthew took a chance and answered the ringing phone.

"My name is Wayne Evans," came the booming voice with a strong southern accent.

"Yeah, I don't know you, so what do you want?"

Ignoring the contempt from Matthew, he continued, "I am looking for Mr. Stockmore, a Mr. Matthew Stockmore."

"What do you want?"

"Who are you, sir? Are you Mr. Stockmore?"

"I am the guy whose phone you just called."

"Sir, I am going to need to know who you are. You will need to identify yourself."

"Look, you called me. I do not know you from Adam's house cat. You either tell me what you want, or we end this call right now. Your choice."

"Well, I am calling about Katie Stockmore. Do you know Katie?"

"Perhaps. What do you want?"

"Well, Katie rented a residence from me. She listed this number and a Matthew Stockmore for her emergency contact information."

"Okay, so what do you want from me?"

"So, you do know Ms. Stockmore?"

"Yeah, she is my mom. Or, was my mom."

"So, are you Matthew?"

"Yes, I am."

"Well, very good then. The reason I am calling is that I understand Katie passed away yesterday. My condolences, by the way."

"Thank you."

"So here is the thing. This is the last day of the month. Rent is due on the first day of the month. So, I need you to come and remove her belongings today."

"Unbelievable! Talk about insensitive. For crying out loud, her body is not even cold yet. Where do you get off calling me the day after my mother dies?"

"Hey, it's just business."

"It may be business to you, but that was, that is, my mom."

"Again, my condolences. But we really do need to get this taken care of, like, today."

"Look, can it not wait until this weekend?"

"Actually, no. We need to turn that place around and get someone else in there."

"I am at work right now. There is no way I can do it today."

"If you need more time, you will need to pay another month's rent."

"Talk about cold-hearted. We have not even buried Mom yet, and you want me to focus on getting her stuff out of your place? How did you even know she died anyway? You are nothing but a vulture."

"Yeah, well, whatever. I need you to get her stuff out of there by 5 pm today. And, um, I need you to clean the place, too, if you want her security deposit back."

"If her rent is paid until the end of the month, the month ends at midnight, not at 5 pm."

"If it is not gone by 5 pm I will remove it myself and set it by the edge of the road."

"Just try that. I will call the police and press charges. Her rent is paid through the end of the day. I will take you to court." The anger in Matthew's voice was abundantly clear. "And, let's not forget about social media. I will blast it all over the place. My mom died yesterday, and you are essentially evicting her before the lease ends at midnight. Oh, that will be great fun! I will destroy you."

Matthew disconnected the call.

The phone immediately rang again. He saw the number on the screen was the same as the previous call. Matthew knew it was Wayne Evans of Capital View Estates. He did not answer.

Less than fifteen seconds later, the phone rang again, and was again ignored.

Fifteen seconds later the phone again rang and Matthew answered. "Leave me alone. Stop calling me. We will settle this legally. I am trying to reach my attorney," he lied, "but you keep calling."

"There is no need for all of that. Let us both just calm down."

"Calm down? You called me back to tell me to calm down?"

"Hang on, just hang on. I will give you until eight o'clock tomorrow morning."

"You are a real prince. I'll see what I can do." Matthew disconnected the call. Wayne did not call back.

Unlocking the door to 113E, and stepping inside, Alex was overcome by a wave of emotion. She had, of course, accepted the fact that her mother had died yesterday. Her death was not unexpected, and truth be told, there was a sense of relief; the cancer had been very aggressive. Katie's last six months had been very difficult, a lot of suffering. So in a way, her passing from this earthly realm was a bit of a relief. At least her mother's pain and suffering were over. Still, there was a tinge of guilt that she should think that of her own mother, that she should think her dying was a good thing. She kept telling herself that Katie was better off, that she was in a much better place. But in the back of her mind, there was a deep little thought that it was wrong to be happy at the death of her mother, of her own mother.

Matthew had called her earlier this morning. Recapping his phone call with Wayne, he asked if there was any way she would be able to get over to Capital View Estates. Being an independent massage therapist, Alex checked her schedule and saw she had no clients booked after two this afternoon.

Alex realized the emotion and guilt was not so much about her mother's death. Rather, it was about the way Katie had been living. It was so sad. The smell, the stench of cigarette smoke. Alex had never noticed how dingy everything was, had never noticed what a drab, dark place it was. Perhaps it was because all the blinds were closed?

Tears began streaming down her cheeks as a fresh wave of guilt washed over her. Why is it she had never noticed how bleak and depressing this place was? Had it always been like this? She had visited her mother every other week for years, for oh so many years, and never picked up on the inherent gloominess.

"Oh dear God, dear Heavenly Father. Please forgive me, forgive me for my blindness. Help remove the darkness from my eyes and from within my soul so I may be more aware of those suffering around me. I am so sorry, Momma. Please dear God, please help me, and please have mercy on my mother's soul. Amen."

Alex opened several moving boxes she had brought with her and began loading the tangible remnants of her mom's life. Alex carried four boxes of Katie's belongings, and three large black garbage bags full of Katie's clothes outside and loaded them into her SUV.

She would eventually go through the boxes, but she really had no use for the clothes; they would go straight to charity. From the back corner in the bottom of the bedroom closet, Alex retrieved a cardboard bankers box labeled `Documents.` She secured the top with a couple of pieces of clear packing tape.

Looking around the empty mobile home, she decided Wayne what's-his-name could clean the place himself. He could keep the eighty-five-dollar security deposit. It was not worth her time, not worth the two or three hours it would take to clean the mobile home. Even then, she had no guarantee the guy would not say the cleaning was not sufficient and would keep the security deposit anyway. So, what was the point?

Carrying the bankers box and the roll of tape out the front door, she turned and locked the deadbolt while balancing the box on her hip. At some point she would open the box and sort through whatever her mom had been keeping in there. But not today. Probably not for several days.

Chapter 23

"Hiya, Matt," Todd said, greeting Matthew with a smile. "Come on in." Closing the door behind them, he followed Matthew down the hallway on the right and towards the kitchen.

Walking into the kitchen, Alex greeted Matthew with a hug. "Hi, Honey."

"Hey, sis."

"Hey, Matt, would you like a glass of wine, or a beer?" Todd asked.

"Oh but of course. It looks like both of you are drinking wine, so wine will be fine."

"Great. What color?"

"Wine colored."

"Give him some of that Merlot," Alex chimed in. "It is very good. A client gave me that. Good stuff."

The doorbell rang.

"Right on time," Todd said as he handed Matthew a glass of red wine, and headed down the hall towards to the door.

"Right on time? Expecting someone else?"

"Just the pizza guy. We are going super easy tonight. Very casual."

"Oh, and paper plates too? I see you brought out the fine china."

"Only the best for you. And no, we are not going to wash them and save them like you do."

"Hey, I am just doing my part. That is my form of recycling."

"Sick is what that is. What was that old commercial? Something like, if you don't get help at Charter, please get help somewhere."

"Very funny! Besides, I do not wash paper plates. Only plastic plates."

"That is just as bad. They are disposable, you know."

"Yeah, but if I paid for them, I might as well use them until they crack or break. I get my money's worth out of them."

"You can be so cheap."

"Only–"

"Get it while it is hot!" Todd exclaimed, walking into the kitchen carrying two large pizza boxes.

"Would you like another slice?"

"Heck no! Thank you though, but three slices was plenty."

Todd countered, "Then you can take a few pieces home with you."

"No problem there. Heck, that might even be breakfast."

"And you will probably even be eating it cold too, won't you?"

"Of course."

"There is something seriously wrong with you."

"Not really. It only needs to be cooked once. Plus, look at the time and electricity I save by not reheating it."

"That is just wrong. Tell him, Todd."

"I gotta tell you, dear, I am with Matthew on this one."

"Good grief. That has to be a guy thing."

"Wait a second. You eat cold chicken from the fridge. And, I've seen you make turkey sandwiches and not heat them."

"Yeah, but that is different. I don't like the taste of reheated meat. But we're not here to talk about eating habits."

Standing and uncorking another bottle, Todd asked as more of a formality, "Would you like more wine? I think another glass of wine might be in order."

"Excellent idea, dear."

"Hey, no more for her. She is not even legal!" Matthew teased.

"Yeah, I try to tell her that too, but she does not listen me to either," Todd said with a laugh.

"Oh just knock it off. I am nineteen."

"Yeah, sis, but the legal drinking age is twenty-one."

"It is our house, and I will drink wine if I want to."

"Lawbreaker. I am married to a criminal!"

"Yeah, right. And what does that say about you, Mr. Andrews? You are my supplier!" Laughing, Alex added, "So, who is the real criminal here? Besides, you are only twenty-two."

"Touché"

"You, you two are a real pair of outlaws. A veritable Bonnie and Clyde," Matthew said with a bit of a smirk.

"Now that we have that settled, will you please pour us some more wine, Mr. Barrow? Your Bonnie is thirsty."

Winking, Todd replied, "Yes, ma'am, Ms. Parker."

"Hey, Matt. Remember when you called me last year right after Mom died, and I went over to get her stuff?'

"Yep, sure do. Sorry about that. I think I was at work or something."

"No need to apologize. Anyway, I donated most of her clothes, remember? And most of her furniture too."

"Yeah, I remember. Hopefully it helped a few people." Matthew did not add what else he was thinking, "Hopefully the cigarette smell did not kill them."

"I am sure they appreciated it. Anyway, Mom also had a cardboard box, you know, one of those bankers box things. She had a bunch of papers and stuff in there. Me and Todd went through it earlier this year. When was it, dear?"

"February. We were looking for stuff to do her taxes."

"Yeah, so in February we went through it. Guess what else we found? Come on, guess."

"I don't know. I don't have a clue."

"Come on. Guess."

"I do not know. Either a bunch of cash, or papers saying we were adopted."

Taking a sip of wine, Todd proclaimed, "Well, you are pretty close on one of those."

"What? One of us was adopted? It would have to be me. I was around when you were born. I was like ten or something." Taking a sip of wine, and continuing with a smile, "And, I do not remember being born myself, so it has to be me." Holding the wine glass up in a mock toast, with a wink of his eye, he emptied the glass in a large gulp.

"You goofball! No one remembers being born. And neither one of was adopted. Mom and dad were our parents, our real parents."

"Okay, so then what *was* in the box? A bunch of cash?"

"In a manner of speaking, yes," Alex said to Matthew and she began explaining as Todd refilled their wine glasses.

When Alex and Todd had gone through her mom's box of papers a few months after her death, they found an old life insurance policy on Frank, a policy that Katie had never redeemed. Redeemed? She was not even sure if that was proper terminology. Well, Alex did not actually know whether or not it had been redeemed, but the policy was there and she knew two things: her mom never mentioned the policy, and her mom certainly never had any money. Oh sure, she always seemed to pay her bills, but she was always pinching pennies; the woman never spent much money on anything, and certainly very little on herself.

Alex still distinctly remembered a day early last year, just a few weeks before she and Todd were married, back when she still lived with her mother. They had gone to a Walmart and her mother briefly looked at dish towels, before deeming them to be too expensive.

"But Mom, you need new towels. The ones you have now are looking kind of rough."

"My towels will do just fine."

"But you said this morning your other towels are thread-bare."

"Are you mocking me?"

"No, Ma. I am not mocking you."

Leaving empty handed, they went to lunch. Alex had told her mom that she would pay. Still, Katie complained about the price of everything on the menu.

"This is highway robbery, that is what this is. My goodness, look at the price of tea, even the cost of coffee. Where do they get off charging these prices?"

"It is okay, Mom," Alex assured her, "Do not worry about it, I am paying. Just get whatever you would like. Enjoy yourself for once."

"Enjoy myself for once? What is that supposed to mean?"

Oh great, it is going to be one of those days, Alex thought. They often seemed to butt heads, especially since Matthew had moved out, what was it, ten years ago now. She was aware that it really seemed to have gotten worse the last six months, ever since she came home proudly displaying the engagement ring Todd had given her just hours earlier. She really did not want to do this today, the whole contentious thing. She really just wanted to have a pleasant day with her mom.

"I did not mean anything by it, Mom. Really. I was just saying not to worry about the prices. I am paying."

"Not worry about the prices? Oh miss I-have-a-big-paycheck-now."

"Ma, let's not do this. Look, I did not mean anything by it. Let's just have a nice lunch together."

Astonished by the price of a salad, Katie opted for a cup of soup and a glass of water. Alex had wanted something more filling, what she really wanted were chicken fingers, but she dared not get that when her mom was eating a cup of soup. About thirty minutes after they had gotten home, Alex told her mom she had forgotten to get deodorant while they were out earlier, and while she did indeed go buy deodorant, she also went through a fast-food drive-thru and got chicken strips and fries. They were devoured in less than five minutes.

A few days later Alex noticed Katie had a new dish towel. She was almost afraid to ask, she could never tell how her mom was going to react. As politely and nonchalantly as she could, she simply said, "Hey, Mom, you got a new dish towel."

Katie was so proud when telling Alex she had gotten them at the dollar store, for a lot less than the seven dollars Walmart wanted. Alex remembered smiling as she told her mom that was great, but on the inside, she was crying, her heart was breaking that her mother had to resort to such measures.

Presuming it had not been redeemed, neither she nor Todd had any idea whether or not the policy was still good. Was there an age limit on those things? Was there an expiration date? Was there a time limit for redeeming? With more questions than answers, they turned to the internet. Opening a browser on her laptop, Alex searched for "how to redeem life insurance policy."

Reading the results on the screen, she learned the proper terminology was "to file a claim." She also quickly had the answers to her other questions, namely that there was no time limit for filing a claim. Not only that, to her surprise, she also learned the unpaid policy actually accrued interest. And, filing a claim required proof of death, usually in the form of a death certificate.

Alex and Todd agreed they needed to call the insurance company the next morning, and needed to start the process of getting a death certificate for Frank.

Returning back to the box, they began digging through the rest of Katie's documents. Frank's life insurance policy was certainly not the only surprise.

"Wow, what is this?" Todd asked while unfolding a tri-folded group of papers.

"What is what?"

"Hmm. I think you are going to want to see this."

"But what is it?"

He extended the papers to Alex. "Just see for yourself."

Skimming the document quickly, "Is this what I think this is?"

"If you are thinking it is a life insurance policy on your mom, then I would say it certainly is."

Reading the pages with deliberation, Alex saw that her mom had apparently taken this policy out shortly after Frank's death.

Noticing the tears flowing down his wife's cheeks, Todd asked Alex, "What is wrong, dear? Is it finding the policy? I know it is a bit of a surprise."

"Well, yeah, sure, it is a surprise, but–" and the tears turned to sobbing. Leaning over and wrapping his arms around her, the dam broke loose.

After holding her for almost a minute, and with the sobbing having subsided, Todd asked, "What is it, dear?"

Handing the papers back to him, she told him to read the beneficiaries. And, both Alex and Matthew were named as beneficiaries, with the distribution at fifty percent for each of them. It was not so much *that* which had caused the emotional outburst, rather, it was just the idea that Katie had been looking out for them and Alex never knew. It was more the wave of guilt that had washed over her for the tumultuous relationship she sometimes had with her mother over the last couple of years.

"And so, Matthew, there really was a bunch of cash in the box. There were two life insurance policies; one for Dad and one for Mom."

Having listened to the story, Matthew was intrigued. "Okay, so what now? What do we do next?"

"I don't want to steal Alex's thunder, but I would say we celebrate. I think this calls for champagne instead of wine, and we just happen to have a bottle of Dom in the fridge."

"You have Dom, in the fridge, in *your* fridge?"

"Yeah, sure. Not normally, but we do tonight. It is time to celebrate."

"Celebrate what?"

As Todd went to the refrigerator, Alex continued, "Well, like Todd said, the next step is to celebrate. Everything else is done. That is why I invited you over tonight."

"I am at a loss. What are you talking about?"

Alex told Matthew she and Todd had already submitted claims for both life insurance policies. The policy for Katie had paid off relatively quickly, while Frank's policy took a little bit longer, but the insurance carrier eventually issued a check which arrived just last week.

As Todd arrived back with the champagne and three glasses, Alex pulled two white envelopes from underneath her placemat on the table and handed one of them to Matthew.

"What is this?"

"Just open it."

Sitting there with a stunned look on his face, he barely noticed Todd set the fluted glass in front of him.

"Are you serious? Are these for real?" Matthew asked, holding the two checks in front of him.

"They are indeed."

"They had insurance policies for $135,000?"

"Not exactly," Todd added. "That is your half. The total was actually two hundred and seventy thousand dollars. Now, how about that toast?"

Following the toast, Alex slid the other envelope across the table to Matthew.

"And what is this?"

In going through some of her mom's other belongings, she found an ATM card. She never knew her mother had an ATM card and had never known her to use an ATM. It took a while at the bank, verifying her mother's identity, verifying her own identity, and providing the death certificate. Still, it was not a done process and there was a bit of paperwork involved. In the end, Alex was able to gain control of Katie's account.

"Open it and find out."

"What, what is, what is this?" Matthew stammered.

The other envelope contained a cashier's check made out to Matthew, a check for eighty-three thousand dollars and twenty-seven cents, exactly half the balance of Katie's account.

"What it is," Todd exclaimed, "is a reason for another toast."

Raising her glass, Alex made the toast. "Here is to Mom, and to Mom for looking out for us."

"I'll drink to that," Matthew replied. "To Mom."

Chapter 24

Matthew awoke in the morning still having difficulty believing last night was real. Getting out of bed and making his way to the kitchen, he saw the two white envelops sitting on the counter right where he left them last night.

Seeing the envelopes was comforting, at least it was not all a dream, still, he had to see the checks again for himself. Yep, it was real. Between the three checks there was a total of two hundred eighteen thousand dollars. Oh, let's not forget the twenty-seven cents!

He was not sure what he was going to do with the money, but he knew he needed to deposit the checks. Picking up his smart phone, he logged into his Wells Fargo account and began to initiate a mobile deposit as he normally did.

However, when asked to enter the amount, he noticed a message indicating the daily limit was twenty-five thousand dollars, and a thirty-day limit of just under one hundred fifty thousand dollars. Oh well, he sighed, it looked like he would be headed to the bank later today.

Picking up the cup of coffee he had just made using a pod, he looked around the apartment. Yeah, he was done with this place. He decided he would soon be finding a better place to live. His own place. A house. His own house. His very own house.

And work, well, he might just quit work. Then again, maybe not. Maybe he would just continue to work; he would be working because he wanted to work, not because he had to work. And if someone, if anyone, annoyed him he might simply walk out the door and never look back. Or, if he woke up one morning and decided he did not want to go to work anymore, well, maybe he simply would not go. The world was his oyster, and he was definitely going to shuck it.

Pulling into the bank parking lot at eight o'clock, he was disappointed to see the bank lobby did not open for another hour. The ATM would have to do.

He did not expect that. Actually, he was not sure he expected anything. But, something about depositing over two hundred thousand dollars in his account caused a wave of, of what, happiness, or was it relief? A wave of something washed over him. After depositing the checks in the slot of the ATM, he waited a few seconds as the electro-mechanical teller scanned and totaled the checks. The total appeared on the screen. two hundred eighteen thousand dollars and twenty-seven cents. He simply sat and stared at the screen for a few moments. A beeping horn from the car behind him got his attention. Without bothering to look in the mirror, he extended his finger and pushed the button to finalize the deposit. Seeing the amount added to his account gave him a huge sense of satisfaction. Granted, the funds would not be available until tomorrow, but they were still *his* funds. He was not sure if the satisfaction was from depositing the money, or if it was from knowing he had financial freedom, from knowing he was not reliant on anyone now for anything. He was not sure, but he would certainly take it.

Arriving at the warehouse fifteen minutes later, Matthew had not noticed until now the deep blue cloudless sky. Wow! What a gorgeous day. Walking across the parking lot he began whistling something that, at least in his head, sounded like the theme song from the old Andy Griffith show.

The kerCHUNK sound emanated from the Simplex timeclock as Matthew inserted his timecard. Being almost ten minutes early, Matthew stopped by the break room and got a cup of free coffee and made his way to the office.

Walking into the office, he said, "Hiya, Cherise."

"Good morning, Matthew," she responded from behind the counter.

"How are you today?" he asked her.

"Depressed."

"Really, why is that?"

"A friend of mine spent over five hundred dollars at the fair. I want to take my kids, but I cannot afford that."

"Five hundred dollars? What did she do? Take the entire neighborhood?"

"No. That is just the thing, she took her four kids."

"How old are your kids?"

"One is three, and the twins are five."

"Okay, here's the thing. Do something cheaper, and just as much fun. They are young enough they really are not going to know anyway."

"What are you talking about?"

"Take them to Kroger."

"To Kroger? Have you lost your mind?" Cherise said emphatically.

Matthew began to explain his plan. "Take the kids to Kroger, it will be every bit as fun. You can take them for rides in the grocery carts. They have those little carts, so you use two of them. And you cart the kids around the store. You push one cart while pulling the other one, and you swap positions at the end of each aisle."

"Dear God, you have lost you mind."

Undeterred, Matthew continued. "And they have those big carts too; you put them all in that one big cart. It will be just like a four-seater ride at the fair. Just push them around the store in that. And in the big open space between the deli and the meat department, well you just spin the cart around in circles there. Oh, oh, oh, and don't forget the electric scooter buggy things. You can put them in those too. Heck, those three rides alone would have been what, five or six tickets a piece at the fair?"

"Have you been drinking?"

"No, at least not so far today." Doing the quick math on that, multiply by three kids across three rides, he told her that came to something like forty-five to fifty tickets, at what something like a buck and quarter each. "That just saved somewhere between fifty-five and seventy-five dollars."

"Matthew Stockmore, I believe you have lost your marbles."

"But wait, there is more." In the front of the store, in front of the full-service registers, they have boxes and boxes of candy like you get at the movies. They are only a dollar a box. Who knows, maybe that is all the candy the theaters could not sell when they were shut down because of COVID. "Who knows, who really cares. The point is, they are only a buck a box. You cannot do that at the fair."

"Good grief."

And there was more. "Let's not forget about the food," Matthew continued. Over next to the deli, they have prepared foods. They have fried chicken, chicken tenders, French fries, onion rings, and they even have corn dogs. You'll be out of luck with the cotton candy, but does anyone really need to eat that stuff anyway?"

"You really are bonkers, Mr. Stockmore," said a smiling Ralph Yadkins, the owner of the company. He had been standing in the doorway behind Matthew ever since the tail end of the four-seater comment. "You know, maybe you should write kids' books."

"Don't encourage him, dear," Cherise said to her husband.

"Oh and one other thing," Matthew added, "Kroger has that cool little jingle too. *Let's go Krogering,* or something like that."

"Encourage him, dear?" Ralph said. "With an imagination like his, of course I will encourage him. Heck, I will even buy the first book," he said, laughing, as he turned and went back into his office.

"You would," she said to her husband's back.

"What do we have for today?" Matthew asked.

Apologetically, Cherise told him there were no trucks due today. He told her there was no need to apologize. And to think about Kroger.

She told Matthew, with a wink and a smile, to think about getting some professional help.

Walking out the through the double glass doors, Matthew smiled and exclaimed, "Can this day get any better?" He began softly singing as he walked across the parking lot,

"Zip-a-dee-doo-dah, zip-a-dee-ay
My, oh, my, what a wonderful day
Plenty of sunshine headin' my way
Zip-a-dee-doo-dah, zip-a-dee-ay!"

Chapter 25

Inside the garage, Matthew picked up the EAGB6. The only thing left to do was to install the actuators and make the electrical connections.

Last weekend Matthew had gone to a salvage yard in Augusta, GA. Sure, there were salvage yards closer to him and around Columbia, but he wanted to make sure things were not traceable back to him.

Stopping at the ATM on the way out of Columbia, he withdrew one hundred dollars so he could pay cash, again trying to ensure his purchase would not be traceable back to him. Looking at the balance on the ATM screen, he debated whether or not fifty dollars would be enough. Money was certainly not an issue; he just gotten paid yesterday, and he had of course deposited the checks from Alex just two days before that. Considering he may also need to get gas and would probably get something to eat along the way, and he would, of course, want to pay cash for that too, so he opted for the hundred bucks.

He told the guy at the front desk in the salvage yard office that he needed a window motor. "What make and model?"

Matthew had done a quick check on the internet to increase his odds. Searching for the most wrecked cars in the United States, on thetruthaboutcars website he was a bit surprised to see the top three: Subaru Crosstrek, Honda's HR-V, and the Hyundai Elantra GT. Granted, it was a 2019 article, but still, those were certainly not the cars he expected to see. He surmised the most wrecked cars might be a higher percentage of the cars in the salvage yard, but he had never even heard of the Subaru Crosstrek.

As he pulled into the parking lot, he could see rows and rows of cars, and even stacks of cars.

About six rows back he could see what appeared to be an old four door Honda Accord.

"Um, a Honda Accord."

"What year?"

"Um, I don't really know. But it looks a lot like that blue one you have sitting out there, about six rows back."

Sam walked around the end of the counter and looked through the glass door in the side of the building as Matthew pointed out the car to him.

"2003."

"I suppose so," Matthew replied. "From what I understand, Honda pretty much used the same window motor from about 1998 through 2009," he lied. He did not have a clue about Honda electric window motors, or lock actuators for that matter.

"I am not sure where you got that, but it is not entirely accurate. They may have used the same motor for a couple of years, but I don't believe they used the same motor for eleven years."

"Maybe not. But that does look like my friend's car that I am working on. So, I'll take my chances with that."

"Fine, as long as you understand we have a thirty-day refund policy."

"No problem."

Getting his socket set, locking pliers, and hammer from the truck, he made his way out into the yard to the Honda in row 305. Matthew had no idea how their numbering scheme worked, nor did he really care. Sam had told him it was row 305, so row 305 it must be.

Setting the tools down next to the driver's side door, he stretched and, feigning a yawn, looked around. He did not see any video cameras, nor did he see Sam or anyone else looking out the door at him.

Walking around the car, he opened all four doors. Matthew set about removing the electric lock actuators from each door, glancing around after he was finished with each door.

He then removed the electric window motor from the driver's side door. After all, he had told Sam that was what he was here for. He really did not want Sam or anyone else to know what he was actually after.

After stuffing the door lock actuators in his socks, he collected his tools and the window motor and made his way inside to pay Sam.

He had four actuators, but he really needed six. He supposed he could either buy two from a parts store, or he could find another salvage yard. He imagined buying new ones would be a bit pricey, but he had not bothered to check any auto parts stores. The next closest salvage yard he knew of was in the Charlotte area. He really did not want to drive all over creation to get the remaining actuators. Two rows over he saw a badly wrecked Honda. Looking at his watch, he decided he had been here too long as it was. The guys inside would probably be getting suspicious before much longer. Why press his luck?

"Take a little longer than expected?"

"Just a bit. I pulled up a video on my phone," he lied. He did not even have his phone with him. To further ensure he was untraceable, he left his cell phone sitting on the counter at home and had driven Kevin's old truck.

That spurred a thought; the hole in the truck windshield. "Oh by the way, I need one more thing. A windshield for an old Ford F150."

Taking Augusta Road out of Augusta, Matthew drove towards Aiken. For some reason he wanted a hot dog for lunch, and he knew just the place: the Midway Grill in Warrenville, about halfway between Augusta and Aiken. He had found that place one day last year while just out cruising around. The food was great, and reasonably priced. He had vowed to come back, and now was his chance.

Fifteen minutes after polishing off a Greg's Favorite and steak fries, Matthew was standing inside an auto parts store.

"Yeah, I need two electric door lock actuators, for a 2003 Honda Accord," Matthew replied after being welcomed to "the Zone," and being asked how the store associate could help him.

"Is that the DX, EX, or LX?"

"Um, the LX," Matthew guessed.

"What size engine? The 4 cylinder 2.4 liter, or the 6 cylinder 3.0 liter?" she asked him.

"Does that really matter? This is for a door lock actuator. What does the engine size have to do with it?"

"We just want to make sure we get the correct part."

"I still do not understand why engine size makes a difference for the door locks."

"Sir, the computer just asks. I need to enter that to advance to the next screen."

"Um, the 4 cylinder."

STEVE MULLANEY

Rotating the screen so Matthew could see, she began rattling off the prices.

He was pleasantly surprised. They ranged in price from around twenty dollars to around sixty dollars, depending on quality and warranty. For his purposes, the model for $21.49 would do rather nicely. He had a fleeting thought that perhaps the trip to the salvage yard was a wasted trip when he could have gotten them new for less than twenty-two bucks apiece. He quickly remembered he had paid Sam twenty dollars for the window motor, yet he walked out of the salvage yard with the motor and with four actuators he had not paid for.

"I need two of those please. By the way, what kind of current draw on those?"

"You have two go bad at one time, honey?" the woman wearing the Cindy name tag asked.

"You know how it is, you have one go bad in a car that old, the other one can't be far behind."

"Ain't that the truth," Cindy replied.

"For twenty something bucks a piece, you might as well replace both of them. Now if they were two hundred each, I doubt I would replace any of them."

"I hear ya, sweetie."

It occurred to Matthew that if he called a female he was not dating "honey" or "sweetie," that would be problematic. He would be labeled sexist, chauvinistic, misogynistic, and every other kind of "ist" or "tic" there was. But it was somehow okay for a, what was she, 30 something? 40 something? year old woman to call him "sweetie." Oh well, just another one of those little mysteries of life.

Asking again about current draw, she said she did not know, but all the door locks were generally connected through that same ten-amp fuse, so it should only be a couple of amps each.

Consulting the internet when he returned home, Matthew learned a D-cell battery could deliver between four and a half amps and six amps, depending on the type of battery. A couple of D-batteries and he would have plenty of current. Ah, but voltage was a different story. D-cell batteries are about 1.5 volts. Heck, he would need eight batteries just to get the twelve volts, and then even more to get the required amperage. Ugh. That was not very practical.

A couple of six-volt batteries? That coul– suddenly Matthew had an idea. Kevin had a couple of DeWalt cordless drills in the garage, as well as a DeWalt compact reciprocating saw. The battery from one of those, from the hammer drill or the saw might work, except it was a twenty-volt battery, and he would hate to mess up a perfectly good DeWalt. "If there is not a rule prohibiting desecration of a DeWalt, there certainly should be," he said to himself.

Another visit to the internet, and a query for twelve-volt drills, gave Matthew the perfect answer: a twelve-volt Warrior drill for a penny less than twenty dollars at Harbor Freight. "Sold," he exclaimed.

An hour later he was standing in the garage holding the EAGB6, with the battery from the Warrior drill sitting on the workbench in front of him.

He opened the IPA he had brought into the garage over three hours ago, and after taking a long drink from the bottle, Matthew stood staring at the finished EAGB6. Truly amazed, he could hardly believe he had made it himself.

Setting the beer bottle down, he picked up the button. Running his thumb over the button, almost gently caressing it, he pressed it.

Simultaneously, each of the actuators mounted behind each of the six barrels clicked. "Hot dog, it is indeed going to work!" Matthew exclaimed, almost giddily.

Picking up the beer bottle, he poured the contents down his throat. It was warm, but he did not really care. The gun board was finished; it was certainly no time to cry over warm beer.

Now he just needed to get some shells: .22, .38, and .45 caliber. And of course, he needed a situation to use it. What good was having a new EAGB6 if it was not going to be used?

Chapter 26

"Realtors! What a frustrating breed they could be," Matthew groaned. He had called a realtor and told her what he was looking for. He gave her a price range and a general location. She seemed to be oblivious to everything he said he wanted, and it seemed she tried to show him everything but what *he* was looking for.

He told her he was interested in the one twenty-five to one forty-five price range. Of the first three houses she took him to, none of them were priced below two hundred thousand dollars.

When he complained, her response was they really needed to look and see what was out there, to see what a few more dollars could buy.

"Ma'am, with all due respect, seventy-five thousand is not just a few dollars more."

With a tinge of self-pity, she retorted, "Fine. I was only trying to help you. I was just trying to show you something better. I guess I wasted several hours trying to find the right house for you. In the long run, you would have been happier."

It became immediately clear she did not care about finding him the house he wanted, instead, all she seemed to care about was selling him what she wanted him to buy, something that would add to her bank account.

"Lady, we are done here. Just take me back to my bike. As for wasting your time, that's not really my concern. I told you specifically the location I wanted and the price range I wanted. What did you show me instead? Houses thirty or forty miles away from where I wanted to be, and way out of the price range I stated."

Sniffling, she said, "I was only trying to help you."

"You were only trying to help yourself. You were only after a larger commission."

The next realtor was not much better. Matthew was not amused as they pulled into the driveway of a house.

"What is this?"

"I thought I would show you this. It is a nice little house," the realtor said, handing him a printed flyer.

"Forty-eight thousand dollars?" Matthew said incredulously looking up from the flyer.

"Well, I thought it might be more in your price range."

"What the heck? You know nothing about me. Because I am wearing jeans and a t-shirt you don't think I can afford a hundred and thirty-five thousand dollar house? Or is it because I ride a motorcycle?" The more he spoke, the louder he spoke. The frustration was clear. "I gave you a price range. I told you the type of house and the general location. I told you I wanted to pay cash, and you bring me to," waving his hand in front of him, "this, this, this piece of junk?"

As requested, the realtor drove back to the office, along the way telling Matthew there were other houses to show him. Matthew declined; he had no confidence in this realtor.

After looking for two weeks on his own, he finally settled on a place. In the Deer Lake subdivision just off of Percival Road in Northeast Columbia, he found a three bedroom, two bathroom, twelve hundred sixty-eight square foot house. In foreclosure, the house was listed for one hundred thousand dollars.

Driving by the house, he found it was vacant, and the grass had not been cut in quite some time. Looking through the windows, the inside appeared to be neat and clean. Around the back of the house, pulling out a pocket knife he was able to gain entry into the house. Wandering from room to room, he liked the house, it was nice, he wanted it.

Once back outside the house, Matthew pulled out his phone and dialed the number on the sign in the front yard. Yes, the house was listed for one hundred thousand. No, they would not take the eighty thousand Matthew offered.

One hundred is the price, the woman from the bank told him. No, they would not take the ninety Matthew countered with. The house is bank owned, and the bank does have room to negotiate. Matthew told her he knew the house had been vacant for some time, and he also told her he would pay cash. She put him on hold for several minutes. She had spoken with the manager she said when she came back on the line and, for all cash, they could do ninety-five. Matthew countered with all cash for ninety, and he could be there within the next fifteen minutes. Placing him on hold one more time, she was back six minutes later, apologizing for the delay. If he was there within the next thirty minutes, they would accept ninety thousand all cash.

Twelve minutes later, Matthew was inside Wells Fargo. He did not actually have ninety thousand dollars in cash in his pocket, but that was a small detail. Since he banked with Wells Fargo, and they were the bank that owned the house, it was a simple matter of them taking the money from his account. Forty-five minutes later, Matthew owned the house on Marshdeer Way. And, he had not needed a realtor.

By the end of the day, he had electricity and water at the house. The internet provider told him he would have service by tomorrow afternoon, but they would ship him the modem, and that would take three to four business days, unless he wanted to stop by and pick it up in person. He told them he would get that tomorrow.

By eight o'clock that evening, most of Matthew's belongings were sitting in the living room of his apartment, stacked by the front door. He was both amazed and a bit disappointed by how little he actually owned.

Earlier in the evening he had transported the single chest of drawers, the dresser, the two nightstands, and the kitchenette in one trip to his new house. On a second trip he took the sofa and the recliner, and pretty much all of the food, except for the food in the refrigerator.

Sitting on the floor of the apartment, drinking a beer and eating a delivery pizza, in retrospect perhaps he should have at least kept something to sit on. He supposed he was really just excited to have his own place, so he really was not thinking about a place to sit this evening. Oh well, on the bright side, most of the stuff was moved.

He needed to move the bed tomorrow, his clothes, the stuff by the front door, and the food in the fridge. There was not a fridge in his new house, and he would not have one until tomorrow. The one in the apartment was the Delatorios'; he could not very well steal their refrigerator. Well, maybe he could, but he really had no desire to wrestle that thing down the stairs by himself. Plus, it was pretty old and worn out; it worked, but it had definitely seen better days.

Matthew had stopped by Best Buy to buy a refrigerator, but their delivery date was seven days away. Lowe's delivery was three to five days, and Home Depot said they could deliver the next day. So, he went ahead and bought a refrigerator, and a washer and dryer all from the orange big box store. He did not particularly mind that the washer and dryer would take three days. Delivery was free, whether they were delivered in one trip or two, and, he actually had plenty of clean clothes. After all, he had just gone to the laundromat last evening. Still, he was looking forward to being able to do laundry in his own washer and dryer, and in his own house.

Chapter 27

Climbing onto his motorcycle, he pulled out of the Delatorio's driveway and headed first to the internet service provider to pick up a modem, and then to his house.

He had left the truck parked where it normally sat, but he did keep his copy of the key. After all, he never knew when he might need the truck again, and it would be nice to have it at his disposal.

Matthew did not bother to tell either Kevin or Margie he was moving. He simply loaded up Kevin's old truck, drove it to his new house, backed up the driveway, unloaded it, and returned the truck back to Delatorio's driveway all within four hours.

The rent was month to month, and there were still five days left in this month. As far as Matthew was concerned, he was paid through the end of the month, and since there was no contract or anything, he did not owe them anything. He briefly wondered whether or not he should be grateful to them for giving him a place to live. He decided no, he should *not* be grateful to them. They used him, just like everyone else has used him. They did not *give* him a place to live, they did not *give* him anything. He *paid* to live there. He paid them six hundred dollars a month, plus he paid them another hundred dollars a month for utilities. They did not need the money. Their house was probably paid for years ago, many years ago. Yet, they were *using him* just to pad their own bank accounts. He did not owe them anything. They would certainly figure out soon enough that he was gone.

Besides, it was not just the Delatorios he had not told. He had not told anyone he bought a new house, not even Alex, his own sister. Oh, sure, he would certainly tell Alex once he got settled, he might even surprise her with a dinner invitation for her and Todd. But for right now, only the bank and God knew, and since he did not much believe in God anymore, it was safe to say only the bank knew. Okay, and the insurance company. He had not yet bothered to do a change of address with the post office, nor had he notified his cell phone provider or Visa. Matthew laughed as he distorted the credit card company's tagline,

"Visa, it may be everywhere you want to be, but they do not know where I might be." As for work, well, work certainly did not need to know where he lived.

After walking through the house, Matthew could not help but notice how empty his house was. "Wow, this place is huge. It is, it is…," he said, searching for the word, "cavernous. Yeah, it is cavernous."

Oddly, the house had not seemed so large and empty when there was nothing in the house. Ironically, it was only after he moved his small amount of furniture into the house that he realized the emptiness, the *cavernousness*, of the house.

Life was funny like that. Sometimes it took a little bit of something to realize how much of nothing there truly was.

Three bedrooms, and there was only furniture, and it was beat-up furniture he had bought used a couple of years ago, in one of the spare bedrooms. Initially putting it in the main bedroom, his furniture looked tiny and out of place. Fifteen minutes later the furniture had been relocated to a smaller bedroom.

Accepting that furniture purchases were in his immediate future, he decided he might as well just go ahead and replace everything. And why not? It was about time he had some new stuff. He deserved to have some new things, some nice things. He was tired of having old used stuff. It was about time. His ship had finally come in. Besides, buying this house at ninety grand was a lot cheaper than the one twenty-five to one forty-five price range he had originally set. Heck, with the money he saved, he could buy all new everything, new clothes, even new underwear, and if he really wanted to, he could even buy a pink flamingo for the front yard! "Out with the old, in with the new!" Matthew proclaimed to the empty house. Having not expected the harsh echo, he added, "Wow. That was loud."

Opening the box of leftover pizza he had brought from his apartment, it was no longer cold and was instead somewhere near room temperature. He thought he might as well heat it up. Oops! Matthew realized he had no microwave, as the one he had been using for the last three years belonged to the Delatorios. Three years? Had he really been living there for three years?

Doing quick math in his head, "Over twenty thousand dollars," he said bitterly. "I paid those old goats over twenty thousand dollars to live there."

As if a switch was flipped somewhere deep inside him, he went from bitterness to anger. "They took over twenty grand from me and they would not replace that hideous linoleum because they said they could not afford it?" His voice was reverberating in the openness as his ranting continued. "And when I asked about painting the walls, heck, they said they could not afford the paint. When I asked about them replacing the eye on the electric stove, they told me they could not afford it and, anyway, it was my responsibility since I was the one using the stove.

Always the same story whenever I asked them to replace anything! Could not afford it? Yeah, right! They could have afforded it. They took over twenty grand from me. They could have afforded it; they just did not want to! All they wanted was my money!"

Picking up two slices of pizza, and having no microwave, Matthew decided to heat them in the oven instead. "Oh, great, just great," he said upon realizing there was no oven in the house. No oven, no stove. Oops! How did he manage to overlook that? Well, apparently his appliance buying was not done. At least the refrigerator should be arriving any minute now, and that would give him a place to keep his beer. And the washer and dryer would be delivered in a couple of days. But he definitely needed a way to heat food. After the fridge was delivered, he supposed he would go get Kevin's truck. Hopefully he could buy both a slide in range and a microwave, maybe even a microwave that mounts above the stove top, this evening and, with any luck at all, he could leave the store with them.

Opening a warm beer, he took his two pieces of room temperature pizza and sat on the couch. The doorbell rang as he was taking his first drink from the bottle. "Oh, great."

In less than fifteen minutes, Matthew had a new refrigerator sitting in his kitchen. But apparently you couldn't just plug it in he was surprised to learn. The delivery guy told Matthew he needed to wait a couple of hours, anywhere from two to four hours, before connecting it to power. "Now what we can do is turn the breaker off, then plug the unit in, and all you will have to do is flip the switch in a couple of hours. That way, the water line can be connected and the unit can be slid into place. You won't have it sitting in the middle of your kitchen." He asked Matthew where the breaker box was and, after following Matthew to the laundry room, he switched off the twenty-amp breaker dedicated to the refrigerator. Putting a piece of tape across the breaker, "Okay you are good to go. That tape is just to discourage anyone from accidentally flipping that breaker. Just pull it off when you are ready to switch it on."

"Two to four hours?" he asked the delivery guy. "Which is it? Two or four? Or, how do I decide when it is ready?" Edmond, the delivery guy, told Matthew that two hours or so should be fine. The timeline really depends on how the refrigerator was shipped. His was shipped vertically, so two hours should be fine. The four hours would only be necessary if the appliance been shipped horizontally, which his was not.

"Okay, but why do I have to wait at all? Why can't I just plug it in?"

Edmund tried to keep it simple, telling Matthew that it had to do with lubrication. A refrigerator has a lot of tubing and a compressor to do the cooling. If the refrigerator was not shipped vertically, or if it was tipped or laid on its side during transport, oil from the compressor could run out of the compressor and into the cooling lines. The waiting period really just ensured there was ample time for gravity to do its thing, to pull the oil back into the compressor. "Now, since your refrigerator was shipped vertically, it should not be a problem. Still, the manufacturer recommends waiting two hours, so we do too."

"So, how long before I can put food in it?"

According to Edmund, once the fridge was plugged in, it would take about two hours to be cool enough to store food in, and it would take about twenty-four hours to make ice. "Oh, and don't forget to throw out the first batch of ice. It's a safety thing. That's in the owner's manual there, but most people just stick the manual in a drawer somewhere and never read it. I recommend you do take the time to actually read it. It's a pretty straightforward refrigerator, but the manual will tell you things about the water filter, where it is and how often to change it."

Ten minutes after Edmund left, Matthew had connected the water line and slid the refrigerator into place, and was once again sitting down on the couch to eat his lunch. Both the pizza and the beer had started out about room temperature, so the good news was they had not gotten any warmer.

Chapter 28

Satisfied with his purchase of both a glass top range and a microwave, he was even happier that he could pick them up now. However, he could not very well take them on his motorcycle. Matthew told them he needed to get a truck and would be back in about an hour. They assured him the appliances would be waiting.

He had decided to do the appliance shopping before getting Kevin's truck, figuring he could get it after he purchased something. He really did not want to take a chance of getting the truck only to find out there were no ranges in stock and it would take a few days to get one.

Riding down Two Notch Road, Matthew realized he did not have the key to the truck with him. Sure, he could have used the spare key hidden under the side rail of Kevin's truck, but he wanted to use his own key. He recognized Polo Road coming up on his left.

About a mile down Polo Road, he decided he would try a short cut. He was not really familiar with Wildewood, but he guessed there had to be a way to weave through that subdivision and wind up closer to home.

On Leaning Tree Road, Matthew was instantly hyper-alert. With the buzzing feeling that was suddenly coursing through his body, he felt like he had consumed twenty cups of black coffee. Not that he had ever actually done that, but it nonetheless was the best way Matthew could describe the electric sensation that had wrapped itself like a blanket over his entire body. He had no idea what was happening, he had no explanation.

At the tan house ahead on the left, he saw a middle-aged guy on a riding mower cutting the grass most likely for the last time this season. Getting closer, he saw the guy was probably in his mid-sixties. Lawn tractor guy smiled and waved at Matthew. He waved back; the tinted face shield on his helmet hiding his face from lawn tractor guy.

Approaching the end of the house, Matthew saw a row of bushes and trees completely obscured that end of the house.

"This is it!" he exclaimed from behind the face shield. Instant clarity; Matthew suddenly understood the energy coursing through his body. His excitement level was off the charts.

A quarter of a mile down the road, he turned around in the intersection and slowly made his way back towards lawn tractor guy's house. Approaching from the opposite direction, he could just barely make out a white door in the brick foundation, just where the bushes ended. Barely able to contain his excitement, he continued on to his own house to get the truck key.

He had thought about taking the gun board with him when he moved, but then he had thought better about it. He figured it would be best to just keep it in Kevin's garage. So, he stuck it in the back corner and covered it with an old paint tarp he had found folded on a shelf. He was not too concerned. Kevin was still in the hospital, and even if he was not, he rarely ventured into the garage. As for Margie, for some reason he doubted she had ever stepped foot in the garage.

In the end, Matthew decided it would be convenient to have the gun board near the truck. That way, he would not need to carry it on his bike. He figured when it was time to use it, well, he would just go get it.

Based on what he had just seen in Wildewood, that time was going to be soon, very soon indeed.

Though it had set about ten minutes ago, the sun had not quite yet pulled all of its light below the horizon. The appliances he had picked up were now sitting in his house.

Waiting to turn onto the interstate so he could return
Kevin's truck, a thought suddenly occurred to him.
Matthew pulled out of the turn lane and continued
on straight to the next traffic light. Turning left, he
eventually made his way back to Leaning Tree Road.
With a plan already forming in his mind, he parked the
truck in front of the house next to lawn tractor guy's
house.

Getting out of the truck, Matthew began walking
around, calling for an imaginary cat, "Here, Fluffy,
come here, Fluffy." He walked between lawn tractor
guy's house and the neighbor's house, calling for the cat
to no avail. Walking towards the row of bushes, he got
a much better look at the white door, the door leading
to a crawl space.

"Here, Fluffy. Come on, Fluffy. Come here, girl."
Still, there was no sign of the cat. Matthew was getting
anxious. "Fluffy, come here, Fluffy. Pleeeease!" Still
no cat.

Looking around, he saw no lights come on, and he
saw no people outside looking at him. Apparently, no
one was paying attention to him. Heck, it was like they
did not even notice him. Bending down, he opened
the crawlspace door and crawled inside. Pulling the
cell phone from his pocket, he turned on the flashlight.
Shining the light around, he saw the plumbing, the waste
line, the drain lines, and the water lines, and surmised he
must be under the master suite. Was he allowed to call

it the master suite, he wondered, or was he supposed to refer to it as the main suite? "This will do," he whispered almost inaudibly, "this will do nicely. Guess I will not need those beer bottles and cigarette butts after all."

Crawling back out through the opening, Matthew closed the crawlspace access door behind him. He stood silently in the shadows for a moment, slowly looking around to ensure he was not being observed.

Emerging from the shadows, he continued the charade. "Fluffy, here Fluffy." His gaze shifted up to the soffit where he saw a set of flood lights mounted on the corner. They were not on. He wondered if they were motion lights. Intentionally walking towards them, he continued calling for the cat. Matthew walked around in a large circle underneath the lights, looking around as if he really was looking for a lost cat. Nothing, absolutely nothing. No response from the cat, and the lights did not come on. Clearly not motion activated. He was liking this more and more.

His search for the non-existent cat ended, he walked back to the truck and continued on his journey to return it.

Chapter 29

The red error message appeared on the screen. "The email and password do not match. Try again, please."

What was that password? Matthew sat on a chair in the kitchen, with his laptop on the table in front of him. Yes, this old dinette set would be gone soon enough.

He had been looking at LED televisions and wanted to order one. He knew he had an account at Newegg, heck he had bought his external disk drive from them earlier this year.

He tried again, and again, using a different password each time. "Ugh. I don't want this account to be locked."

A thought occurred to him. "Maybe, just maybe." Clicking near the top right of the web browser, Matthew found where passwords were stored.

Scrolling down through the list, he found the site he was looking for. Clicking the eyeball icon, the unencrypted password appeared.

But then he scrolled back up to the screen to something else that had gotten his attention.

Matthew did not have a Facebook account, yet there was one listed right here, along with the encrypted password. That certainly was not his email address associated with the account. "Hmm. Whose email account is that?" he wondered, rubbing his chin.

"Ah ha. Heather. That has to be you, Heather. Who else would it be?"

Matthew and Heather had hung out together for a few months earlier this year. That woman was the queen of social media. She had accounts with Facebook, Twitter, Instagram, Pinterest, Snapchat, TikTok, and half a dozen other social media platforms he had never even heard of.

Scrolling through the password list in the web browser, he saw accounts and passwords for all of them.

But that Facebook account, that suddenly gave him an idea.

Matthew actually still used her Netflix account to watch videos. So, he figured, why not have a look at her Facebook account?

Having forgotten for the moment about buying a television, enabling his VPN – no sense in having his IP address be tracked – he opened a new browser window and logged into Facebook using the credentials stored in his browser. He was now Heather Winslow.

One of the things Matthew could not quite figure out is why people insisted on posting on social media sites where they currently were. To Matthew's way of thinking, if he knew where someone was, then he also knew where they were not.

And the people that posted their address and phone number on social media sites like Facebook? Really? What were they thinking? How could people be so naïve, he wondered.

Logged in as Heather, he scrolled through statuses and postings. One after another, when he saw someone checking in somewhere, or otherwise posting where they currently were, he would then look at their profile.

"Well, hello there, Amy." According to Amy's profile, she was thirty-four, had a cat, and her profile conveniently included her address and phone number.

The status Amy posted included a picture of her and three of her female friends at a brew pub celebrating Rachel's birthday. He presumed Rachel was one of the people in the photo, but that really did not matter to him.

There was that feeling again. That itch he needed to scratch.

He looked at the time on the computer, and he looked at the post; there was about a twenty-minute difference. Opening another browser window, he pulled up Amy

Afton's address on the map. Ms. Afton's house was only about twenty-one minutes away.

Like a dog with fleas, he was not going to be comfortable until he scratched that itch. No time like the present. Scratch away, scratch away, scratch away now!

Matthew, are we going to do what we think we are? I definitely am. Do we have a plan? I am working on one in my head right now. Good, we do not want to get caught. I won't get caught. I think I have just figured something out. We like that.

"Where is it, oh where is it? I think I know." Matthew walked into the spare bedroom and began opening a box. There were really only three boxes it could possibly be in, and he was pretty sure it was this one.

Seeing what he was after, he gently lifted three clear resealable plastic bags from the box. The larger bag contained four beer bottles, while each of the smaller bags contained an ashtray, cigarette butts, and ashes. The original plan when he collected these was to use them to stage the scene of the victim of his EAGB6. He would use them outside to make it look like the multiple perpetrators, assassins even, were lying in wait outside under a tree, waiting for the victim. Then he came across Larry, and the crawlspace. It would not make much sense for the perpetrators to be waiting outside, only to enter through the crawlspace. And so, the bottles and cigarette butts were not needed and he had no idea what he was going to do with them, except he figured he could still use them one day to confuse the police. He thought now was as good a time as any to use them.

He was not sure what type of a weapon he should use, maybe he would improvise. Maybe a lamp cord.

Matthew, we do not like that. Do not like what? Using a lamp cord. What is not to like; it is clean, it is simple. We think that could be trouble. I do not agree. We think a lamp cord will be viewed as weapon of opportunity. So, it is. We have a problem with that. You have a problem with everything. Please, listen to us. We will not steer us wrong. Ok, what? We are going to plant the bottles and the ashes outside her house, right? Yep. We are going to make it look like someone was waiting for her, right? Right again, except several someones. See the problem? Nope. We see a problem; if someone is waiting to kill her, would they not have a weapon with them already anyway? We want us to think about that. We do not think it makes sense. That is the whole point. I do not want it to make sense to the police. I want to confuse them. I want them to think there were several people waiting for her, but I want to leave enough room for confusion and doubt. We think we understand. I think you worry too much.

Driving past Amy's house, Matthew scanned the area. He had a pretty good idea what he was going to do from looking at the on-line map; the street-view had been very helpful. He just wanted to verify it in person. He liked what he saw. There was sufficient tree cover. Across the street was some semblance of a park. He had seen that on the map. Somehow, he thought there would be lights. Instead, the park was lost in the dark of night.

Two houses past Amy's, Matthew killed the engine, and coasted to stop fifty feet later. Getting off the bike, he collected the plastic bags from the right saddle bag and walked in the shadows back to her house.

Stopping underneath the large tree in front of Amy's house, Matthew walked back and forth, trampling the ground under the tree. Pulling two plastic shopping bags from his pocket. He pulled one over each of his shoes and began the trampling anew.

He set the plastic bags on the ground. Picking up the larger of the three zipped bags, with his latex glove covered hands, he opened the bag and scattered the empty beer bottles around the ground. Yeah, the beer bottles were empty, bone dry, and that should confound the detectives. He had thought about swishing a little bit of beer inside the bottles to freshen them up, but what fun would that be? Why not keep them dry and mess with their heads? Opening one of the smaller bags, he squatted down and gently dumped the cigarettes and ashes in about a one-foot arc in front of the tree. With the plastic bags still covering his shoes, he took a few steps back and forth through the debris. Removing the plastic bags from his shoes, he again took a few steps. The appearance of people being here waiting, smoking cigarettes and pacing back and forth in the shadow of this tree. He opened the other bag and sprinkled those contents in a tighter arc.

Ensuring he had all the plastic bags, and the ash trays too, he made his way back to the motorcycle and returned them to the saddle bag.

Matthew slowly scanned the front of the house in the dark. He walked around the side of the house. The windows on that side were a bit high, and there was nothing to climb on, except perhaps the trash can. On the other side of the house an air conditioning unit set below a window. Bingo! Climbing onto the unit, he drew back his knee and was ready to drive it into the window pane until he noticed the glazing. Bending close to the window, he saw the glazing was severely cracked. This was, after all, an older house. He imagined it had to be a fifties or sixties vintage home, which meant, wow, it was sixty or seventy years old? Pulling out a pocket knife, within a minute he had a pane of glass removed. Reaching inside, he unlatched the window and raised it.

Climbing down from the air conditioner, he made his way to the front door. With a credit card slid into the doorjamb, he verified the deadbolt was not locked, and with the same card, was able to pop the front door open. Walking down the hallway to the bedroom where the open window was, he made sure to stomp around and knock a few things over. Best to make it look like some clumsy galoot came in this way.

Back outside under the tree, he pulled a cigarette from the pack he had bought at the store. He wanted fresh ashes to add to the mix. He knew he could not smoke the cigarette himself because that would leave usable DNA. But he also knew he could not simply light it and let it burn down because then the filter would not only have no DNA, but it would also contain no tar or nicotine; no brownish-yellow streaks in or on the filter. They would surely cut it open in an attempt to extract saliva. They would know the cigarette was not smoked. The solution? Tear the filter off, light the cigarette and let in burn down. They would never know, and there are already plenty of filters on the ground.

Deception done. A good investment of ten minutes. The cops should think several people waited outside for this woman to come home. They will naturally collect the beer bottles and the cigarette butts. They will find DNA on all of them, DNA from multiple sources. They will of course see the window and will know one or more of the perpetrators came in through the window. Maybe they all did, or maybe one did and opened the front door for the others. Yep, he was going to confuse them and keep them guessing.

Matthew made his way back inside the house and closed the front door. Going to a back bedroom, he picked up a lamp from the nightstand and, yanking the plug from the wall, ripped the cord out of the lamp.

Returning to the living room, he patiently sat and waited.

Sitting in the mostly dark room, a hint of glow came from the nightlight down the hall. Sitting. Thinking.

Through the window he watched the lights of a car slowly pass by. The third one in the last two hours. Not a heavily traveled road. Where was she? Matthew was beginning to get annoyed. He had been sitting in this woman's house patiently waiting for her, and she did not have the decency to come home?

Sitting. Pondering. Biting his bottom lip, he slowly wrapped the lamp cord around his palm, unwrapped it. Repeat. "Some people are just so inconsiderate," he fumed. Wrap, unwrap. Repeat. Again, and again. A metallic taste formed in his mouth; the taste of iron, the taste of his own blood. Annoyance turning to anger. Casually wiping his finger across his lip, he held it up in the ambient glow in front of him. A smear of red. A slight amount of blood. His blood. She did this. She made him bite his lip. This was her fault, all her fault. She would pay for this.

Thinking. Well, he might as well be productive. Matthew stood up and began walking down the hallway. Might as well add to the confusion.

In the bedroom, he began opening dresser drawers. He quickly riffled through the clothes in the drawer. He knew better than to dump the drawer contents in the floor. He had seen far too many episodes of *Forensic Files* where people did just that and, on top of that, then they threw the drawers onto the floor. Stupid, stupid, stupid.

Of course, the police saw through that and surmised the scene was staged.

Opening the closest doors, he pulled a few select boxes from the top shelf. Setting them on the floor, he removed the lids and tossed them aside on the floor. He did not bother looking inside the boxes; he did not care what Amy kept in them, this was all for effect.

Back down the hall to the living room. She still was not home yet. "Does she not know I have things to do tomorrow? I need to get to bed. Does she not care?"

Walking into the kitchen, it was dark, very dark indeed. He opened the refrigerator door and light flooded the kitchen. Peering inside the fridge, he saw the top shelf of the door was loaded with bottles of water; the middle shelf held numerous bottles of soda.

Removing three bottles of water and two sodas, he carefully placed them into the sink. One at a time, he opened each one, slowly, methodically, emptying the contents into the drain. He turned on the water and let it run down the drain for fifteen seconds. "We can't have them finding traces of soda in the trap, now, can we?"

Picking up the empty bottles, he returned to the living room. Placing a couple on either end of the coffee table, he also set one on the floor next to the chair. Sitting on the chair, he bounced up and down a few times. Might as well make it look like someone was sitting here too. Will the cops think these people waited outside under the tree, and then decided to come inside and waited a bit longer? Will they think the perpetrators waited outside, then after the deed was done spent a considerable amount of time in the house with the body? Matthew really did not care what they thought, as long as they were confused. And if he ever was caught—not a chance of that ever happening, he was just too smart for them—the confusion and conflicting evidence would work in his favor. The cross examination by defense counsel would be epic. The scene played out in his head.

"How many sources of DNA did you find?"

"Five."

"And was my client's DNA among those?"

"No."

"But you did check my client's DNA?"

"Yes."

"And there was no trace of it found in the house?"

"I see. And the DNA you did find. Who does that DNA belong to?"

"We don't yet know."

"And that, ladies and gentlemen of the jury, is what we call reasonable doubt."

She still was not home. Did she not have any idea what time it was? Looking at his watch, only ten minutes had passed since he first gotten up to stage the bedroom; it seemed like it was thirty minutes. Time was moving slowly; Matthew's frustration growing as he waited.

Back to the kitchen. Opening the pantry door, he needed food for the illusion. No light in the pantry?

She really should put a light in there. Then again, after tonight it would not matter anymore anyway. "In that case, the next homeowner really should put a light in there," he chuckled. Opening the refrigerator gave him the light he needed.

From a shelf in the pantry, he picked up an unopen bag of barbequed potato chips. "Oh, and she has cookies too. Oreos. Great choice." He picked those up as well. He carried the packages over to the sink. Opening each package, he carefully put handfuls of each into the garbage disposal. Turning on the water, he flipped the switch on the wall. The disposal roared to life, eagerly eating what it had been fed. "Wow, you must have been hungry. Does Amy not feed you?" He pulled three ice cubes from the bin in the freezer, and dropped those into the running disposal. Flipping the switch off, the house was again deadly silent. With the ice having cleaned the disposal blades, there was now no trace of what had happened to the chips and cookies.

Closing the refrigerator door, the kitchen was again plunged into darkness.

In the living room, Matthew set the food packages on the coffee table. He was sprinkling crumbs on the table when the living room was suddenly awash with light. A car was pulling into the driveway. "She is home."

Picking up the lamp cord, he took a position behind the front door. "Places everyone."

The house was again dark. Like an alligator lying in wait, he waited.

Where is she Matthew? How should I know; still in the car maybe. We are worried. Don't be. We are wondering, what if she comes in the side door? The side door?

It suddenly occurred to Matthew that she could indeed come in the side door, the door into the kitchen. He now remembered seeing that as he walked around that side of the house.

A faint glow of a light near the front window. The sound of keys in the front door. Nope, she was not coming in the side door.

Matthew wrapped the lamp cord around the palm of each hand, leaving three feet in between.

The door started to open. He licked his lips. The taste of blood long gone.

Wider, wider, the door opened.

The sound of a switch.

The room was instantly illuminated by the four LED bulbs in the ceiling fan.

A woman staggered inside, dropping her purse on the table beside the front door.

With the front door still open, she stood dumbstruck, staring at the scene on the coffee table. "Wha—"

Matthew kicked the door shut.

Before she could even turn around, he was behind her, quickly slipping the lamp cord over her head and around her neck.

"Hello, Amy," and he began tightening the cord.

Her hands flew up to her throat, grasping, clawing helplessly.

Struggling to breathe. Feet shuffling. Hands still clawing.

Loosening the tension momentarily, Matthew turned her around to face him and, again, increased the tension in the cord. "Do you have any idea what time it is?" Anger increasing. "I have been waiting for you, have been waiting hours. Hours! Do you have any idea how inconsiderate that was?" He gave a sharp tug on the cord.

An odd sound emerged from her throat. Her lips were pulsing. Matthew thought she looked like a fish. Well, except for the tongue that was flicking about like a lizard.

Those eyes. "You have beautiful eyes, you know that? Such beautiful blue eyes."

He increased the tension more. The terror, the sheer terror in her eyes was unlike anything he could have ever imagined.

Her struggles started to decrease.

"Do you have any idea how stupid it is to post your whereabouts on social media?" Another quick tug on the cord. "You never know who might see that."

Hands dropping. Eyes bulging. Head lightly lolling from side to side.

Matthew thought it was simply amazing, watching her eyes. It was exhilarating, watching the transition in this woman's eyes, the transition from fear to resignation was almost mesmerizing. The look of death in her eyes, the looking of dying in her eyes, was electrifying!

"And posting your address on social media. Really? Do you have any idea how irresponsible that is?" Another quick tug on the lamp cord.

All resistance had ceased. Her eyes rolled backwards.

"Hey, hey, not so fast there, Amy." He slightly eased the tension on the cord. "Just one more thing. Those sodas. Really? Don't you know how bad those things are for you?" Matthew increased the tension in the cord once again. "Oh yeah, one final thing. There really should be a light in the kitchen pantry." He jerked violently on the cord.

He watched intently as the last remnants of life left her eyes. "Whoa. Cool."

She was done.

So was he.

He turned off the lights as he exited the front door, gently closing it behind him. Walking quietly in the darkness, he made his way back to his motorcycle. "Hi ho hi oh, it's off to home I go."

Chapter 30

Matthew was sitting on the front porch, smiling, holding a cup of coffee and rocking in the wooden chair. He felt alive, so completely alive. What a beautiful morning. A crisp forty-five degrees, brilliant deep blue sky, plenty of sunshine, and not a cloud in sight. "Fall is definitely here."

Rocking. Sip of coffee. Rocking. Reminiscing. Sip of coffee.

Last night, he thought with a sigh. Last night was simply amazing. More like absolutely incredible. Watching the life leave her eyes was insane. The intensity of the feeling, the sense of pleasure, it was all almost indescribable. It was like a slow burn. Actually, it was more like a pot of water. Apply the heat, and it starts to slowly warm at first. Then warmer, and warmer.

Bubbles form, rising from the bottom. Wisps of steam slowly swirling. The water begins to move. Then a ripple. Then another. And another. The surface of the water breaks. A gentle boil begins. Boiling rapidly increases. More. More. More. The water roils. Intensity increasing, reaching a fever pitch. The water erupts over the edge of the pot. Release. Water landing on the hot burner sizzles, immediately evaporating.

Matthew took another sip of coffee. He was quite proud of last night. It came together so quickly. None of it was really planned. He did not wake up yesterday morning and think, "Gee, today would be a good day to kill someone." Nope, it just happened. Kind of like the girl in Lexington. "Ol' bobble head," and he burst out laughing. The couple walking on the road past his house turned and looked. He smiled and waved. Without stopping, they politely waved back.

Some of last night, he could use some of that with Larry. The bottles inside were a nice touch. He needs to remember that. He needs to take them with him. And they needed to come from someplace across town. Nowadays, they could trace the codes on the bottles and find out when and where they were made. It would be easier to trace if they were all the same type of drink made in the same batch at the same place. So, each of the drinks would need to be of a different type. And he would need to stage the inside, would need to make it look like several people were inside waiting for Larry.

Oh, and the eyes. Looking into the eyes. That was so cool. He wondered if he would be able to do that with Larry. He would like to, but it did not really seem possible. He may just have to do that another time. After all, Larry was going to be eight to ten feet in front of the gun board, and Matthew would be several feet behind it. Only a fool would stand in front of the gun board. "Sorry, Larry, I am not calling you a fool. You sort of need to be in front of the board." He laughed and took a sip of coffee. "I was talking about me. I would be a fool if I stood in front of it. Do you have any idea how dangerous that thing is? Well, Larry, I guess you will find out soon enough." Taking a sip of coffee, Matthew began laughing so hard he snorted coffee out of his nose.

"Thank you, Heather," he said aloud. "Thank you for a wonderful evening. I could not have done it without you."

Ah, yes, Heather. Talk about inconsistent. "She changes her mind more often than I change my underwear," he thought, "and I change that at least daily."

She would say something one day that completely contradicted something she said just one or two days previously. By the next day she would be saying something else, denying she had even made the other statements.

He remembered she had a bicycle, a pretty nice road bike. Heather told Matthew she wanted to sell it, and maybe buy a standup paddleboard. A lot of her friends had gotten into SUPs and she thought she might like to try it too. He recalled suggesting she sell the bike on Craigslist, telling her eBay could work, but then she might be responsible for shipping. She said she might try Facebook marketplace, as she had sold a few things pretty quickly on there. When he said he knew nothing about that since he did not use Facebook, that was when she logged into his laptop and showed it to him. Two days later he asked Heather if she had any luck selling her bike. She had looked at him like he had three heads or something as she responded she was not selling her bike.

"Well, I guess I thought you were. Thought you said you were going to sell it to buy a paddleboard."

"I never said that. I am not sure whatever gave you that idea."

"Well, we sat right here and talked about it two days ago. You even showed me Facebook marketplace."

"I did not, I did no such thing," followed by her predictable refrain, "that must have been one of your other girlfriends."

There it was, that subtle jab, "one of your other girlfriends." It did not matter if he was not dating anyone, she would still make that comment. It surely was not jealousy. Was it insecurity on her part? Was it she had feelings for him but was uncertain regarding his feelings towards her? Though it did make him wonder, he usually pushed it aside. But it always seemed to be lurking just below the surface.

"No, I am pretty sure it was you."

"Me doing standup paddling? With my bad back? Are you kidding me? My back is why I do not bike anymore."

And that was the end of that. Except he had her Facebook login and password on his laptop.

Still, she was not as bad as that other woman, old what's her name. He had kind of tried to forget her. Jean. What a real piece of work she was. Oh, sure, she was very attractive, and she had a body that would not quit, and they had a lot in common; similar tastes in food, in music, in alcohol, the outdoors, and they both seemed to enjoy each other's company. But the lying, the constant lying just drove him crazy.

It was quite ironic really, the ease with which he lied. Non-truths rolled off his tongue like silk, just as smooth as could be. However, he had no tolerance for someone else lying to him. How was he supposed to control situations, to manipulate things, if he could not believe what was around him? Then again, perhaps it was his adeptness at lying that enabled him to so quickly pick up on Jean's lying. On the other hand, it seemed her friends and even her own family were well aware of her penchant for side stepping the truth, or even twisting it like a pretzel. Her own sister had once told him, "Be careful, you cannot believe anything that girl says."

She did not just lie about the big things, nor did she lie just to cover up or deceive, but she lied about small things, trivial things. At times, it seemed she could not help herself. She was by all accounts a habitual liar. Still, he did kind of like her and they did have some good times together. He naïvely thought he could perhaps change her. That certainly turned out not to be the case.

One day he had stopped at Pizza Inn in Lexington for lunch. Coincidentally, Jean and a few friends came in a few minutes later. Since she was with friends, he opted not to disturb her, and since he was sitting the corner and they were on opposite sides of the room, she did not see him. They spoke by phone that evening.

"Hey, how was your day?"

"Busy, very busy. I was stuck at my desk all day. Never really even had a chance to eat lunch."

Did he just hear that? "Really, you did not get a chance to eat lunch?"

"No, not really. I just grabbed something from the vending machine and ate at my desk."

Matthew could not resist. "Bummer. I ate pizza for lunch. Went to Pizza Inn, you know, over in Lexington. About twelve thirty or so."

Busted. The ensuing silence was priceless.

"Hey, um, I have got to go. Incoming call. Mom is calling." The call disconnected.

Why would she lie about that, about something that did not really matter, he wondered.

One day, Matthew got a call from Rob, a guy he vaguely knew, more an acquaintance than a friend, who also knew Jean. He said she called and was asking a lot of questions about Matthew. "And then, it was the weirdest thing, dude, she asked me if I wanted to go canoeing, in the Congaree Swamp, like this weekend or something. What's up with that?"

"I don't have a clue. What did you tell her?"

"I told her I would have to let her know. So, is she like just wanting to pump me for information about you? Are you two like dating or what? I do not want to get in the way. But if you're not, I'd kind of like to take my shot."

Matthew suggested Rob text Jean now, telling her he was interested in canoeing on Saturday.

In less than thirty seconds, Rob reported back. "Here, I will read it to you. `Great. Saturday it is. 9:30. Can you pick me up? Maybe we can have dinner and a drink later. I know a cozy Italian place.`"

Matthew asked Rob to hang on a second. He sent Jean a text, asking if she wanted to go for a hike on Saturday. She replied back immediately. "Would love to. But busy Saturday. Promised my sister I would babysit for her all day."

"Hey Rob, you go right ahead. Load up your guns and fire way. Take your shot."

And that was the end of that.

"Well that sure went downhill in a hurry," Matthew said, draining the last of his coffee. "God, how depressing. What the heck happened? Things were going great and then I had to start thinking about that crap. Time to forget about that nonsense." He stood up. "Besides, I need more coffee."

Waiting for the Keurig to work its magic with the pod, he tried to change the mood. "Happy thoughts Matthew, think happy thoughts," he said to the empty kitchen. "Now last night, last night was fun. Think about that."

Last night was fun? Satan be gone. I do not want to do this. Please, dear God, help me. If you really do exist, I beg you to help me. I need you. Please help me change my ways. Pleeeeaaase! Please help me push away the thoughts of violence and anger. What is happening to me? Please God, help me. I pray to you, I beg you, I need you. Amen.

How is that working out for you? That whole praying to what's his name thing? Satan, be gone. You are not here. You have no power over me. Well, there you are right and wrong. Actually, wrong and right. I am here. God may not be here, but I am. As for me having no power over you, that may be true. You have power over yourself. Satan, be gone. God is the one that is gone. He has abandoned you. He has given up on you Matthew. No! Yes. Are you having a conversation with God right now? He is not here. Yes, He is. Well then, where is He? Demand he show himself to you. Leave me alone. Demand he at least speak to you. Go way. Demand he at least act like He hears you. Dear God, please help me. Please hear my prayer. Please hear my cries of anguish. Protect me from me from evil, please protect me from Satan. Amen. Hah! There you go again praying to a God you are not sure even exists, and still nothing. God exists. Are you sure? In Jesus name, I demand you leave me now. Desperately, he began rapidly

praying. "Our Father who art in Heaven, hallowed be thy
name. Thy kingdom come. Thy will be done ..." Matthew
was alone; a sense of peace washed over him.

What has happened to me? When did I become so
filled with hate and rage, Matthew wondered. He used
to be so happy, so happy go lucky. He thought about a
night a few months ago. He and Elaine were camping
with friends for the weekend. The eight of them were
sitting around the camp fire drinking wine and enjoying
life. With the orangish light of the flickering fire casting
shadows about, they sat around spinning yarns.

"Okay, your turn Matthew," Elaine announced. "Tell
us a story."

"Yeah, Matt," added Darrell, "and make it good one."

"Alrighty then," Matthew said. Taking a drink of wine,
"Let's see," and he began.

"There were these three little pigs, and this big bad
wolf, and some chick named Red, Red Riding Hood,
great grand-niece of some dude name Robin Hood.
Seems he lived in a forest and had this thing for wearing
tights and sticking feathers in his cap, but that is not
important right now. Nope, we were talking about Red.
Most peeps in the `hood just called her Lil' Red.

"Anyway, Lil' Red was of the gullible type. You see, she
was headed over to visit her granny when she happened
upon this guy name Jack, Jack Sprat, a real skinny dude
that had nary an ounce of fat on his bones, and he was
selling beans, supposedly magic beans that would grow

a beanstalk. No wonder he was so darn skinny, eatin' nuthin' but beans while his wife was getting just as fat as could be. It seems that silly boy Jack had traded the family cow for those beans, and well, that did not go over very well on the old home front. Magic beans! That boy with the fanciful imagination. He was a character! He certainly was not the crispiest chip in the bag, but he did make his fat wife laugh. And, let's face it, he was kinda cute too, and out here in the countryside the pickings were kinda slim. Besides, he had gotten her out of traveling with that circus. Oh sure, she was no Dolly Dimples, but hey, it was a living and paid the bills for a while. Still, she was tired of living on the road and was ready to settle down and along came Jack.

"Anyway, Lil' Red saw those beans Jack had and she just had to have some. I mean, after all, we are talking 'bout magic beans and beanstalks! She could just imagine how jealous her cousin, Alice, the one that lived in Wonderland, just down the street from Michael Jackson's Neverland, would be. Oh sure, Alice had a rabbit hole and all that jazz, but she certainly had no beanstalk!

"So, she bought herself some beans! It may not have been the best deal, and she really was not sure what she would do with them, but they were so colorful, and just so darn pretty! Meanwhile, the pigs, remember the pigs? They were not too terribly ambitious, and apparently not too terribly bright either. You see, along came this wolf, a gnarly looking character. He walked right up to the pig pen and said: `Yo! Little pigs, little pigs, I'm gonna come in. I see you in your stye, and now you are gonna die!` The little pigs replied: `Die? Die?? Oh my!`

"Did I mention these pigs were not too terribly clever? Well, they decided to hide. So, the first little pig pretended to be a ham sandwich. The second little pig pretended to be a slab of bacon. The third little pig pretended to be a cupcake. A cupcake? Yep. Don't ask me, I have got no explanation either. I just make this stuff up. So, the wolf gathered them up and took off down the road. Getting hungry, he ate the cupcake.

"How disgusting! A pork flavored cupcake. The wolf starting hacking, but it was just a furball. A lumberjack looking on from the other side of the road told him not to water it or feed it after midnight. The wolf walked right up to him and said, 'Who the heck are you? Hoyt Axton? I mean, I mean, I mean that whole after midnight thing was in the movie Gremlins. I would eat you too, but you are too stupid to eat, you old silly lumberjack.'

"Well, the wolf, you see, was a high-school dropout. Unfortunately, for him, he did not quite realize what lumberjacks do. Which, also means he did not realize it is not very smart to call someone with a very sharp ax stupid. Anyway, the lumberjack went walking home with a ham sandwich and some bacon. But along the way he met this chick named Lil' Red. She was kinda hot looking and had a bunch of beans. Hmmm. He was thinking they could cook dinner together. But she was already involved, it was complicated she said and, besides, she seemed a little flaky talking about beanstalks.

"You see, the lumberjack was actually a local cobbler turned toy maker. As a shoemaker, though he was very honest and worked very hard, he just could not seem to make a living as a cobbler. Let's face it; he was not really very good at it. About the only thing he really knew about "cobblering" was eating his wife's peach cobbler. The only way he managed to get any decent work done was with a bunch of magical elves. Feeling a bit dismayed and unfulfilled with his career choice, Geppetto decided to try his hand at making toys. A woodsman had given him a chunk of wood, and he decided to make a little boy. But the silly thing got up off the table, ran out the door, and got swallowed by a fish. Feeling like that whole toy thing did not turn out very well, Geppetto decided to try his hand at lumberjacking. If a woodsman could bring him a piece of wood, and all they really did was cut down trees, they did not seem to chop them, or stack them, or deliver firewood, all they seemed to do was sit around waiting for a Fairy Tale in need of a lumberjack, well that sounded like a job for him. So, after leaving Lil' Red, he sat down against a tree and waited to be called upon, and fell asleep.

"Just before Lil' Red had encountered the old lumberjack, she had been underneath this tree, this very tree, looking for berries and she accidently dropped a few beans. This is the very spot where Geppetto, Geppetto Van Winkle, his friends called him Rip because of his poor wood whittling skills, had fallen asleep. Meanwhile, a brief rain shower passed by and Rip slept right through it. Lo and behold, the beans sprouted and grew into a giant beanstalk! Whodathnukit! The beans were magical after all! Either that, or they were some new breed of Kudzu, which is a pretty scary proposition. So, let's go with them being magic beans.

"When old Rip awoke, he saw this big green giant of a guy. Rip was having a bit of trouble processing what he saw. A giant? A green giant, walking into this castle. He was wondering if it was something he ate? Maybe it was the wolf? He had never eaten wolf before. Suddenly, he thought of another green giant he knew. A jolly Green Giant, that has this thing for vegetables, especially frozen vegetables. But this guy, this guy he was looking at, did not seem to be the vegetarian type. Rip had made his way over to the castle and was peeping through a window, a trick he had learned from his cousin, Tom, and he was truly amazed as he watched him eat a goat, a chicken and half an ox. All of a sudden a chicken, yes, a chicken, squatted down and out popped a golden egg. Really, a golden egg! Just because I am making this story up does not mean I would make up something like a golden egg laying chicken. That was made up by the dude that wrote the story about Jack and the beanstalk about a thousand years ago. Actually, the story itself is over 5,000 years old, but that really isn't important right now."

"Yo, dude," said Darrell, "that's pretty warped."

"Well, you said to tell you a story and make it good one."

"I am not sure if it was good," Elaine chimed in, "but it was certainly different!"

Chapter 31

Reaching down, he grabbed the old paint covered tarp and removed it from the EAGB6. He cast the tarp aside on the garage floor, the thought of folding it and returning it to the shelf he took it from weeks ago never crossing his mind.

Picking up the gun board, he carried the contraption over to the workbench.

Removing the twelve-volt lithium-ion battery from the charger, he secured it to the gun board and made the two electrical connections.

With no shells in the barrels yet, Matthew picked up the triggering device and, after a brief pause, pushed the button. All six actuators engaged and all six barrels dry-fired.

Disconnecting the battery, he set it aside on the workbench. He would reattach the battery when he got to his destination. He really did not want to chance one or more of the guns actually firing.

He walked out to the truck parked in the driveway, returning a minute later with a zipped plastic bag containing six pieces of ammunition.

One barrel at a time, he moved off to the side the firing pin attached to the actuator, and inserted a cartridge. Two .22 shells, two .38 shells, and two .45 shells.

Making the homemade guns was easier than he thought it would be. Each of the barrel and actuator combinations were essentially an improvised firearm, a zip gun.

The simplicity and ease of construction was due to the simple fact they were single shot guns. There was no clip, there was no repeating mechanism; there was simply a barrel holding a single shell, and a firing mechanism.

Matthew himself made the barrels, made them right here in this very garage. The barrels were each six inches long and relatively smooth on the inside.

Picking up the EAGB6 and the battery, he stuffed the empty plastic bag in his pocket and made his way out to the truck.

Placing the gun board contraption on the floorboard on the passenger side, he put the battery into the glove compartment. Walking around to the driver's side, he opened the door, and climbed inside. He was just shifting the truck into reverse when he froze. "Uh oh. I almost forgot a little something."

Putting the truck back into park, he went back into the garage. He pulled the DeWalt reciprocating saw off the shelf, and pulled a yellow and black DeWalt battery from the charger at the end of workbench. "Yeah, I think I'll be needing this," he said aloud as he walked out of the garage.

Chapter 32

He was being very careful to obey all the traffic laws. Matthew generally viewed things such as speed limits as recommendations, as mere suggestions. But today, today was different. He seriously doubted any police officer that might stop him for some sort of minor traffic infraction would have a clue about his contraption. They are not that smart. Well, some of them may be smart, but they certainly were not smart enough to figure out his little EAGB6.

Oh sure, they could read, they could read the word EAGB6 at the top of the board, but they would have no idea what it was or what it meant. They just simply were not smart enough; they simply were not as smart as him. Still, why take a chance, especially since the barrels were loaded. So, he followed their silly little laws tonight.

But he was going to show them just how smart he could be, and they were not even going to know it. He was going to confuse them, make fools of them all, and they would not even know they had been played.

Pulling into a convenience store near his former apartment, Matthew parked in front of a gas pump at the end of the island. He got out of the truck and began walking towards the store. As far as anyone knew, he might be opting to pay cash and needed to go inside to pay and have the pump turned on. However, he had no intention of getting any gasoline, he simply wanted to be in a spot that minimized the possibility of people looking into the truck.

Looking through the glass doors of the drink cooler, he decided on three different drinks: a bottle of water, a sports drink, and a soda. Reaching to open the door, he suddenly stopped.

Um, Matthew, stop. What? Gloves Matthew, we need gloves. We do not want to leave finger prints.

Walking to the front of the store, Matthew asked the clerk, "Um, yeah, do you have any gloves, for like pumping gas? I try not to get any gas on my hands."

Oh well, it was worth asking. He knew he had several pair in the truck.

Setting the bag of drinks on the floorboard of the truck, he closed the passenger door. Matthew removed the blue latex gloves and dropped them into the trash can.

Chapter 33

After backing into the driveway next to Larry's house, Matthew turned the engine off. He had lately been referring to lawn tractor guy as Larry. Lawn tractor guy was a bit wordy, so he had tried referring to him at LTG, but that did not exactly roll off the tongue. And so, LTG had become Larry.

Matthew had learned the house next to Larry's, this very house, was for sale. Using Zillow to find out more about Larry's house, he found out the vacant house next door was for sale. The price was apparently reduced by ten thousand dollars on September 21st, and was now listed for only five hundred ninety-nine thousand nine hundred dollars. "Wow, what a bargain," he remembered thinking sarcastically, "it is a good thing they came off the price by ten grand."

Rolling down the window, Matthew took a deep breath, and then sat stoically in the seat for several minutes. There was silence, complete silence, broken only by the ticking of the engine as it cooled.

Rolling his head to the right, he glanced over at Larry's house. The house was dark. From his surveillance of Larry, was it surveillance, or monitoring, or was it observing? Matthew preferred to call it observing. Not that it really mattered what it was called, the only thing that mattered was that he knew lawn mower guy's schedule for the evening. Larry should be home in about an hour.

"Let's go," Matthew said aloud to the empty truck. "Let's go have some fun," he said, pulling a pair of blue latex gloves onto his hands.

Placing the battery into the reciprocating saw, he set the saw on the hood of the truck. Removing the EAGB6 and the twelve-volt battery from the passenger side of the truck, he set those on the hood too.

Removing the plastic bottle of red Gatorade from the bag, he unscrewed the cap and poured half the contents into the grass next to the driveway. Next was the bottle of soda. Removing the cap, he poured all of the liquid into the grass. Putting the cap back on the bottle, he returned the bottle to the plastic bag. And with the water bottle, he poured out about a third of the contents.

He stuck his hand through the loops of the plastic bag, and picking up the other three items, he carried them to the edge of the bushes. At ten thirty on this cloudless Saturday evening, it was dark. And a bit nippy. "Fall is definitely here," he thought as he glanced around.

Squatting down, he opened the crawlspace entry door and placed inside the doorway the items he carried from the truck. Climbing inside himself, he pulled the door shut. Using the flashlight on his phone, he located on the wall the light switch he had seen when he was under here the last time. Flicking the switch on, the crawlspace was illuminated with LED lights. "Now that is what I am talking about," he said aloud.

Pulling a piece of pink insulation down, Matthew picked up the reciprocating saw and made a two-foot cut along the inside edge of two floor joists. He then cut perpendicularly at each end of the long cuts. Reaching up, he lowered the rectangular piece of subfloor. "I won't be needing this," he said as he cast it aside.

What are we going to do now Matthew? What do you mean? I am going to climb into that hole and do what I came to do. Have we really thought this through? You know I have. So, we are just going to climb through the floor, just like that? Yep, just like that. We have a suggestion. I don't have time for this. We think you should listen. You are not going to just shut up and leave me alone, are you? We just have an idea to keep us safe, to make sure we are not caught. I really do not have time for this. We think you should make time. Okay, great, what is it? We think you should take the saw back to the truck now, and we think you should turn these lights off too. I was going to turn the lights off. Good, we like that. But now take care of the saw. The saw is fine. We disagree, take it back to the truck now. Why? We think it could be problematic if we are trying to leave in a hurry after we do the deed and if we have to carry the gun board and the saw. Actually, that is not a bad idea.

From out of the darkness below, the EAGB6 slowly rose and then was laid onto the carpeted floor. He reached up and put a hand on either side of the hole. Standing up, Matthew climbed through the hole. He was indeed in the master bedroom. Light filtering in from somewhere down the hallway provided a hint of illumination in the bedroom. Coming from the darkness under the house, it did not take long for his eyes to adjust. Standing, listening, waiting, he heard not a sound from inside the house.

Walking out of the bedroom and into the hallway, lights began flashing as a shrill sound erupted. He had triggered the alarm system, a development that was not at all unexpected. Matthew had actually planned for this.

Stopping in his tracks, he looked around. In the corner above his head, he saw what appeared to be a video camera. Reaching into his pocket, he pulled out another blue latex glove. Hmm. The ceiling had to be nine or ten feet high; there was no way he could reach the camera. Think Matthew, think, and do it quickly. Stepping directly beneath the camera, he jumped straight up with his hand extended. Once, twice, making contact with the bottom of the camera each time. Three times was not a charm; the camera was still on the wall. The fourth jump was the payoff. The camera rotated up and was now angled towards the ceiling. Not exactly the outcome he had hoped for; he was planning to pull the camera off the wall and put the glove over the lens, but this would work just fine.

The flashing lights continued and lacking entry of a security code to type into the keypad, the continuous shrill beep transitioned after thirty seconds to a whoop-whoop-whoop from the alarm system.

Matthew walked into the living room and stood near the front door, looking out the window, and patiently waited. After three minutes, the alarm had ended its quest to frighten away any intruders. "Right on schedule," he whispered. Two minutes later he saw the police car arrive and park in front of the house. "Great response time, guys. Must be a slow night. Or the doughnut shop has not yet turned on its red neon light proclaiming fresh and hot donuts."

Watching the officer get out of the car and begin walking across the yard towards the front porch, Matthew backed away from the window and stood directly behind the steel front door.

He heard the footfalls on the front porch, heard the rattle as the officer jiggled the door latch; the door did not open. A moment later he saw a beam of light coming through the dining room window and sweep across the room. The light disappeared, followed by the sound of retreating footsteps. Sneaking a peek out the window, Matthew saw the officer walking along the sidewalk towards the garage.

Standing silently, he waited, and waited. A minute later he saw a beam of light coming in through the glass of the rear door, and he heard the sound of the officer verifying that door too was secure. The light was gone.

Peering discreetly out the front window, he watched the officer approach his patrol car. "Now's the time," Matthew said, moving into the hallway and flapping his arms about until the motion detector was again triggered. Quickly making his way back to the sanctuary of the backside of the front door, he waited. Footsteps on the front porch, rattle of the door latch, light through the dining room window, light gone, shrill beep transition to whoop-whoop-whoop, wait, wait, wait, light through back door glass, sound of doorknob being checked, light disappear, wait, wait, wait, officer reappear at the car.

"This is fun, let's do it again." Again, into the hallway and the entire process repeated itself.

"Okay, one more time." Waiting behind the door, he heard no footsteps on the porch, there was no rattling of the doorknob, and there was no light through the window. Cautiously, slowly, he looked through the edge of the window. There was no officer, there was no police car. Any future triggering of the alarm for the remainder of the evening would likely be treated as a nuisance alarm and would be ignored. The house was now his.

Retreating back to the bedroom, he retrieved the gun board and the bag of drinks. He carried them down the hallway and placed the gun board on the floor about ten feet away from the door that led to the garage. He knew this was the door Larry would use.

With the EAGB6 in place, he unwrapped the trigger module and stretched the eight feet of red and white bell wire down that hallway.

Matthew had considered putting a wireless trigger device on the gun board, but there were two real problems with that approach. The first was that he did not want the guns to accidentally fire. He was afraid a stray signal from somewhere could either cause the guns to fire unexpectedly, or could interfere with him trying to fire them. The second problem, and perhaps the biggest, was that he simply did not know how to do it. He was not exactly an electronics genius. Mechanical things he could do, and some light electrical such as the simple wiring of the EAGB6 he could do, but trying to figure out something electronic? Do not count on it. And, as Matthew was fond of saying, quoting Harry Callahan, "A man's got to know his limitations."

Now the waiting began. It should not be long now. Lawn tractor guy should be home soon. Time for a few last-minute preparations.

In the dining room adjoining the hallway, he placed the plastic bag of drinks on the floor. Matthew then pulled three chairs several feet out from the table. He turned two of the chairs to face the hallway.

Removing the bottle of water from the bag, he placed both the bottle and the cap on the table in front of one of the chairs.

He pulled the other two bottles from the bag. He stuffed the empty plastic bag into his pocket. Removing the caps, he set the bottles and caps in front of the other chairs. He did not know how often Larry dusted, so it was best to momentarily set those two bottles on the table and hope to make a ring, if nothing else, in the dust.

Leaving the bottle cap on the table, he walked into the bedroom and dropped the empty soda bottle onto the carpet next to the hole in floor.

"The stage is set, let the show begin," he whispered as he made his way back down the hallway.

Sitting on a dining room chair, he waited. And waited.

Matthew knew the guy was in a Fall bowling league, and he had an idea what time the guy should be home. But, would he be home earlier? Did the police call him about the alarm? Did he have remote access to the alarm? Would he be alarmed the video camera was just showing white? Would he leave his teammates and rush home? Surely he would know it was a nuisance alarm, or would he?

Regardless, it did not really matter to Matthew. Larry would be here when he got here.

He heard the rumble of the garage door opener as it came to life. Larry was home. "It's show time," he exclaimed.

Picking up the opened bottle of Gatorade, Matthew nonchalantly tossed it on the floor down the hallway, somewhere between the gun board and the bedroom.

Taking the trigger mechanism, he placed his thumb on the button and patiently waited.

The rumble of the garage door opener again, as it presumably began lowering the door.

He heard the sound of keys in the deadbolt and realized he had been holding his breath. Exhaling, he told himself, "Be calm, Matthew, stay calm. Any second now."

The sound of keys now in the doorknob.

Wait for it.

This sight of the knob turning.

Excitement building.

Light pouring in from the light in the garage opener as the door opened.

Anxious. His body tingling.

Larry was lit from behind; he could not yet see Matthew in the hallway. Setting the bowling bag on the floor, he reached over for the light switch.

The entryway by the door was instantly illuminated by the LED bulb in the overhead light.

"Hello, Larry," Matthew announced.

Lawn tractor guy looked up.

Smiling, and waving, Matthew pushed the button. Time slowed. He was transfixed; everything was registering.

Six barrels all firing at once.

Six flashes combining into a single blinding flash.

The deafening sound of six explosions melded into one.

The gun board kicking three feet backwards.

The sight of Larry falling to the floor.

The smell of burnt propellant.

The screaming.

The smoke.

The screaming of a woman.

Larry laying motionless on the floor.

Larry is screaming like a woman?

Crying, "Patrick, Patrick."

Who is Patrick?

The woman draping herself over Larry's body.

Woman? Who is that woman?

Matthew was startled out of his transfixation. He was confused, on the verge of panicking. This was not in the plan. The woman most definitely was not in the plan. *Who is she Matthew? We do not who she is. I don't know. Who is she, Matthew? Please, we do not like this. I don't like it either. Just let me think. But who is she, Matthew? I already said I don't know. Where did she come from? I don't know. Matthew! What are we going to do?* "Stop, just stop," Matthew yelled aloud.

Not only did the voice in his head stop, but the screaming and crying immediately ceased. Matthew saw the woman staring blankly up at him.

He was not even aware he had been walking towards her and was now standing over her.

"Who are you?" he demanded.

No answer. She lowered her head and began sobbing, "Patrick, oh Patrick."

"Who are you?" he demanded again, the anger quickly rising.

Uncontrollable sobbing was the only response.

Matthew was acutely aware he was spending too much time in here. He should have been gone by now. Surely neighbors heard the gunshots. Surely they had called the police by now. He had to put a stop to this and he had to do it now.

Reaching down, his blue covered hand grabbed her hair near the scalp. "You want something to cry about? I will give you something to cry about!" His voice conveyed the anger he now felt. He slammed her head against the wall. Again, and again. She lay whimpering on the floor. Quickly making his way into the kitchen, he riffled through the drawers, until the butcher block of knives sitting on the counter caught his attention. He was not so much thinking as acting instinctively, driven by pure adrenaline and a sense of self preservation.

Back to the woman near the door. Except, she was not where he had left her. She was about two feet away

STEVE MULLANEY

from Larry, reaching for the cell phone he dropped when he had been shot.

"Oh no, no, no," Matthew said as he kicked the phone away from her. Squatting down, he again grabbed her by the hair. "I do not know who you are," anger dripped from every word, "but you are going to ruin everything. And I certainly cannot have that."

Standing, but staying bent over, Matthew raised her head by the hair. "At least have the decency to look at me when I kill you." The fear in her eyes was clear. The terror on her face was exciting.

The chef's knife he was holding in his other hand now moved into view. She closed her eyes, which further enraged Matthew. He remembered Amy. Remembered the elation, the euphoria of watching her face, of seeing Amy's eyes as she died. He wanted that again, oh how he wanted to feel that again. "Open your eyes, and you open them now," he yelled. "Maybe you do not want to watch, but I do. I want to look into your eyes when you die."

Her eyes slowly opened and Matthew immediately dragged the edge of the eight-inch knife across her throat. There was no gargling noise as there had been with Sam, the old guy down by the river. But there was a strange guttural gasping as she tried breathing with a slit throat.

"I do not have time for this. I really do not. I have got to go." Rolling her on to her back, "You. Ruined.

310

Everything." He slammed the knife into her abdomen. Again, and again. Getting angrier with each thrust of the knife, and still he continued stabbing her lifeless body another ten times.

"Well that certainly made a mess," he said as he stood up straight. "That will teach you not to mess with my plans." Tossing the knife on the floor, he grabbed the gun board and ran down the hallway to the bedroom. Turning around briefly, barely able to control his laughter as he tried mimicking Jed Clampett, "Y'all have a good night, y'hear?"

Throwing the gun board into the bed of the truck, Matthew pulled the latex gloves off and stuffed them in his pocket. Sure, the blood on the gloves would transfer to the inside of his pockets but it would not be in or on the truck.

The sound of sirens in the distance was discernable, "Time to go." He quickly got in the truck, started the engine and pulled out of the driveway.

The sound of multiple sirens was approaching from the direction he was headed. Towards the end of Leaning Tree Road, he could see the glow of flashing lights approaching from down the road on the right. Nope, not that way, change in plans. Not knowing where it would take him, he turned left and, reminding himself to stay calm and not to do anything to draw attention, he slowly accelerated.

Chapter 34

The fire flickered in the ceramic pot in the center of the Delatorio's garage as his pants and shirt were burned to ash. He would have burned the shoes too, but he really did not want to deal with the stench of burning rubber. The shoes sat soaking in bleach in the mud tub in the corner. Matthew sat on the stool drinking a beer, while the EAGB6 lay disassembled on the workbench in front of him.

Picking up a saw, he cut the board into six pieces. Not seeing any lighter fluid, he retrieved the red two-gallon gas can. Placing the pieces of wood on the floor, he doused them with gasoline. They immediately erupted into flames as he dropped them into the blue ceramic flower pot.

Returning to the stool, Matthew saw the gun barrels laying on the workbench. "Oops, I almost forgot you guys." He picked up the two wooden barrels and cut them in half. He doused them in gasoline, making sure to pour plenty into the barrel pieces, and dropped them into the fire. "Don't worry, it won't hurt for long," he laughed, and made his way back to the stool and his beer.

He would worry about the metal barrels and the actuators later. They were not really traceable. For now, he would just stash them in a box of scrap pieces in Kevin's garage.

On the way back from Larry's, Matthew had stopped at a Walmart. Maybe he was being paranoid, maybe not. He had seen too many episodes of *Forensic Files* where someone was eventually tied to a crime because of microscopic blood drops, either from blood spatter or cast off. He was not going to be one of those people.

At the store, he bought a pair of jeans, a plain black tee shirt, sneakers, a large flower pot, two gallons of bleach, and a lighter. As an afterthought, he also picked up a six pack of beer.

Taking a long drink of beer, "What was she doing there?" he asked the empty room. "She ruined everything," he exclaimed as he suddenly stood up and threw the half empty bottle across the garage. Striking the wall, the bottle violently exploded.

That woman, whoever she was, was the whole reason he was sitting here in new Walmart clothes while his own clothes were burning in the pot and his shoes were drowning in bleach. He was, of course, going to have to throw those shoes into the woods or something on his way home, and it would need to be on this side of town. Maybe this would be a good time to get rid of the metal barrels and actuators too? "Nah, I will take care of those later."

Matthew. What? Who was she? I told you I don't know. We want to know. I don't care. What was she doing there? How should I know? How could we not know? What is that supposed to mean? We thought we were doing research; we did do research, did we not? Yes, I did research, of course I did research. If we did research, then why is it we did not know his name, why did we not know his name was Patrick? Why did we have to find that out from that woman? Because I like the name Larry better. Then, we want to know why we did not know about her, about the woman. I don't even know who she was. We are not happy about that; how could we not know who she was if we did research. Lay off. Was she his wife? I don't know. A girlfriend? I don't know; she could be a woman he picked up at the bowling alley for all I know. We think there seems to be a lot we do not know. Give me a break. We were put in danger tonight, Matthew, real danger. Hey, it all worked out. Just barely; we almost got caught. But I did not get caught. But we almost did. But I did not. We still cannot understand how we could not know about her. It all worked out. We do not want to do this anymore. Great, we agree on something; I do not want to do this anymore either. I just want to drink a beer, finish up here and go home. We think perhaps we do not fully understand; we do not want to do this anymore. This? What does that mean? Killing people, we do not want to do that anymore. But I am good at it. Tonight was a fiasco. It turned out okay. We thought our plan was to kill the guy, that was the plan. We thought the plan was to make a gun board and use it to kill the guy. I did that. Explain the woman to us. I already told you I do not know about her. That is what we are not happy about; it was not just sloppy, it was beyond sloppy. We think it was irresponsible. It was not irresponsible; it all worked out. It endangered us; what if they tie us to her? They will not; they cannot. Look on the bright side, she was a bonus. We do not care; we do not like it.

Matthew was convinced he was in the clear. Sure, the woman was an unexpected twist, but he improvised and it all worked out. The cops were not smart enough to figure any of it out. He was too smart for them. They would see. He imagined how things might play out.

The detectives are going to look at the crime scene, and will look at Larry's body. They are going to find three different caliber bullets. They will not find any shell casings; they stayed in the barrels on the gun board. What are they going to immediately think? That there were three different guns, that is what they will think. And there were indeed different guns, sort of, except the cops will not be smart enough to think of something like his EAGB6, that is for sure. And then what will they think? They will think there had to be at least two shooters, but they will most likely decide there were probably three. The detectives will consider there could have been two shooters if one of them held a gun in each hand, but they will settle on three shooters. Why? Because of the three bottles he left. See? He was too smart for them. They will never think it was single person, because with their small little minds and their simple way of thinking they will say a person with three hands does not exist, and that is what it would take for there to be three different guns, so it could not be a single person. And because of the bottles, they will think the killers, the three killers, must have been lying in wait to ambush this guy. They will think it was some type of a hit, some type of a payback for something.

He was playing them, playing them like a fiddle, like a cheap fiddle at that. And, it would only get better. They will have bullets, but they will not find any lands or grooves on them because there are not any, because there was no riffling or any other type of marks in the barrels. Matthew had made the gun barrels himself, and the barrels were smooth. As for finger prints, they will not find any of those either. Neither the bottles nor the caps have finger prints on them, at least not his, because he wore gloves every time he touched them, even when he bought them. See? He was just too smart for them. They would never figure it out. They would be convinced there were three people so they were going to be looking for three people not one, and with no finger prints at all to work with.

Matthew's self-aggrandizing continued. And the woman, the woman was an added bonus. They would look at her, would look at her sliced throat, and then look at the dozen stabs in her abdomen and be confused. They would think the slit throat implied some type of hit or something, maybe even a gang killing, while all the stab wounds, the viciousness of the attack, would leave them to believe it might be a crime of passion. For Matthew, it was more like rage, but they would not know that. They will take Larry into account, and will decide these were executions, rapid executions carried out by a group of people, a group of angry people.

"Let us not forget about motive; the police always had to have a motive," Matthew said as he opened another beer. In fact, he thought, the cops could not conceive of a murder without a motive. Well, he had news for them: sometimes there simply was no motive. In this case, there really was no motive, except that he just wanted to have a bit of fun.

Matthew knew he had nothing to worry about, but still, being careful never hurt.

The fire was gone, having been reduced to smoldering embers. Matthew picked up an empty beer bottle from the workbench, walked over to the utility sink and filled the bottle with water.

There was a long-drawn-out hiss as the water Matthew began pouring on the embers was instantly turned to steam. Emptying the remainder of the bottle extinguished the embers.

He carried the pot to the utility sink and set it on the floor. Matthew reached into the sink and removed the stopper. The aroma of bleach would cling to his forearm for the next several hours, but there were worst things in life. Besides, he kind of liked the scent of bleach; it was the smell of clean. Matthew rinsed the shoes off and set them aside.

He set the flower pot in the sink and ran water over it to ensure the embers were completely out. After all, he could not risk starting a fire in Kevin's trash can. Matthew could not very well take the flower pot on his motorcycle. Well, he could, he just did not want to. If the embers were not completely out, well that would pose a problem in the saddle bag. Plus, the other consideration was that after dousing the pot with water, well that would just make a mess in the saddle bag. He thought momentarily about just putting the pot in a trash bag and strapping it to the back of the seat, but why bother?

Chapter 35

Waking up to the sun pouring in through the window, Matthew stretched and turned his head to look at the clock. Seven thirty-three. Sitting straight up, "It is going to be a great day. G. R. E. A. T." Last night was, well, last night was simply amazing. And tonight, dinner with Alex and Todd. "Yep, it is going to be a great day indeed," he mused as he got out of bed.

Matthew was taking a sip of coffee when the sound indicating an incoming text message emanated from his phone. Sitting the cup on the counter, he picked up the phone.

"Whasup?"

He laughed as he thought, "Oh, not much. I just killed a guy last night." He figured that was probably not the best thing to text to his sister.

"Not much," Matthew wrote back.

"Are we still on for tonight?"

"Yep," he replied to Alex.

"Time and place?"

"5:30 or 6 work?"

"Sure. Where?

Matthew had called his sister a few days ago and casually asked if she and Todd would be interested in meeting for dinner and a bit of wine on Sunday. She agreed. When asked where, he said he would let her know. It was now time to do that. He texted her the address.

"Where is Marshdeer Way?"

"NE Columbia."

"What restaurant is that?"

"No restaurant."

"?"

"It is where I live."

"Where u live? Did u move?"

"Yep. I bought a house."

"OMG! When?"

Matthew barely had time to read her response before the phone started to ring.

"Hi, sis."

"Mmm. Smells good. What's for dinner?" Alex inquired, as she and Todd stepped into Matthew's house.

"Lasagna."

"Homemade?" asked Todd.

"Yeah, right," Alex laughed lightly. "If I know Matt's cooking abilities, it is probably Chef Boyardee. Just like mom used to make."

"Ouch. That hurts. It is not Chef Boyardee."

"Oh yeah, I forgot, you would still need to actually cook the noodles."

"Now that really hurts. It pains me. Deeply, I might add."

"You nut."

"Besides," Matthew said, "did you know they quit making that? Years ago."

With a playful jab of his elbow into Matthew's side, Todd chimed in, "So what is it? Stouffers?"

Laughing, he said, "Don't you know it. Alex is right, I can't cook worth a darn."

"Well then," his sister laughed, "it is a good thing we brought the dessert."

"Whoa," Matthew said as he attempted his first bite of lasagna. "You might want to bless this again, sis, because it is still hot, too hot to eat."

"You are not funny, Matthew Stockmore," Alex chided him. "And, you better not even think about laughing, Todd Andrews," she playfully added, "I see you over there snickering."

"Or what?" Todd asked with a smile.

"Or it's going to be a long walk home."

Taking a sip of wine, Todd grinned widely. Reaching into his pocket, he retrieved the keys. "I hope you brought some good walking shoes," he said, jangling the keys in front of him, "because I've got the keys!"

After the ensuing nice bout of relaxed laughter, Matthew could not help but reflect on how nice this was. Time with family was to be cherished. And, Alex and Todd were his only family. True, Alex was his only *real* family, but he considered Todd family too.

With dinner finished, Todd asked, "So Matt, when are you going to get a girlfriend or something."

Matthew tried a quick deflection. "Um, hey, how about dessert?"

"Are we really ready for dessert now, or do you want to wait a bit?"

Matthew told Alex he was actually pretty full from dinner, but the chocolate cake and another glass of red wine actually sounded pretty good. Todd agreed.

"Now, about that girlfriend thing, Matt," Alex said with a smile while setting the cake and plates on the table.

"Yeah, Matt," Todd said, "do not think for a moment that we did not see through your little dessert ruse."

"Oh, do not even get me started."

He regaled them with the story of a recent date. "I picked her up to go see a movie. When we got to the theater, she saw the movie was rated R. So, she called her mom to ask for permission to see the movie. Her mom said no, so we had to see something else. Not a very good first date."

"Nah ah! No way! You are making that up."

Taking a sip of wine, Matthew smiled. "Yeah, I stole that from the Jimmy Fallon show."

"You goof!"

"Seriously though, no prospects?" Todd asked.

"No, not really. I've been so busy. Plus, it is hard to meet anyone. I have gone out with a few people here and there, but none of them really floated my boat, if you know what I mean."

The next few minutes were pleasant enough as Matthew regaled Alex and Todd with stories of his dating adventures and misadventures.

He claimed he met a woman through an on-line dating site, and they agreed to meet for dinner. It all happened very quickly. It was one of those swipe-left or swipe-right sites, within a few minutes they agreed to meet, and forty minutes later there they were meeting in person.

He was pulling into the overflowing parking lot when she sent him a text message stating she was already inside and had a table. Walking up to the door he realized he could not recall what she looked like. Rather than look silly by texting her to ask what she was wearing, he decided he would wander around the restaurant until he found her. And there she was. Young single woman, very attractive, sitting at a table for two by herself.

Two place settings, two red napkins wrapped around silverware, two glasses of water, and only one person.

He sat down opposite her and introduced himself. She smiled and softly said her name was Tina, but, Matthew said, she was apparently a bit shy, and a bit nervous, because she kept looking around.

He picked up the glass of water and took a long drink, just as the wait person arrived to take a drink order.

"Wine?" he asked Tina.

Hesitantly, as she looked around the restaurant. "Um, yeah, I guess."

"Red or white?"

"Red?"

"Chianti or cab?"

"Um, look, I really don't know—"

"Okay, I will decide. Please bring us a bottle of chianti. Ruffino."

"Um, I thin—"

"Don't worry, I have this, I will pay for it. Boy, you sure seem nervous."

"It's just that, I tried to—"

"Hi, honey," said the guy standing next to the table. "Who is this?" he asked turning to look at Matthew.

"And when I asked who he was, he said he was her husband," Matthew laughed as he told them, "He was outside parking the car! I was at the wrong table."

"No way! That did not happen," Alex protested.

"Really, it did."

And then there was the time where the young woman just kept talking about everything she was doing. They went on a few dates, but it was always about her. Her, her, her. The tone of Matthew's voice changed. "It was always about her. I might as well have not even existed."

Susan, who he casually knew found out he knew how to fix a few things. She would call and play nice, even maybe want to meet for a drink, but it was always the same. She would mention some problem she was having and he just knew that meant she wanted *him* to fix it. "Oh, she never came right out and said it, but that is what she meant."

Todd offered, "Maybe she did not want you to fix it. Maybe it was just common ground?"

"Yeah, sweetie," added Alex. "Maybe that was just what she was using to be with you."

"Nope, not a chance. It seems the only time she wanted anything to do with me was when she needed something done."

"Did you ever think maybe she did not really need your help, but she acted like she did as an excuse to spend time with you?" Todd asked. "Women do that," he said, to which Alex nodded, and added, "Yep, we do." "No, not at all," his emphatic response startled them.

For ten minutes they sat patiently listening to Matthew, listening and watching him grow more animated by the minute, that animation slowly turning to anger. Ten minutes of listening to him play the victim, blaming the women he had dated for things not working out. It was, of course, always their fault, and they were all just using him, taking advantage of him.

Alex tried to diffuse the situation. "Whatever happened to, to that cute girl, what was her name? The one you brought to our neighbor's cookout a few months ago."

"Heather."

"Yeah, Heather. I liked her."

"And she was smokin' hot," Todd chimed in, eliciting an icy glare from his wife.

"Man, she was nutty as a fruit cake," and he expounded from there.

Wiping any traces of chocolate cake from his mouth, he dropped the napkin on the plate in front of him. Todd sat back in the chair, holding the glass of wine in his hand. He was but an innocent bystander as Matthew and Alex engaged in a discussion about vaccines. Matthew voted for Biden, but he did not agree with the government forcing people to get vaccinated, and he himself was not about to be poked. Besides, he had COVID-19 about ten months ago, and said it was not that bad for him. The best part of it was losing his sense of taste for a few weeks. Matthew had heard a lot of people complaining about that, but he looked at the bright side: he could eat food that he would have normally thought tasted bad. The real benefit was that he could eat the cheapest food he could find and taste had no bearing on that decision.

Alex told Matthew he was not being funny, that it was very serious, even fatal, for some people.

Alex was a Trump fan and did indeed get the vaccine. She thought Matthew was perhaps being a little bit selfish. He should get the vaccine to help protect other people; this was not about protecting Matthew. In her opinion, everyone needed to get vaccinated to move the country forward.

Todd knew better than to get in the middle of one of their discussions. Todd quietly mused how ironic it was. The Dems were anti-vax because Trump was the one that got the vaccine going and got it to market. There were large numbers of people who said they would not trust a vaccine developed under the Trump administration, and they certainly would not take a vaccine if Trump was recommending it. Oddly, as soon as Joe took office, things turned upside down. The Dems embraced the vaccine and it was not long before the Biden administration was using strong-arm tactics to force people to get vaccinated. Alex, the Republican, supported the vaccine, while Matthew the Democrat did not. Go figure. Todd found it interesting that Joe and the Dems often blamed the GOP, and particularly Trump supporters, as being the problem for the lingering pandemic because they did not like anyone mandating they get a vaccine. For them it was choice. How ironic, he thought, when these same people were trying to restrict choice in so many other aspects of life. Choice to own a gun? Nope. Choice in what is taught in schools? Nope.

Choice to make money? Nope. But, the decision to get or not get a vaccine was not a choice. Amused by it all, Todd just shook his head.

Todd was happy indeed when Alex asked Matthew about Thanksgiving. A change of topics, finally.

"So, what are you doing for Thanksgiving? Any plans?"

Matthew had no plans whatsoever. Alex said they should all get together. This would be their first real Thanksgiving without their mother. Sure, there was last year, but everything was still so raw then, it was surreal. It was all so sad; it was more like mourning. This year would be happy. They had all gotten over Katie's death by now. The money from the life insurance policies certainly helped, but it was more them believing that Katie had lived a difficult life and was indeed much better off. They each had a different perspective.

Alex thought their mom was in a much better place, that she most certainly was in heaven, enjoying the afterlife in the presence of the Almighty God. Matthew thought that was utter nonsense. There was no God, and there was no heaven. There clearly was no common ground there. Regardless, they could both agree Katie was a good woman, that she had suffered enough, her suffering was over, and she would suffer no more.

"Sounds good. Your place or mine?" Matthew asked.

Alex thought either place sounded fine.

Matthew offered his house.

"That will work, but one condition."

"Yeah, and what is that?"

"That I do the cooking," Alex said.

Matthew said that was not quite right, that he could do the turkey and Alex and Todd could do the side dishes.

"That is sweet, Matt, but I can do the turkey."

"Seriously, sis, I can provide the bird."

"Look at what we are eating tonight."

"What does lasagna have to do with turkey?"

"Well," said Alex, "we are eating Stouffer's frozen lasagna because you could not cook noodles. And you want to cook a turkey? I'm just sayin'."

Todd asked Matthew if he had ever cooked a turkey.

"No, but how hard can it be? I just stick it in the oven and cook it for one or two hours."

"One or two hours?" Alex asked.

"What is wrong with that?"

"Oh, Salmonella and E. coli come to mind," Todd replied with a grin.

Alex ignored Todd's witticism. "At what temperature do you plan on cooking this turkey?"

Matthew responded that he did not know, but he could read it on the turkey packaging or look it up on the internet.

Alex told her brother that it should take about thirteen or fourteen minutes per pound at three hundred and fifty degrees. Unfrozen of course. And the general rule of thumb was fifteen minutes per pound and that was about three hours for like a twelve-pound bird.

"You do know you have to thaw it first, right?" Todd inquired.

"Yeah right. I do not thaw frozen pizzas or frozen chicken tenders when I cook them."

"And that, Matthew, is why Alex wants to cook the turkey."

"Okay, okay," Matthew reluctantly agreed, "in that case do you want me to do the sides?"

Alex again told Matthew that was sweet of him to offer, but she would take care of it.

"Okay, you can cook everything. But at least let me buy the food. And if you want, you can just cook it all here."

Alex told Matthew she appreciated the offer, but it might be easier if she just did it. She would be able to put the turkey in the oven, and even be able to program it to come on later.

"Why can't you just cook it here?"

"Well, we decided we are going down to the soup kitchen on Thanksgiving morning this year."

"Why are you going down there if we are going to have food?"

"Not to eat, silly. We are going down to help feed the homeless and anyone else who is hungry. We have never done that, and thought it might be a good idea."

"Why would you do that? What's the point?"

Alex explained that sometimes people just needed help. Matthew responded that maybe people just needed to help themselves.

"Not everyone has that opportunity, Matt. They can't just go get a job."

Matthew responded there are thousands of jobs that were going unfilled. Fast food restaurants were closing dining rooms because of a lack of employees. Full-service restaurants were reducing hours, or operating at partial capacity because of a lack of employees. Litter was piling up along roadways because local governments did not have employees to collect it. Maintenance was going undone at parks and facilities because of a lack of employees. From warehouses to garbage collection, the list went on and on. "And you are going to tell me your homeless people cannot find a job? Yeah, right." Matthew was on a roll now. Even a local grocery store had a sign on their door, "We are currently experiencing a cart shortage. Sorry for the inconvenience." However, the corrals in the parking lot were overflowing and stray carts littered the parking lot, but there were none at the entryway of the store. The manager complained they had no one to collect the carts. The obvious question was why did the manager not take five or ten minutes every couple of hours to collect carts themselves? But that was a whole different story. Employers were having problems finding hourly workers, presumably because the pay, incentives, and benefits of not working outweighed the benefits of having a job. "So, why don't these homeless you are going to feed just go get a job?"

"It is not that easy," countered Todd

"Why not?" Matthew asked. Employers can't find people to work. They are losing money because they don't have employees. Surely they would hire them. It is a no-lose proposition for them. They get employees, and they get to stay open and make money."

"Yeah, but they just need help," Alex added. "Right now, they are just hungry and are looking for someone to feed them."

"Why don't you go down there with us, Matt," Todd asked him. "It might give you a different perspective."

"Not a chance," Matthew replied. "Let them fend for themselves. That is what I have had to do in the past. It is not going to kill them to help themselves."

"True, Matt, maybe letting them fend for themselves will not kill them, then again, maybe not helping them will. But helping others is not going to kill you either."

"I will take my chances. You two can have all that touchy feely stuff."

"That is just so sad, Matthew."

Todd ended the conversation by asking what time they were getting together with Matthew on Thanksgiving. After all, that was only four days away.

Alex said they could be at Matthew's by about one o'clock, and they would be able to eat by five or five thirty. Matthew thought that was a bit late to eat, and he again offered to cook the turkey. Alex reluctantly agreed. The evening ended with Alex giving Matthew instructions on both thawing and cooking a turkey, and Matthew promising to call if he had any questions.

Chapter 36

Matthew took the turkey from the refrigerator and put it in the sink. He filled the sink three quarters of the way with water, and the remainder with ice.

He had gotten the frozen turkey yesterday afternoon and put in the refrigerator, as Alex had instructed. She told him it would take about a day per four or five pounds for the turkey to thaw. The turkey Matthew bought was just over 10 pounds, so it would require just over two days to thaw. His sister had also told him he could alternatively thaw it in cold water. But her suggestion was to thaw in the fridge the first day, and then move it to the sink Wednesday evening. So far so good.

Alex had told Matthew to figure on eight ounces of cooked turkey –half of a pound– per person, and one pound per person if they wanted leftovers.

"Great, so I will just get a three or four-pound bird and we should be good."

"Not so fast," Todd chimed in.

"What? Do you want more left overs? No problem. I can just get a five or six-pound turkey."

"Dude," Todd said while shaking his head, "at 3, 4, 5, or 6 pounds, you are talking about a chicken, not a turkey!"

"Matthew, Matthew, my dear brother. We really need to talk," Alex laughed playfully. She then explained there was about a thirty-two percent yield from a turkey. "There is the skin, the liquid, the carcass, the legs bones, the neck, the giblets, that all go into the weight of the raw turkey, but those are things that do not count as meat for most people." So, if they wanted three pounds of cooked meat, they really needed to have about a ten-pound turkey.

Matthew did not have a roasting pan, and could not really see buying one. His sister told him to just buy a large aluminum pan, a deep full size foil steam table pan, and a roll of wide heavy-duty aluminum foil to make a tent. She had to explain the concept of the tent to him; join two pieces of foil together on the long side, and then place that over the turkey and crimp the edges onto the lip of the aluminum pan. Then he would pour a can of chicken broth into the pan with the turkey. The foil tent would keep the moisture and steam in the pan, keeping the turkey from drying out, and it would also help the skin to crisp.

He had gotten the pan, the foil, a can of chicken broth, and everything else Alex had asked him to get. He even picked up an apple pie and a pecan pie for dessert–the pies were his own idea. The one thing he did forget though was the ice cream.

Matthew was hungry and wanted something to eat. He did not have anything at home that interested him. That was okay, he would just take a quick trip to the grocery store at Sparkleberry Square. After all, he did need to get ice cream for tomorrow.

Chapter 37

Thirty-seven minutes ago, Matthew left his house, headed to the grocery store to pick up something for dinner. He was not sure what he wanted, but he knew he did not want any of the fast-food offerings that were all around. He ate too much of that stuff; he knew it was not good for him, but it certainly was convenient.

Sometimes he just wanted to cook, though Matthew was by no stretch of the imagination a gourmet chef. In fact, his "cooking" usually amounted to following the instructions on something he found in the grocery store freezer or some canned offering sitting on the shelf. His contribution was to add a spice or two from his collection of garlic powder, chili powder, oregano, basil, minced onion, and black pepper. Sometimes he might even add a bit of shredded cheddar or mozzarella cheese. Matthew's idea of homemade pizza was buying a Mike's frozen pizza and then sprinkling it with every one of his spices and covering it with a layer of shredded mozzarella.

He had salt in his spice collection too, but rarely used it. He thought there was entirely too much salt in most foods and even beverages. It seemed it was in everything. He once picked up a bottle of natural apple cider and he was quite surprised to see 4% sodium listed on the label. It was in everything from the soda he sometimes drank to the ice cream he ate. He came across something a while back that perplexed him, though he admittedly had not bothered to use "the Google on the Internet machine." The "Internet machine." He loved that. Where was that from? Ah yes, it was from `Blades of Glory.` That movie was a classic in Matthew's humble opinion. Anyway, the thing that perplexed him was sodium. He recalled learning in school that sodium is a highly reactive metal, so reactive, in fact, that it is never found in nature in its free form, and is always found as a salt. Sure, sodium chloride is table salt, and there are many other salts, but if sodium is always found as a salt, then a salt is a salt is a salt and sodium listed on food labels simply equates to salt he reasoned. A few months ago, he had picked up a bottle of soy sauce. He was surprised to see it contained 1577mg of sodium, 68% of the USDA recommended amount, based on a 2,000 calorie per day diet. He picked up a container of iodized table salt and was stunned to see it contained 590mg of sodium, which was about 25% of the USDA recommendation. How could soy sauce possibly have more salt than salt? How could soy sauce possibly have more than two and a half times more salt than salt? He was confused.

Matthew did not necessarily think sodium was completely deserving of the bad rap it got. He had read somewhere years ago about the sodium potassium pump in the human body. He surmised at that time that perhaps it was not an increase in sodium that was a problem for people, rather it was a lack of potassium that merely manifested itself as an abundance of sodium. But, what did he know? He certainly was no expert. Regardless, he still thought there was too much sodium in foods and did try to minimize his use of it.

He wandered throughout the store and, as usual, concluded that cooking a frozen meal was no healthier than eating something from a fast-food establishment. Still, there was just the satisfaction that he cooked it at home, and he would therefore convince himself it must be healthier. He pondered something Mexican. He looked at container of a frozen enchilada casserole. Wow! He was stunned as he read the label: 135% of the total USDA recommendation for fat, the percent of saturated fat and trans-fat were mindboggling, and the percentage of sodium was 225%. The cholesterol was 115%, and the calories of 2795 in a single serving far exceeded the

USDA's 2,000 daily calorie recommendation. How could they even be allowed to sell this stuff? He was not for government intervention and regulation, but still, this simply should not be allowed. He put the toxic waste back in the freezer and continued on.

Frozen pizza? Nope, not tonight. Soup? Nope. Canned pasta? Nope. He settled on a 32-ounce package of frozen vegetable medley. Even that had 40grams (2%) of sodium, yet the ingredients listed only broccoli florets, carrots, and cauliflower. He guessed perhaps the sodium came from the fertilizer, or even the soil itself since free sodium was not naturally occurring, but was always found as a salt. Perhaps that explained the sodium in his apple cider too?

He did not think any more about sodium or chemicals or ingredients or reading labels as he picked up a half gallon of ice cream. Thinking the container was a little small, he read the weight and sighed. A quart and a half. A mere 48 ounces. When did this happen? The amount in the container had decreased by 25% but the price certainly had not. He happened to notice this change several years ago, he guessed while there was still older stock on the shelves, because there were two identical looking jars of pickles on the shelf except that some of them were sixteen ounces while the others were fifteen ounces. Same price, fewer pickles.

"Companies are robbing us blind," he said to the couple standing next to him. "They make the containers smaller but charge us the same amount."

"Oh, don't you know it. We were just talking about that."

The guy's wife held up a container of orange juice. "Since when did a half gallon of orange juice become fifty-two ounces? Where are the other twelve ounces? It's not like it is a convenient size or a standard size thing because it is 1.6 quarts. And it is not like it is a metric thing either because it is 1.53 liters."

"Show him the container, Joan," he said to his wife. "You see that?" addressing the question to Matthew. "You see it? It is not even full! They kept that same container. Just changed the label, put less in it, and then charge more for it anyway."

"That's not right, man," Matthew replied. He started to put the ice cream back in the freezer, paused, and then added, "and they can get away with it because they know we are going to buy it. Just like with this ice cream. I do not need it, but I do like it. They know no one really needs it, but they are going to buy it anyway. Y'all have a good night," he said as he turned and started walking towards one of the self-serve checkout lanes.

Matthew turned the key and the V-twin engine of his Vulcan 900 roared to life. He liked the low sculpted seat. He felt like he was sitting in the motorcycle instead of sitting on it. It reminded him of an old 440 LTD he had once ridden. He bought this bike about a year ago. Granted it was a 2015, but it only had about 9,000 miles on it and, for $6,000, the price was right. The owner originally wanted $6,500, or best offer. Matthew originally offered $5,000, but they met somewhere in between. One thing he really liked were the black leather saddle bags, trimmed out in brass studs. His frozen vegetables and ice cream were tucked safely in the right saddle bag.

He pulled out of the Sparkleberry Square parking lot, and turned left onto Sparkleberry Lane. He was already in the third gear of the five-speed transmission before he was even into the straightaway. The very first time he rode it on the test drive he noticed the bike definitely had some get-up-and-go. Maintaining the speed limit, he continued on through the green traffic light and past the fire department.

"Hey hon, it's me," Kitty Barnwell said into the phone she was holding to her left ear. Kitty did not much care for using the speakerphone feature. She thought there was something so impersonal about it.

Ed knew it was his wife calling, the caller ID made him aware of that. And, after having had these phone numbers for twenty years he would recognize her number even if there was no caller ID. Still, Kitty always said, "Hi hon, it's me." It was sort of like her trademark. He kidded her about it from time to time, asking who else it would be calling him on her phone, but the practice continued.

"Where are you?" he politely asked. "Jack and Bess stopped by a few minutes ago."

"Oh really? What a nice surprise," she said, making the right-hand turn onto North Lake Point Drive. "I will be home is less than ten minutes. I just left Carol's."

"Okay. They invited us to dinner. We are going to have a glass of wine first."

"You go ahead and get started on the wine without me. I have already had three glasses with the girls," she said while completely ignoring the stop sign at the end of North Lake Point.

"Be careful. We will see you in a bit then."

"Love y—"

The left corner of the front bumper of the maroon Mitsubishi Outlander turning right onto Sparkleberry Lane hit the right thigh of the motorcyclist. Kitty never saw the motorcycle, and never really felt the impact. It seemed like a glancing blow, except the sound. There was a definite thud as her car struck the black motorcycle.

Matthew never saw the SUV. He felt a heavy thud against his right thigh. It happened so quickly. The impact of the turning Outlander drove the motorcycle across the center line. It was at that instant Matthew saw the front grill of the oncoming dump truck.

Chapter 38

The light was blindingly bright. It was like staring into the sun, except infinitely brighter. And quiet; it was deathly quiet. The peace was simply indescribable.

The light slowly transformed to sheer white, which gradually was recognizable as clouds. The clouds slowly parted. He was standing at a fork in the middle of a dirt road. The right fork continued through a lush valley and then into the gently sloping hills, while the left fork strewn with rocks continued down a dangerously steep hill to the edge of a cliff.

"Hello Matthew, my child," he more felt the voice than heard it. The voice was not too loud or too soft; it simply was.

"Um, hello?" he replied aloud. "Where are you?"

"I am here, my child."

"I cannot see you. Where are you? Who are you?"

"I am here. I am all around you. I am in you. I am."

"You am? You are who?"

"I Am."

"I am? As in God?"

"I am."

"I do not believe in God."

"Well, God believes in you."

"God does not exist."

"God does exist, and so do you."

"What is going on? There is no such thing as God. If you really are God, show yourself to me."

"Oh ye of little faith."

"Faith? You do not exist. If you do exist, let me see you."

"Do you think you are having a conversation with someone or something that does not exist?"

"This is not happening. It is all in my head."

"This is happening. It is not in your head; *it is in you.*"

"Am I dead?"

"You are in the process of dying."

"The process of dying? So then this is not final?"

"It is final for the body. What is done is done."

"If I am dead, then why am I here?"

"The process of dying is over for the body. Now it is time for the soul."

"Time for the soul? I do not believe in any of this. There is no soul. There is only a body and once we are dead, we are dead."

"Be that as it may, this is real. I believe in you. I created you, both body and soul."

"So then, what is next? I mean for my soul? Is this like judgement or something?"

"There is a time for everything. There is a time when all beings will be judged. That time for you is now."

"Whoa, wait a second. If I recall, is not Jesus supposed to be the judge? I think I remember hearing something about Jesus, not you, doing the judging. Where is he?"

"Where I am He is. Where He is I am. Where We are the Spirit is. Where the Spirit is We are.

"Well, since I do not believe in you, and I do not believe in any of this, none of this applies to me. There is nothing after death."

"Whether you believe it or not, it does apply to you. It applies to everyone. There will be a day of reckoning for both believers and non-believers. That time for you is now." A montage of Matthew's life began to reveal itself. Was it in the air around him, or was in it his mind's eye? He could not begin to tell. It began to occur to him that if his body was dead and this was truly his soul, then there was no distinction between what was around him and what was in him, simply because there was no physical him. He was, he was, he was but a spirit.

"But if I do not believe you exist, then what difference does it make? You cannot judge me; you do not exist."

"Ah, but my child. I am very real and I most certainly *do* exist. Whether you believe in me or not has no bearing on my existence. Believing in Unicorns does not make them exist, no more than believing the earth is flat will make it be so. A penny falling from the top of the Empire State building will not kill a person it strikes below standing on the ground, and gum does not take seven years to digest." There was something familiar about what he was hearing, like he had heard it before. Perhaps from Alex? "No matter how much you chose not to believe those facts, your lack of belief will make them no less true. Whether or not you believe in me will in no way alter my existence. Thusly, you can and you shall be judged. As it is written in Hebrews 9:27, 'And just as it is appointed for man to die once, and after that comes judgment.'"

"God quoting scripture? Using someone else's work? Is that not kind of like plagiarism? Well, I guess you did at least cite it. But still."

"At least you have accepted I am I Am. As for scripture, I did not write it, but it certainly was divinely inspired. I inspired it."

"Yeah, well, I never much read scripture. As for this judging thing. I am being judged on what? On all the bad things I did? I am no worse than anyone else."

"Yes, there are people worse than you, just as there are people better than you. This is not about comparing them to you or you to them. There are two parts; accounting and judgement. Accounting is as much about the things you did do as it is about the things you did not do. It is reckoning. It is being held accountable. Final judgement is based on you, who you really are, your essence, your relationship with me, your acceptance of me, your belief in me."

"Yeah, I remember some of that nonsense. Something about clothing the naked and feeding the hungry. Well, no one ever bought me clothes or fed me. What about the times I had nothing? Where was anyone to help me? Where were you? You just stood by and watched it happen. Heck, you probably entertained yourself by making it happen. Or was it all just some kind of a test?"

"I was there. I did not cause those things to happen to you. It does not work like that. Life is like a Venn diagram, where lives are represented by circles, and those circles sometimes overlap. People make choices; every choice has consequences and impacts. Lives intersect. Things happen. That is no test, that is life, a life of free choices. However, there is indeed a test. The test is not the events themselves; sometimes you have control over those events and other times you do not. The real test is how you choose to respond to those events."

"So, this still is about what I did or did not do?"

"Consider this. How many times did you blame me for your struggles? How many times did you take my name in vain in anger? How many times did you take my name in vain against me?"

"Um, I do not really know."

"There it is right there in front of you, being revealed for you. There are so many times that you lost count of them."

Matthew just stood and stared, transfixed by the montage appearing like a hologram right before his very eyes, except it was not a hologram. He somehow felt that if he reached out and touched it, he would touch actual people, he would actually touch himself. But that was crazy; it could not possibly be real.

"Matthew, my child. How many times did you cry out to me for help?"

"I honestly do not know. A few I guess."

"My child, you have cried out to me many times, oh so many times. I heard every one of your cries for help."

"So, all that proves is that you were never there for me."

"I was there for you in ways you cannot comprehend. I did not leave you. I gave you the strength to endure, the strength to carry on. I did not cause those events, I helped you overcome those events. Remember those times when you cried out to me in despair and desperation? Do you not remember the tranquility you felt afterward? That was me. Do you not remember those times you acted in anger, yelling and taking my name in vain, only to feel remorse later and apologize to me? Do you not remember the peace you felt after that? That was me. Each time was a fresh start for you, but each time you chose to forget about me shortly after that and to revert to your previous ways."

"That was not you. That was just venting. Just getting anger out of me. That is why I felt better, I just let the pent-up anger out is all."

Was this actually happening? Was all of this in his head? Was he merely imagining all of this? God spoke again.

"You are pretty good at blaming me when things go wrong, and you are pretty good at crying out to me when you need help. That shows you do believe in me."

"Yeah, a lot of good any of that did."

Unfazed by the interruption, God continued. "You are pretty good at crying out to me when you need help, and blaming me when things do not go your way. But how many times have you bothered to thank me when things went well, when things turned out better than you expected?" There was no montage, there was no recollection; there was just silence.

"Well, I am waiting. Show me that too."

Still there was no montage, nothing flashing before Matthew.

"I am showing you."

"Your, your, your projector or whatever it is must be broken. I cannot see anything."

"You are seeing nothing because there is nothing to see. There is nothing broken, except you."

"Did you, the great I Am, just say I am broken?"

"You curse me in your anger and you blame me when things do not go your way. Yet, you have never thanked me during the good times. You believe in me, yet you refuse to acknowledge me. Fear not, for I am a compassionate God. Broken can be repaired. All you have to do is believe in me and show remorse for your sins, for your actions and for your lack of actions."

"But I do not believe in you. As for my actions, hey, I did what I needed to do to survive."

"Still you deny me?"

"You do not exist."

"Matthew, my child. How many times did you take my name in vain? How many times did you cry out for me to damn someone?"

"That means nothing. It was only words, only an expression. Even atheists yell out goddamn. It is only an expression for Christ's sake."

"And that you reference both God and Christ in your expressions shows no acknowledgement of either God or Christ?"

"They are just words, just expressions. If you truly exist, prove it to me. Do something. Convince me you are real."

"Faith is believing even when you have not seen. Faith is believing in me. Faith is trusting me."

"Then put me down in your little judgement book, or whatever it is, as having no faith. I do not believe in you, and I certainly am not going to trust something I do not believe in. And, I do not believe any of this is happening. I will wake up soon and this will all be over."

"My child, do you not understand? You are not merely sleeping. This is not a dream. You will not be waking up. You are dying. This is your last chance."

"Okay, then judge away and let's get this over with. What's the big deal anyway if I am already dead?"

"You are not quite dead yet, but you are dying. You still have time to choose me. Once your dying has completed, once your life has ended, there is no more choice. The fate of your soul is to be determined. It will spend eternity in either heaven or hell. You still have time to determine the outcome, to decide on eternal heaven or eternal hell. We are alone, Matthew. You, your essence and I. Free of earthly distractions and free of the voices in your head, no outside influences. You have time to accept me. You have time to show remorse."

"Big deal. I do not believe any of this. Heaven and hell do not exist. That is some made up nonsense."

"Matthew, my child, there is heaven and there is hell."

"Oh yeah, I know the fairy tales, about heaven with streets of gold and hell with a pit of fire. But you know, if hell was really like a fiery furnace, souls would burn up and it would all be over with pretty quickly."

"Hear me. I am love and love is me. I am pure perfect love."

"So?"

"Hell is the absence of me. Hell is the absence of love. Choosing to not accept me means choosing to reject love and, in doing so, banishment to hell means never knowing love again."

"Love never did anything for me anyway. I can live without it. I told you, I did what I had to do to survive. I have no remorse. You should know that if you are God. You are God, are you not?"

"I am."

"You said that before, I am. You said, I am I Am."

"I am I Am."

"What does that even mean. I am? I am what?"

"I am everything. I am the beginning and the end. I am the Alpha and the Omega. I am infinite. I am truth. I am light. I am things you cannot comprehend. I am I Am."

"I don't quite get it. You are everything, and you are nothing?"

"I am Love. I am pure perfect love. Everything else revolves around that."

"I can do without love."

On the pavement in front of the dump truck, almost imperceptibly, the forefinger on the motorcyclist's left hand twitched slightly a single time. He was dead.

He noticed he was drifting down the left fork of the dirt road. In doing so, he heard God one last time.

"Matthew, your time on earth has ended. You have denied me for the final time. You have chosen to not accept me. You have chosen not to know me, to not know love. So let it be done. You shall spend eternity in a place without love."

His pace began to pick up and, within a blink of an eye, he was at the edge of the cliff. "Wait!" But there was only silence. That is, until he fell over the edge of the cliff, and fell from God's grace.

Chapter 39

"In other news, a 28-year-old motorcyclist was killed earlier this evening in a traffic accident on Sparkleberry Lane near Spring Valley High School when a car driven by an unidentified 63-year-old woman pulled out of North Lake Point Drive, striking the motorcycle and forcing it into the path of an oncoming dump truck. The highway patrol is investigating and charges are pending. The driver of the car failed a field sobriety test. When we come back, Weather is next and we will see what changes are in store for the weekend. We will be right back."

ACKNOWLEDGEMENTS

Thank you to all the fictional characters that gave their lives in the writing of this novel. This book could not have been written without you.